WHISK ME AWAY

Whisk Me Away

Praise for Georgia Beers

Can't Buy Me Love

"Everything about the story and the characters was exciting and I adored every minute. It had everything from the magical moments of instant attraction to the misunderstandings that cause all the drama that every great romance needs…A great story, lots of humorous moments, some heartfelt ones, and lots of cute getting to know one another ones as well. I really, really enjoyed the story and will definitely be reading it again."—*LesbiReviewed*

Aubrey McFadden Is Never Getting Married

"Georgia Beers has become a household name in the world of LGBTQ+ romance novels, and her latest work, *Aubrey McFadden Is Never Getting Married*, proves she is worthy of the attention. With its captivating characters, engaging plot, and impactful themes, this book is a pure delight to read. Its enemies-to-lovers narrative tugs at the heart, making one hope for resolution and forgiveness between its leading ladies. Aubrey and Monica's push-and-pull dynamic is complicated and knotty, but Beers keeps it fun with her quick wit and sense of humor. The crafty banter ensures that readers have a good time."—*Women Using Words*

Playing with Matches

"*Playing with Matches* is a delightful exploration of small town life, family drama, and true love…Liz and Cori are charming characters with undeniable chemistry, and their sweet and tender small town, 'fake-dating' love story is sure to capture the attention of readers. Their journey reminds readers of the importance of love, forgiveness, family, and community, making this feel-good romance a true triumph."
—*Women Using Words*

Peaches and Cream

"*Peaches and Cream* is a fresh, new spin on the classic rom-com *You've Got Mail*—except it's even better because it's all about ice cream!… [A] delicious, melt-in-your-mouth scoop of goodness. Bursting with tasty characters in a scrumptious story world, *Peaches and Cream* is simply irresistible."—*Women Using Words*

Lambda Literary Award Winner *Dance with Me*

"I admit I inherited my two left feet from my father's side of the family. Dancing is not something I enjoy, so why choose a book with dancing as the central focus and romance as the payoff? Easy. Because it's Georgia Beers, and she will let me enjoy being awkward alongside her main character. I think this is what makes her special to me as an author. While her characters might be beautiful in their own ways, I can relate to their challenges, fears and dreams. Comfort reads every time."
—*Late Night Lesbian Reads*

Camp Lost and Found

"I really like when Beers writes about winter and snow and hot chocolate. She makes heartache feel cosy and surmountable. *Camp Lost and Found* made me smile a lot, laugh at times, tear up more often than I care to share. If you're looking for a heartwarming story to keep the cold weather at bay, I'd recommend you give it a chance."—*Jude in the Stars*

Cherry on Top

"*Cherry on Top* is another wonderful story from one of the greatest writers in sapphic fiction…This is more than a romance with two incredibly charming and wonderful characters. It is a reminder that you shouldn't have to compromise who you are to fit into a box that society wants to put you into. Georgia Beers once again creates a couple with wonderful chemistry who will warm your heart."—*Sapphic Book Review*

The Secret Poet

"[O]ne of the author's best works and one of the best romances I've read recently…I was so invested in [Morgan and Zoe] I read the book in one sitting."—*Melina Bickard, Librarian, Waterloo Library (UK)*

On the Rocks

"This book made me so happy! And kept me awake way too late."
—*Jude in the Stars*

Hopeless Romantic

"Thank you, Georgia Beers, for this unabashed paean to the pleasure of escaping into romantic comedies…If you want to have a big smile plastered on your face as you read a romance novel, do not hesitate to pick up this one!"—*The Rainbow Bookworm*

Flavor of the Month

"Beers whips up a sweet lesbian romance…brimming with mouthwatering descriptions of foodie indulgences…Both women are well-intentioned and endearing, and it's easy to root for their inevitable reconciliation. But once the couple rediscover their natural ease with one another, Beers throws a challenging emotional hurdle in their path, forcing them to fight through tragedy to earn their happy ending." —*Publishers Weekly*

Fear of Falling

"Enough tension and drama for us to wonder if this can work out—and enough heat to keep the pages turning. I will definitely recommend this to others—Georgia Beers continues to go from strength to strength." —*Evan Blood, Bookseller (Angus & Robertson, Australia)*

One Walk in Winter

"A sweet story to pair with the holidays. There are plenty of 'moment's in this book that make the heart soar. Just what I like in a romance. Situations where sparks fly, hearts fill, and tears fall. This book shined with cute fairy trails and swoon-worthy Christmas gifts…REALLY nice and cozy if read in between Thanksgiving and Christmas. Covered in blankets. By a fire."—*Bookvark*

The Do-Over

"You can count on Beers to give you a quality well-paced book each and every time."—*The Romantic Reader Blog*

"*The Do-Over* is a shining example of the brilliance of Georgia Beers as a contemporary romance author."—*Rainbow Reflections*

The Shape of You

The Shape of You "catches you right in the feels and does not let go. It is a must for every person out there who has struggled with self-esteem, questioned their judgment, and settled for a less than perfect but safe lover. If you've ever been convinced you have to trade passion for emotional safety, this book is for you."—*Writing While Distracted*

"I know I always say this about Georgia Beers's books, but there is no one that writes first kisses like her. They are hot, steamy and all too much!"—*Les Rêveur*

Calendar Girl

"A sweet, sweet romcom of a story…*Calendar Girl* is a nice read, which you may find yourself returning to when you want a hot-chocolate-and-warm-comfort-hug in your life."—*Best Lesbian Erotica*

Blend

"You know a book is good, first, when you don't want to put it down. Second, you know it's damn good when you're reading it and thinking, I'm totally going to read this one again. Great read and absolutely a 5-star romance."—*The Romantic Reader Blog*

"This is a lovely romantic story with relatable characters that have depth and chemistry. A charming easy story that kept me reading until the end. Very enjoyable."—*Kat Adams, Bookseller, QBD (Australia)*

Right Here, Right Now

"[A] successful and entertaining queer romance novel. The main characters are appealing, and the situations they deal with are realistic and well-managed. I would recommend this book to anyone who enjoys a good queer romance novel, and particularly one grounded in real world situations."—*Books at the End of the Alphabet*

"[A]n engaging odd-couple romance. Beers creates a romance of gentle humor that allows no-nonsense Lacey to relax and easygoing Alicia to find a trusting heart."—*RT Book Reviews*

Lambda Literary Award Winner *Fresh Tracks*

"[T]he focus switches each chapter to a different character, allowing for a measured pace and deep, sincere exploration of each protagonist's thoughts. Beers gives a welcome expansion to the romance genre with her clear, sympathetic writing."—*Curve magazine*

Lambda Literary Award Finalist *Finding Home*

"Georgia Beers has proven in her popular novels such as *Too Close to Touch* and *Fresh Tracks* that she has a special way of building romance with suspense that puts the reader on the edge of their seat. *Finding Home*, though more character driven than suspense, will equally keep the reader engaged at each page turn with its sweet romance."—*Lambda Literary Review*

Mine

"Beers does a fine job of capturing the essence of grief in an authentic way. *Mine* is touching, life-affirming, and sweet."—*Lesbian News Book Review*

Too Close to Touch

"This is such a well-written book. The pacing is perfect, the romance is great, the character work strong, and damn, but is the sex writing ever fantastic."—*The Lesbian Review*

"In her third novel, Georgia Beers delivers an immensely satisfying story. Beers knows how to generate sexual tension so taut it could be cut with a knife...Beers weaves a tale of yearning, love, lust, and conflict resolution. She has constructed a believable plot, with strong characters in a charming setting."—*Just About Write*

By the Author

Romances

Turning the Page	The Do-Over
Thy Neighbor's Wife	Fear of Falling
Too Close to Touch	One Walk in Winter
Fresh Tracks	Flavor of the Month
Mine	Hopeless Romantic
Finding Home	16 Steps to Forever
Starting from Scratch	The Secret Poet
96 Hours	Cherry on Top
Slices of Life	Camp Lost and Found
Snow Globe	Dance with Me
Olive Oil & White Bread	Peaches and Cream
Zero Visibility	Playing with Matches
A Little Bit of Spice	Aubrey McFadden Is Never Getting Married
What Matters Most	
Right Here, Right Now	Can't Buy Me Love
Blend	This Christmas
The Shape of You	Whisk Me Away
Calendar Girl	

Visit us at www.boldstrokesbooks.com

WHISK ME AWAY

by

Georgia Beers

2025

Acknowledgments

I love to bake. Of course, loving to bake and being good at baking are two different things. It took me several years, but I finally understand why I love to bake but I don't love to cook. It's because baking is about rules. You can't wing it when you're making chocolate chip cookies or an apple pie or a soufflé, not like you can when you're making dinner. Measurements in baking are there for a reason. There are rules. And I was raised to be a rule follower. It's something I fight against a bit now (hi! lapsed Catholic here!), but not when it comes to, for example, my famous rum balls. No way. The sugar, the Nilla wafers, the chocolate chips, their measurements are precise, and I follow them to the letter (though I admit to measuring the rum with my heart). I love baking shows. I love watching people learn how to make something from scratch and the pride on their face when they get it right. The research for this book was so interesting (and made me sooooo hungry), and writing it was the most fun I've had in several books. Ava and Regan are a pretty smooth pairing, but also one of my spicier ones. They're like chocolate with cayenne pepper. I really loved writing them, and I hope you enjoy them as much as I did.

Now for my never-ending gratitude:

The last couple of years have encompassed a lot of change, loss, and grief for me, but it's been mixed in with immense joy, and that's been a hard combination to reconcile. As I write these acknowledgments, it's still early in the year, and I'm praying for a calmer, less stressful stretch this time around. I feel like I'm finally coming into my own (a weird thing to say when you're slightly past middle-age, but it's true) and learning exactly who I am. I've been confused about a lot of things in my life, but my career has never been one of them. So this time, first and foremost, I want to thank my readers, old and new. Whether you've read every book I've written or this is your first of mine, I thank you. Whether you follow me on social media, belong to my Patreon page, or have never heard of me before, I thank you. It's because of you that I'm able to continue what has turned out to be the very coolest job that little Georgia, sitting in her room writing stories in notebooks with a #2 pencil, ever could have dreamed of.

As always, thank you to everyone at Bold Strokes Books who keep things running smoothly behind the scenes. In a world where it seems recently that most of the recognition goes to the Indies or the Big Publishers, as an author at a small press, it's become suddenly easy to be overlooked or even forgotten. I'm so lucky to have a publisher that knows this and does its best to help me not get lost in the very large shuffle.

And finally, to my very unconventional family…the ones who keep me grounded while also covering me in drool, crumbs, peanut butter, and hugs. I am forever grateful for all the love in my life.

To all the people who want to bake but don't
because they're not perfect at it.
A lopsided cake is still cake. And cake is delicious.

CHAPTER ONE

L ove is baking made visible.

That's what Regan Callahan's grandmother always told her when they'd bake together. Regan would stand up on one of her grandma's kitchen chairs so she could reach the counter, her own little pink apron with the ruffles tied around her waist. She'd help Grandma frost cupcakes or ice cookies or sprinkle powdered sugar onto lemon bars. They were always baking something. From the time Regan was old enough to help, they were always baking something.

What had made her think about that now?

She searched her memory banks and realized quickly it was the last step in the rustic cherry tarts she'd made: the gentle sprinkle of powdered sugar. She tipped some into the small mesh strainer, then tapped the side of it softly against her hand over each of the tarts. Just a little. Too much would get sticky and clumpy and make things too sweet. Too little and, well, why even bother, what would be the point? It needed to be just right. Enough to show up and give the tarts a little extra zhuzh, as her roommate Kiki would say.

"Those are beautiful. My God, you're an artist." Billy Jergenson, owner of Sweet Temptations Bakery and Regan's boss for the past four years, spoke softly, just above a whisper. It was as if he was afraid of breaking some spell Regan had cast, some magical cherry tart wizardry floating around in a sparkly, sugary haze in the kitchen.

"You always say that," she said and glanced up at him with a grin.

Billy was tall and lean like a runner, and at sixty-three, he was still very attractive. He often joked about how he used to turn all the heads at the men's bars in the eighties, but Regan knew he probably still would. He had a dancer's body, a full head of silvery hair, and only recently had a tiny bit of a bulge start to appear around his middle. Less gym time, a slowing metabolism, and more sampling of the goods in his shop, Regan surmised, but happily. If the owner loved your stuff, you were in good shape, right?

"I say it because it's true," Billy went on. "Those are gorgeous. You went with the rustic. Good call. They have so much more personality than the traditional tarts." He picked up one of the two trays and took it out to the front display case where the tarts would live until sold.

So...where they'll live until about five o'clock tonight, Regan thought with a tiny burst of ego.

She surveyed the remaining tray. Billy was right. Her rustic tarts didn't sit in a simple round dish like traditional ones. They didn't have simple crimped crust edges and cherry pie filling inside. No, sir. Hers had fresh cherries that she'd cooked down with a little brandy until they were thick and sweet and syrupy and had a lovely, shiny gloss to them. Her crust was wraparound, flaky and buttery, and it had taken her almost a year to get the method of folding just right. And when they came out of the oven, all bubbly and hot, they were irresistible.

Serves one, gone in about five bites.

Her mouth was watering now, so she slid one off the tray as Billy returned for it, and he gave her a knowing smile. "Save me a bite," he tossed over his shoulder as he bumped through the swinging door.

"I make no promises," she called back and dug a fork into the tart, wishing she had warmed it up first. They had to cool completely before the dusting of sugar or it would melt and run and look messy, but they really were best when hot from the oven. But still...she made a humming sound of approval as she chewed the bite. Oh, yeah. They were fabulous.

Billy came back into the kitchen, and she held up a fork for him. "Sold two already," he said, cutting into the tart and then making very similar sounds as he chewed. He pointed at her with the fork. "I'm telling you. Artiste." Then he made a chef's kiss gesture and headed into the back where his office was, leaving Regan with her fork and the rest of the tart. Which she finished easily, happily, and with pride.

It was after two in the afternoon, and she'd been there since before five, so she was ready to punch out. She tossed her flour/egg white/batter-covered apron into the laundry bag in the back and got her stuff out of her locker. Then she changed from her ratty flour/egg white/batter-covered Nikes into her newer ones and, not for the first time—or the last—wondered at the hot pink Crocs her coworker Kiley wore. Regan had been very vocal about never being caught dead in a pair of Crocs, let alone hot pink ones, but her aching arches put thoughts in her head, visions of a fun white pair. Or maybe red. With—what were those little decorations called? Giblets? Goblins?—shaped like a rolling pin or a whisk or a layer cake. And then reality set back in because if she ever gave in, she would never, ever hear the end of it from Kiki. Her roommate was a nurse and lived in her Crocs, and the harassment Regan would have to endure would be the endless kind. Probably funny, but also endless.

With a sigh, she swung her backpack over her shoulder, waved goodbye to the staff that remained to man the bakery until it closed at nine, then peeked in Billy's office. He was on the phone and glanced up at her as he spoke.

She waved and stage-whispered, "Good night, sweet prince."

He grinned and waved her on.

She was going to miss the 2:34 subway, so she waited for the next one, plugging her wired headphones in since she hadn't been able to find her AirPods and hadn't wanted to wake up her roommates by rifling noisily through the apartment at three in the morning. Once in her seat, she settled in for the hour-long ride that would get her to within a handful of blocks of her tiny Brooklyn apartment. Luckily, the April weather was free of rain and not freezing, so the walk was no big.

She was the first one home, which was often the case. Both her roommates were nurses at New York Presbyterian, and currently, Kiki was on the day shift and Brian was working some funky shift with a surgeon, so they were both gone. Kiki would be back around dinnertime, and Brian would follow an hour or two later. And while Regan had grown to love her roomies—they were the best friends she had here in the city—she also loved whenever she got their tiny place to herself.

Arms full of three days of mail, because Regan was the only one who ever thought to empty the mailbox, she climbed up to their third-floor apartment. Her legs chose that moment to let her know just how tired they were, and once inside, she collapsed onto the worn couch before she even set anything down, mail and her backpack taking seats with her. She leaned back and closed her eyes.

She heard King Arthur's purring before she felt his featherlight steps on the back of the couch, and she turned her head to meet his clear green eyes. "Hi, Artie. Tell me about your day. How were things at the office?"

He bumped his head against hers, and she let go of the mail to reach up and give him a scratch. It slid to the floor where she left it. Artie's purring changed to a little chirp. "Oh, yeah? Did you have to fire anybody today?" He climbed gently down onto her shoulder, then chest, and settled his petite gray and white form into her lap. "Oh, buddy, I haven't even set my stuff down yet." The cat looked up at her with those eyes—the eyes that had won her over when she'd found him near the dumpster behind the bakery—and she just didn't have the heart to move him. Plus, he was warm and soft and his purr was so relaxing...

The next time she opened her eyes, Kiki's nose was practically touching hers, and she jumped in surprise, making a startled little gasping noise and sending Artie flying off her lap to hide under a chair.

"Jesus, Mary, and Joseph, I thought you were dead!" Kiki's big blue eyes were wide, and that was saying something, considering she had the biggest eyes of anybody Regan knew.

Regan pressed a hand to her chest and gaped at her roommate. "Why the hell would you think that?"

Kiki straightened up and folded her arms across her tall frame. She still wore her blue scrubs and light gray Crocs, her blond hair pulled into a haphazard ponytail, and she arched an eyebrow as she gave Regan a poignant scan.

Regan looked down at herself, still wearing a jacket, backpack on the couch next to her still with one strap looped over her arm, shoes still on her feet, mail scattered on the floor around them. She shot Kiki a sheepish, crooked grin. "Ah. I see. I must've fallen asleep."

Kiki snorted and blew out what was likely a relieved breath. "You think? I was ready to start CPR, for fuck's sake."

"I'm sorry," Regan said, as Kiki bent to pick up the mail. "I haven't been sleeping great, and work has been so busy and..." Her words stopped because Kiki had stopped moving. "What?"

The wide blue eyes were back as Kiki met Regan's gaze and held up a manila envelope. They stared at each other in silence for a full five seconds before Kiki whispered, "I think this is it."

Regan swallowed so hard, anybody standing in the room would've heard it. As if she was moving in slow motion, she reached out and took the envelope, then glanced down at the return address.

Whisk Me Away.

"Holy shit." It was a whisper that matched Kiki's, like they were afraid the room was bugged and they didn't want to give away the details of the mail. She rolled her lips in and wet them, then swallowed again, because the lump in her throat wouldn't go down. Her heart pounded in her ears as she looked back up at Kiki and slowly handed the envelope to her. "I can't look."

"I got you." Kiki took the envelope, stood up, and turned her back. Regan listened to the tearing of heavy manila, the shuffle of papers, then silence as Kiki must've been reading. But that only lasted a few moments before she turned around with a squeal and huge smile. "Baby, you're in. You're in!"

"No way."

"Yes way. *All* the ways. You did it. I told you. *I told you!*"

Regan finally pushed herself to her feet, taking a moment to shake her now-tangled arm out of her backpack strap. With a shaking hand, she pointed at Kiki. "Read it." As Kiki spoke, Regan paced.

"'Dear Ms. Callahan, we are pleased to inform you that you have been selected as one of six attendees to the *Whisk Me Away* eight-week retreat sponsored by renowned pastry chef Liza Bennett-Schmidt.'"

"Oh my God," Regan whispered as Kiki went on.

"'The retreat will begin on May twenty-first and run through July sixteenth. The location is Chef Bennett-Schmidt's residence in upstate New York, where you and your fellow attendees will be housed for the duration. This is also where all pastry creation and apprenticing will take place. Chef Bennett-Schmidt was impressed with your résumé, your credentials, and your creations. Please bring your knowledge, your creativity, and your willingness to learn. Any details you'll need to know are contained in this package. Chef looks forward to meeting you for this once-in-a-lifetime opportunity.' Then there's a bunch of other papers and forms, what looks like a nondisclosure agreement, and a pamphlet." There was a beat where the apartment was silent, and then

Kiki added, "Holy crap, Regs, you did it. You're going on a retreat at freaking Liza Bennett-Schmidt's house!"

Regan stood and stared, and a part of her felt like she would stay there forever, simply frozen in permanent disbelief. This was—at the risk of sounding incredibly clichéd—a dream come true. Liza Bennett-Schmidt had been an idol of hers, a mentor of sorts, despite having never met her, and now? Now she was about to spend eight solid weeks learning from her, listening to her, gleaning everything she could about her craft from the very person she'd been following and listening to for literal *years*.

Once-in-a-lifetime opportunity didn't even begin to cover it.

❖

She was in.

Ava Prescott sat at the foot of her neatly made bed in her tiny studio apartment and stared at the letter in her hand. The corner trembled slightly as she read for the fourth—fifth?—time.

> *We are pleased to inform you…eight-week retreat sponsored by renowned pastry chef Liza Bennett-Schmidt… where you and your fellow attendees will be housed…Chef looks forward to meeting you for this once-in-a-lifetime opportunity…*

Jiminy Cricket pawed at her leg, gently, as if he didn't want to disturb whatever it was that Ava was doing. She glanced up at the clock next to the bed. It was almost one in the morning, and she'd been sitting there staring for nearly twenty minutes.

Giving herself a mental shake, she pushed to her feet. "Sorry, Jims. Mommy got a little caught up. Are you starving?" Jiminy meowed his exuberant response and followed her to the kitchenette. Yes, one in the morning was a pretty unconventional time for a cat to have dinner, but that's how Ava's schedule worked. She went in midafternoon and was rarely home before midnight. The joys of working in the kitchen of a high-end restaurant.

She set the glass bowl on the floor and stroked Jiminy's back as he chowed down on his wet food. "I got in, Jimzy," she said quietly, knowing if she said it out loud, it was closer to being a reality and less likely to be a dream she would pop awake from at any moment. "I got into the Bennett-Schmidt retreat. Can you believe it?"

Jiminy paused in his eating long enough to look her in the eye, and she smiled at him.

"That's right. Your mommy's a rock star. Pretty cool, huh?"

She really needed to sleep, but her brain was buzzing. She felt slightly electrified, like she'd had about four too many Red Bulls, the way she felt when she came up with a fantastic new dessert idea. Excited. Wired.

She really wanted to call her mother, but it was still one in the morning, and while her mom didn't sleep nearly as much as she once did, she generally wasn't awake at that hour. She briefly entertained texting, but if her mom hadn't remembered to put her phone on its night setting, it would definitely wake her up. The only people she knew who were most likely still up were those she'd left work with, but she hadn't told any of them that she'd applied for the retreat.

With an irritated sigh, she peeled off her work clothes, dropped them in the hamper in the corner so the entire apartment didn't end up smelling like onions and fried food, and walked naked to her teeny bathroom to shower off the day's work.

Always a little bit keyed up when she got home, Ava never went to bed right away, despite the hour. She'd shower, make herself something to eat if she hadn't eaten at the restaurant (she hadn't tonight), watch a show or two. But tonight, she felt keyed up and then some. Still buzzing, even after a hot shower that was meant to relax her, she padded to the counter in blue and white striped pajama pants and a blue tank top, her hair piled on top of her head, got out a couple pots, and set to making herself some midnight spaghetti. Having something to do with her hands would help calm her nerves.

One of her professors in culinary school had taught her midnight spaghetti, named because it was a common dish chefs made at the end of their shift, often midnight or later. She boiled salted water and tossed in some spaghetti, then sliced fresh garlic and got it sautéing in olive oil. While those things were cooking, she pulled a bag of fresh parsley out of her tiny fridge and chopped some up, and added a bit of chicken broth to the garlic. Before long, she'd drained the pasta, added some of the water to the frying pan, and was transferring it to the garlic sauce so it could absorb it. She added a healthy helping of parmesan, salt and pepper, then the parsley, tossed it all together, and put it in a bowl. She carried it over to her bed, where Jiminy had already made himself a spot on one of the pillows, as if waiting for her to start their show.

She got comfortable. She did have a chair and a love seat in the small studio, but she rarely used them at night after work. She preferred to set her laptop up on her breakfast-in-bed tray and eat her dinner while watching. Which her mother would be mortified by. Dinner in bed? Spaghetti? Horrifying.

She smiled thinking about it, then hit the keys on her laptop and navigated to YouTube, where she searched episodes of *Whisk Me Away*. It had been a while—well, it had been a good six months, when she'd watched as she filled out the application to the retreat—since she'd watched, and she found herself immediately caught up. Liza Bennett-Schmidt was attractive, yes, but it went beyond that. Ava always thought this must be what they meant when they said somebody had "camera presence." The camera loved her. And she was a natural. Smiling at the camera made it feel like she was smiling right at you, the viewer. And in addition to that great camera presence, she knew what she was doing as a pastry chef. Her show was always twofold. First, she'd make something gorgeously complicated, something no home baker would have any reason to try other than curiosity. But after that, she'd take an element of that dessert and craft something simpler from it, something her viewers could make in their own kitchens without struggle. She made home bakers feel like pastry chefs in Paris, and that was how she'd become such a success. Her following was enormous. She had her own line of bakeware. She'd published something like eight cookbooks so far. She did commercials for mixers and ovens and utensils and a brand of flour and had her own clothing line of chef apparel. The woman was a world-famous gazillionaire. A household name akin to Martha Stewart.

And Ava was going to be learning from her in less than six weeks.

She swallowed the mouthful of spaghetti and sat still, letting that sink in.

Holy shit.

She slept fitfully because her mind wouldn't stop racing, and when she opened her eyes at seven thirty—a full two and a half hours earlier than normal—that was it. There was no more sleeping. She reached for her phone and texted her mom.

You up?

Of course she was up. She'd likely been up for a few hours now, and Ava could picture her on the little screen porch of her modest modular home in the retirement community in Florida where she lived for half the year, sipping her tea and watching the birds flit around her feeders. She spent as much money on bird food as she did on food for herself, but it made her happy, so Ava tried not to give her too much of a hard time about it.

The phone rang in her hand, and Ava grinned. "Hey, Mom."

"Am I up? What a stupid question. I'm always up."

"Listen, my mama raised me to have manners. I needed to check first." Ava pushed out of bed and headed to the kitchen counter to turn on her coffee maker. "How are the birds this morning?"

"Lots of warblers today," her mom said. "I think the two from last year told their friends. And the cardinal couple is back."

Ava smiled as she put a tea bag into her mug and waited for the water to boil. "Warblers. They have yellow tummies?"

"Yup. And I think I finally have bluebirds in the birdhouse."

Ava let her mom go on about the birds, simply reveling in the sound of her voice, her excitement clear, the way it always was when she talked about her birds. They hadn't seen each other since before the holidays, and listening to her talk helped Ava not miss her quite so much.

"And what's new with you, my girl?" her mom asked after an explanation of what was in the new suet she bought. "You don't usually text this early. Everything okay?"

"I have news." And with those three words, Ava's heart rate kicked up again. Her elation built again. Her disbelief surged in again. "Remember the Bennett-Schmidt retreat I was telling you about just after you left for Florida?"

"Of course I do. You said the application was going to take you hours to fill out, but you were practically coming out of your skin with excitement."

"I got in." Three more simple words. And maybe it was because it was daylight now rather than the wee hours. Maybe it was because several hours had passed since she'd read the acceptance letter. Ava didn't know, but somehow, it felt even bigger, even more important. So she said it again. "I got in, Mom."

The shriek of delight that came out of her mother right then made Ava pull the phone away from her ear. "Oh my God! Oh my God! Oh my God! Uh-oh, Connie's looking out her window. Probably thinks I fell in my driveway again. I'm fine, Connie! I'm waving to her now. My daughter just gave me some great news! I'm okay!"

Ava couldn't help laughing and shaking her head at the two separate conversations happening at once, both from her mother.

"Oh, baby, I am *so, so* proud of you! This is amazing. Give me all the details."

"Well, I don't know a ton," Ava said, pulling out the package she'd received and looking it over for what felt like the hundredth time. "It starts in May and runs through mid-July. It's on the grounds of Liza Bennett-Schmidt's home upstate. There are five other attendees besides me. And we're gonna learn directly from her." She took a breath. "I'm going to learn from somebody who's not only a master at what she does—at what I do—but I'm going to learn from somebody I've *idolized* for my entire career, Mom." She swallowed a lump as unexpected tears welled up in her eyes. "I can't even believe it. This is a dream."

"Nobody deserves it more, my girl. Nobody."

Once she hung up from her mom, she called up Courtney's number and shot her a text.

Let me know when you're up. Have some news.

She set her phone down and busied herself doctoring her cup of coffee. Tonight's shift was gonna be rough because she was too wired to go back to sleep. Might as well start with the caffeine now. She was going to need it.

Her phone pinged and she turned to regard it with surprise, which only increased when she saw it was Courtney. As the head bartender at Pomp, her hours were nearly the same as Ava's.

I'm up, the text said.

OMG, why? Ava sent back.

Courtney's response was to send a GIF that featured a woman

dressed in club attire, carrying her high heels and tiptoeing out of a room.

"Oh my God," Ava said aloud, then sent a laughing emoji and typed, *ARE YOU DOING A WALK OF SHAME?* It was not at all unusual for Courtney to go home with—or take home—a customer she met at the bar during her shift. It always made Ava a little nervous, but Courtney was a badass and could take care of herself—which she'd mentioned to Ava more than once.

No shame in my game. Just don't wanna do morning small talk. Don't worry, I left a note. This was followed by a winking emoji. *Why are you up? What news? Everything okay? Your mom?*

Courtney was probably the closest thing to a sister Ava would ever have. They'd met at Pomp nearly eight years ago now and had hit it off immediately. They had the same taste in music and movies, and a healthy pride in their work. Courtney didn't call herself a bartender. She was a mixologist, and she took that title just as seriously as Ava took hers of pastry chef. There was a love and respect between them that was hard to come by in a city like New York.

Her phone rang in her hand, and she answered.

"Okay, I'm in the lobby of this dude's building. What's up? You okay?"

"You paused your escape for me? I'm honored," Ava said with a laugh. Then she told Courtney all about the retreat.

"Oh my God," Courtney squealed, and Ava could picture the doorman of the building—assuming there was one, though Courtney only went home with the kind of guys who had doormen—widening his eyes at her volume. "Holy shit! That's incredible! I thought you said it was a long shot."

"It was, trust me. I still can't believe it. I read somewhere that this year, they had nearly fifteen hundred applicants."

"And they chose you? A. Seriously. This is amazing. I'm so fucking proud of you. When is it?"

They spent a few minutes going over the details, the whole time Courtney throwing in little comments about how proud she was. Ava couldn't keep the smile off her face.

There was a moment where they stayed on the phone together in silence before Courtney spoke again. "So...how do you think Goldie will take it?"

Goldie was the restaurant manager of Pomp and Ava's boss. There was only one answer to that question, and they both knew it, answered simultaneously.

"Badly."

CHAPTER TWO

To say Regan felt like she was floating on a cloud the next morning was an understatement.

Nothing could get to her. Not the early hour. Not the guy on the subway who openly leered at her. Not the pile of garbage she had to walk around on the sidewalk. Not the gray, overcast sky or the threat of rain. Nothing could crap on her mood. She couldn't remember the last time she'd felt this light.

She flitted through the day, smiling, joking, and just basically feeling alive. Proud. Confident. When her lunch break hit, she asked Billy if she could have a word with him in his office.

He sat at his desk, his expression serious when she stepped inside and shut the door behind her, like he was waiting for a horrendous diagnosis from his doctor. "You're quitting, aren't you? Say it quick. It'll hurt less."

She shook her head and grinned at him as she pulled out a chair and sat. "I'm not quitting."

His whole body melted down to the surface of his desk in obvious relief. He looked up at her with his cheek still on the wooden surface of it. "Oh, thank God. I had no idea what I was gonna do."

"You're silly," she said. Then it was her turn to look serious. She swallowed, and it was loud.

Billy lifted his head, his relieved expression morphing into one of concern. "Are you all right? You're not...sick or something? What can I do? What do you need?"

The flood of love Regan felt for this man threatened to swamp her, and not for the first time, she wondered what she'd done in some other life to get so lucky. "No, I'm not sick, but I do need to take some time off."

Billy's thick brows met in a V above his nose. "Okay." He drew the word out, clearly waiting on more explanation.

Regan took a huge lungful of air and dove in. "I was accepted to the Bennett-Schmidt retreat this year."

Billy blinked at her. Blinked some more, and Regan could almost see the words and their meaning get absorbed into his brain, knew exactly when he understood by the way his eyes lit up. He practically jumped out of his chair, throwing his arms out wide. "What? *What?* Holy shit, Regan. I mean, *holy shit.* Do you know how hard it is to get into that retreat? She gets thousands of applicants. *Thousands.* Holy shit. You did it. *You did it!*" And then he was around the desk and wrapping her in his lanky arms, and before she could say a word, he tore open the door to his office and yelled out, "Everybody! Listen up. Regan was accepted to the Bennett-Schmidt retreat this year. Can you believe it?"

A rumble of conversation rolled through the bakery, which then transitioned into applause and cheers that grew in volume as employees from different parts of the building got the news and joined in. Soon, the entire work force of the bakery was cheering for her, coming up to her to shake her hand, give her a hug, congratulate her in some way. She knew all of them—the early-morning workers a bit better than the afternoon/evening workers—and her pride swelled as each of them showed how proud they were of her.

If she thought she'd been floating on her way to work, it didn't compare to the rest of the day. Billy told anybody who would listen about the retreat, explaining to longtime customers what it took to be accepted to the retreat, how proud he was of her. Billy didn't have kids, but Regan had always thought he would've made a great dad. Today only solidified that.

Despite the festive atmosphere in the bakery, she still did her job, spending the day making a list of things she was low on so Billy could get his order in on time, thinking up fresh ideas for next week's Deal of the Day, and then baking more rustic cherry tarts—because they'd been a huge hit yesterday—along with her signature lemon bars, some basics the bakery carried every day that included three kinds of cookies, some brownies, and blueberry muffins. And all day, her coworkers came up to her, hugged her, asked her questions about the retreat, told her how proud they were.

Regan had never felt such confidence or pride.

When two o'clock rolled around and she knew she needed to punch out, Billy stuck his head in the break room. "Hey, can you come down to the basement before you go? I want to check something with you quick."

"Sure. Lemme just change my shoes."

Billy gave a nod and disappeared, and Regan shook her head with a grin. Two lockers down, Jo, the cake decorator, shook her head, too.

"He loves to run things by you," she said, not unkindly. Jo had been with Billy since he opened the bakery more than twenty years ago, and she knew him better than pretty much anybody.

"He really doesn't need to," Regan said. "I rarely disagree with him."

"He trusts you. It's his way of showing you that." Jo slammed her locker shut and turned a gentle smile toward Regan. "You're like a daughter to him, you know." Then she squeezed Regan's shoulder as she passed her and headed out the break room door.

Regan cleared her throat of the unexpected lump that parked itself there. Alone in the break room, she took a second to gather herself. What a day, right?

Clean shoes on, white apron tossed into the laundry bag in the corner, she slung her backpack over her shoulder and headed for the basement, wondering if she should celebrate by ordering some Thai food for dinner.

The basement served many purposes. It was used for the storage of dry goods, it held the walk-in freezer, and it contained Jo's cake-decorating station. Regan reached the bottom of the stairs, and before she could register that there were more people down there, she was hit with an enormous cheer that startled her, making her take a step back, her heart pounding.

The entire bakery was there. Everybody, if Regan's eyes were correct. And then Billy was next to her, his arm around her shoulders. When she looked up at him in question, he bent down to her ear and said, "I put the Closed sign up for few minutes. This is more important."

By the time Regan made it home that day, she was a combination of so many things, she could hardly keep her thoughts organized. She was proud. Beyond-belief proud. She was happy, that was a given. Who wouldn't be? She was thrilled, because this was going to be incredible. She also felt more loved than she'd felt in a very long time, thanks to Billy and her coworkers. Billy had told her to take all the time she needed, that he'd find a way to make do until she returned.

She was pretty sure her feet never touched concrete on her way home, her arrival much later than normal. Artie was waiting at the door, meowing his disapproval of this new return time.

"I know, I know," she said, bending to scoop him up and lavish him with kisses of apology. "I'm very sorry, but it was a crazy day."

"Don't let him fool you." Brian's voice came from the kitchen. He entered the living room with a grin and a bottle of champagne. "This starving cat thing is an act. He ate dinner at his usual time. And you, my friend, are late." He was tall and handsome, a husky guy with a neat brown beard and the greenest, kindest eyes Regan had ever seen. She always told him that if she was in the hospital and he showed up with those eyes, she'd relax in a heartbeat. "But Kiki told me about the retreat, and I am so proud of you." He bent to kiss her cheek, then held up the bottle. "Celebration?"

"Why not?" Regan put her stuff down and slid off her jacket.

"Kiki ran to pick up Thai for dinner," Brian tossed over his shoulder as he went back to the kitchen for glasses, and Regan was reminded how much she adored her roommates.

"I'm gonna take a quick shower and call my parents, okay?" she called out, headed to her tiny bedroom. Once there, she closed the door and leaned back against it, still unable to fully absorb what was happening. She pulled out her phone and FaceTimed her mother, then propped the phone on her dresser so she had both hands free to give attention to Artie.

"Hi, honey," her mom said into the screen. She was clearly making dinner, her phone propped in the kitchen while she looked to be sautéing something.

"Hi, Mom. I have news."

She barely finished telling her mother about the retreat before the entire household was trying to cram their faces into the shot. Both of her parents, her little brother, her little sister, and her grandfather were all trying to talk at the same time, and Regan could see at least a sliver of each person's face. By the time Kiki knocked at her door to tell her the food was ready, Regan was laughing so hard, her sides hurt.

"All right, I've gotta go eat dinner. I'll tell you more when I find out more."

"We are so proud of you, honey," her father said, and she could see that his eyes were wet.

"Oh, Dad, don't cry. Okay? You're gonna make Mom all uncomfortable again." Still laughing, she said her goodbyes and hung up.

Artie was still hanging around, waiting for more attention, and she obliged him, putting her nose right up to his face so he could boop her with his. Then she sighed happily.

"What a day, huh, buddy?"

❖

Much as Ava was dreading talking to her boss, she knew she had to do it. She preferred to wait until the end of her shift, but that wouldn't be until after midnight, and Goldie was usually gone by then.

Ava sighed quietly as she hung her purse and jacket in her locker and donned her white chef's coat with the Pomp logo embroidered on the left breast in black and gold thread. It wasn't that Goldie Schaefer was bad at her job. She wasn't. She was actually a pretty excellent restaurant manager, and that wasn't an easy achievement at a five-star restaurant in New York City like Pomp. It was that Goldie was simply a miserable person in general. Nothing made her happy. She complained *a lot*. And making her employees feel less-than was something she seemed to shoot for on a daily basis. Kind of an "if I can't feel good, then nobody should" type of attitude. Ava had become pretty good at flying under the radar and avoiding any need for Goldie to seek her out, but today could change all that.

"Goldie? Hey." She rapped on the door frame of Goldie's open office door. "Can I talk to you for a sec?"

"That's about all I've got," Goldie said, not looking up from her phone. "Come."

Ava entered the office and stood with her hands clasped behind her back. She didn't take a seat because she'd done that once without being invited to, and she'd been called out on it.

Seconds ticked by and Goldie finally set her phone down. Her dark blond hair was pulled back in a neat though severe bun, and she was dressed in her usual black suit with a skirt and pumps, Ava knew even though she couldn't see below her waist, because Goldie wore the exact same thing every day. Ava imagined her closet at home, filled with black blazers and skirts, all lined up on hangers, the exact same amount of space between each one, probably measured precisely with a ruler, several pairs of black pumps in matching cubbies. But the suits gave Goldie the air of a person in charge, and she wore that well. Ava couldn't argue it.

"What's up, Prescott?" Goldie didn't call anybody by their first name. Ava always suspected it was her way of dehumanizing her employees so it was easier to be an asshole to them.

"Well," Ava said, tightening her hands behind her back in hopes of calming her nerves, "I have some good news."

"Oh, God, tell me you're not pregnant."

The words caught her off guard, and she blinked a couple times before saying, "Um, no. Nope. Not pregnant."

"That's a relief. I was afraid you were going to need an extended leave."

Shit.

"Well…" Ava cleared her throat. Goddamn it, she hated the way this woman made her feel. *Pull it together, Ava! You're a confident professional. Be one.* "I've been accepted into the Bennett-Schmidt retreat." At Goldie's perplexed expression, Ava reminded herself that if somebody wasn't in the pastry business, they might not know of the retreat, so she explained, finishing with, "It's a pretty big deal. Thousands of people apply, and only six are chosen. To learn new techniques from somebody as accomplished as Liza Bennett-Schmidt is…it's a once-in-a-lifetime opportunity." She almost said more but knew she'd be gushing at that point, so she had to make a conscious effort to stop talking right there, to let the words sit and to wait for Goldie's response. And to not smile too much because Goldie certainly wasn't.

It took a moment, and then Goldie took in a long, deep breath and let it out slowly. "Well," she said, then took another moment before she went on. "Eight weeks is a very long time. I'll need to figure out who takes your place. Probably Jen. I mean, who else knows the menu, right?"

Jen was Ava's pastry sous chef, and she was very capable. "Jen could definitely do it."

"You can get her trained on the big stuff, right?" Goldie tapped her finger against her lips, demonstrating how she was thinking. "She'll need help, which means I'll probably have to hire a temporary sous chef for her..." Goldie seemed to be thinking out loud rather than conversing with Ava, but she continued to stand there, not yet dismissed. "When will you need to leave?" They talked dates, Goldie doing more lip tapping, then she picked up her phone and scrolled what Ava assumed was her calendar. "Jesus, right into summer." She murmured that line, though not quietly enough that Ava didn't hear it, and sighed again, loudly.

Ava swallowed to avoid clearing her throat. And waited. And waited some more.

"Okay," Goldie finally said. "Got it."

Ava stood there and gave a nod, then wasn't sure what to do next. "Great. Okay. Thanks." She turned to leave, but a thought occurred to her then and she turned back, lifting her finger as she asked, "I...will still have a job afterward, won't I?"

Goldie lifted one shoulder in the most nonchalant of shrugs. "I guess we'll have to see."

"Oh." Ava swallowed again. "Okay then. Thanks." She left the office, and her blood began to boil, for so many reasons, but mostly for thanking Goldie after she basically told her she might not have a job to come home to. She got to her station and began doing her setup for the evening. One of the dessert specials was a chocolate soufflé. She'd made the batter ahead of time but now needed to work on the elements of presentation. It would be a good way to take her mind off what had just happened.

Jen normally arrived about an hour after Ava, mostly because Ava always showed up early. She liked getting a jump on things.

"Hey," Jen said when she'd sidled up next to Ava. "What needs to be done?"

Ava said hello and slid the list she'd made for Jen across the counter to her. She liked Jen. She was competent and did as she was asked without complaint. Once she had the cherry topping for the New York cheesecake warming in a pot, she turned her blue eyes to Ava. "What's new with you? You're quiet. Everything okay?"

Ava met her gaze. Jen was pretty in a plain sort of way. She had straight brown hair that she always wore in a ponytail. Her blue eyes were bright and free of makeup, and she had great skin. She was prone to smiling for no reason. Often, Ava would glance over at her while she was whipping cream or slicing fruit, and she'd have this soft smile on her face. She was easy to be around, and Ava liked her. "I got accepted into the Bennett-Schmidt retreat," she blurted, no introduction or preamble. Just a blurt.

And Jen, God bless her, her eyes went wide, and her mouth formed the shape of an O, and she clapped her hands together once, then threw her arms around Ava. "Oh my God! No way! That's so hard to get into. Ava! That's incredible!" She did nothing to keep her voice down or her excitement contained, and, for a brief moment, Ava almost shushed her, almost told her to keep it down. But she didn't. And now the chefs were looking, and the servers were watching, and a couple came up and wanted to know what the cheering was for and finally...finally...Ava felt proud. And she knew her coworkers were proud of her. It was the reaction she'd hoped to get from Goldie—which was stupid of her. But Jen had taken care of it, and soon Darren, the head chef, was popping a bottle of champagne he'd gotten from Courtney at the bar, and the whole kitchen and waitstaff lifted little plastic cups in her honor.

"What is going on here?" Goldie asked when she walked in on the toast.

Before she could express her disapproval, Darren shoved a plastic cup into her hands and said, "Our Ava has accomplished something huge. Toast her." And he gave her a look that Ava had seen him use on her before. It basically said *just shut up and smile and be nice for five minutes.* She suspected they were sleeping together, as Darren was the only member of the entire kitchen staff who didn't cower when she walked in. He was also the only one who immediately smiled at Goldie. It was kind of cute, even if it was her.

The celebration didn't last long, as they all had work to do, but Ava appreciated it so much. A bit of congratulations had been all she'd wanted from Goldie, but also, she should've known better. She was shaking her head at herself when Jen spoke up.

"I am so envious of you," she said as she mixed the batter for the cheesecake the cherries would be drizzled over. "Liza Bennett-Schmidt is, like, the idol of every pastry chef I know. She's a legend."

"Right?" Ava said, putting sugar into a pan to make a caramel sauce to go with the soufflés. "I'm ridiculously excited about it. And so, so nervous."

Jen gave a soft laugh. "Really?"

Ava stopped to look at her. "Of course. Why?"

"I mean, you're just always so stoic and put together. It's hard to know if you're excited or nervous or whatever."

Ava nodded and forced herself to smile. Jen wasn't wrong. She'd been raised to be calm, always. Getting boisterous about things didn't do any good, nor was it a good look, her father had always said. Calm, cool, collected. That's what he'd taught her. He was gone now, had been gone for a couple years at this point, and she knew her mother was doing her best to undo some of those habits he'd instilled in her, loosen her up, but they were hard to break, and both she and her mother knew it.

Jen came up closer to her and lowered her voice. "How did Goldie take it?"

Ava lifted a shoulder. "Fine, I guess. She was mostly annoyed." She met Jen's gaze. "She's gonna move you up, I think, have you cover my stuff and hire you a sous chef." She nibbled on the inside of her cheek before adding, "And it might end up permanent for you, I don't know."

Jen furrowed her light brow, and she shook her head. "Nah. That would be stupid of her." She kept shaking her head as she spoke. "Like, really stupid. She wouldn't fire you after you went to a famous, high-end retreat that's *literally* going to make you even better at what you already kick ass doing."

"I'm sorry, have you met Goldie?" Ava asked the question with a sly grin, but she was also serious. Goldie didn't take kindly to being inconvenienced, famous pastry retreat or not. There was a very good chance Ava would return after eight weeks and be unemployed.

CHAPTER THREE

"Oh, wow." Regan said it on a whisper from the back seat of the black Lincoln Town Car that had been sent to pick her up from the train station. As the driver turned through an open wrought iron gate with a sign that read Black Forest Hills, she could see glimpses of the house she'd be staying in for the next eight weeks. Well. House was an understatement. It was more the size of a mansion, but modern. Like a high-end resort, all wood and glass, sitting at the top of a set of rolling hills. "Wow," she said again.

"It's something, isn't it?" the driver asked. His name was Charlie, and he seemed to be a nice guy. He'd been waiting for her at the train station holding a sign with her name on it, just like in the movies. Kind of surreal.

"It's magnificent," she said, the awe clear in her voice. That wasn't a word she used often, but it felt appropriate here. She met Charlie's eyes in the rearview mirror. "Am I the first to arrive?"

"You're the third. Two are coming from the airport and one more arrives at the train station in about an hour."

She nodded and turned back to the view out the window. The property was gorgeous, and clearly well-maintained. She wondered how many gardeners Liza Bennett-Schmidt had to keep things so pristine. It was spring, mid-May, and a long row of lilac bushes were in full bloom alongside the driveway. The scent wafted into the car, even with the windows closed, sweet and lovely. Then the trees ended in a clearing, and the driveway led them around in a circle to the front steps of the most gorgeous house Regan had ever seen. She sat there gaping, even after Charlie had cut the engine and gotten out.

He opened her door and held out a hand to help her out. She stood, still staring at three stories of chestnut-colored siding and windows that were bigger than the entire bakery she worked in. She wondered if there were similar windows in the back and what the view must look like with the rolling hills of Rhinebeck stretched out back there.

Charlie got her bags out of the trunk of the car, then held his arm out to let her go first up the wide stairs to the front door, which opened before she had a chance to knock.

The woman was not Liza Bennett-Schmidt, but her smile was wide and kind. She wore black pants and a white shirt, and her brown hair was pulled back in a rather severe bun. She held out a hand and grasped Regan's.

"You must be Regan Callahan. It's so nice to meet you. I'm May. I run the household for Ms. Bennett-Schmidt. Come in, come in." She stepped back and allowed room for Regan to come into the most glorious...foyer? Entryway? Whatever it was called, it was straight out of a movie, with a grand staircase in front of her and ceilings that loomed higher than she could even guess at. The sunshine flooded in through the windows, and not a single speck of dust was visible. The place was grand, beautiful, and spotless.

"Let me show you to your room," May said, with a nod at Charlie. He went up the stairs first, carrying Regan's bags. To the left, down a hallway, and through an enormous wooden door that had to weigh hundreds of pounds. Inside, the bedroom was huge. Bigger than her entire apartment.

"Oh my God," she said before she could catch it.

May seemed pleased by that. "I trust the room meets your approval."

"And then some," Regan said. There were two queen-sized beds, one on either side of the room. Straight ahead was a doorway to a bathroom. The room was decorated in what Regan would describe as modern ski lodge chic, with an old pair of snowshoes on one wall and a landscape painting of deer out in the snow on the other. A heavy-looking dresser of maybe oak seemed to anchor each side of the room, accented by matching bedside tables. Thick, fluffy duvets blanketed each of the beds in clouds of softness. Each bed had at least six pillows. "This is incredible," Regan said, turning back to May. Charlie must've slipped out while she was gawking because her bags were next to the bed, but he was gone. "Thank you so much."

May shook her head with a wave. "Don't thank me," she said with a grin. "Take some time and freshen up, get used to your room. It's going to be yours for the next two months. There are two to a room, and your roommate will be here later." May glanced at the thin gold watch on her wrist, and Regan was surprised to see it was old-school and not a smartwatch of some kind. "Dinner is at six. Don't be late. Ms. Bennett-Schmidt doesn't like to be kept waiting."

Regan nodded. "Got it."

"Welcome to Black Forest Hills," May said, then turned and left, pulling the door closed behind her.

Regan turned back to the room. "Holy shit," she said, and kept her voice down, despite how much she wanted to shout the words at the top of her lungs. "Holy shit," she said again. And then she started to laugh.

She laughed and laughed until she fell onto the bed, still laughing, because holy shit, how had she gotten here? This was going to be incredible.

She spent the next half hour unpacking a few of her things and getting them organized. The bathroom was just as impressive as the bedroom itself, with both a glass-enclosed shower and a large garden tub. The tub had a huge window next to it. "Nothing like soaking your troubles away while taking in the view and the wildlife," she murmured as she unpacked her toiletries. There were two sinks, so she organized all her things near one of them, leaving the other for her roommate.

At almost five o'clock, she took a very hot shower, amazed by how much room there was. Way more than the tiny shower she shared with Kiki and Brian, where she basically had to become a contortionist just to shave her legs. She took her time, enjoying the space and the hot water and the view, which she could see from the shower if she looked toward the tub. She'd never been somebody whose goal was to be rich, but seeing how the rich lived was pretty eye-opening already, and she'd literally only been in three rooms so far.

She'd read all the literature that had come with her acceptance multiple times, signed all the required forms and turned them in, and packed accordingly. While there was no dress code for dinner, she wanted to look neat, so she stepped into a lightweight pair of yellow pants, then put on a white short-sleeved button-up. She'd made sure to have her highlights done before she arrived, knowing she wouldn't be able to get back to her hair stylist for two months, and now she fluffed it up, checked it in the mirror. Her hair had always been a plain, boring brown, but two years ago, when she'd turned thirty and had a bit of an existential crisis, she'd found that putting some blond highlights in it made her feel a bit hipper, a bit younger. So now she did that regularly and really liked it. Her hair wasn't long, just long enough to tuck behind her ears, a length she'd chosen because it was perfect with the oval shape of her face, and also because it was kept out of the way when she worked. Nobody wanted to find a hair in their tiramisu.

The bed on the other side of the room was still untouched, and no bags had shown up while she was in the shower, so she figured her roommate hadn't arrived yet. A glance at her phone told her it was almost six, so she tucked it into a pocket, hung up her wet towel, then pulled her door open, and realized she had no idea where the dining room was.

"How hard can it be to find?" she murmured to herself just as another door opened across the hall and a gorgeous Black woman in white pants and a floral print top met her in the hallway. Behind her, Regan saw a flash of pink hair, along with a purple bandanna tied around her neck, and then another woman joined them in the hall. "Hi," Regan said. "Are you guys here for the retreat?"

The Black woman nodded and extended her hand. "I'm Vienna. This is Maia," she said.

"Regan." She shook both their hands, then asked with a grin, "Any idea where the dining room is?"

Deciding they could likely find it, they headed toward the huge staircase together. "Don't you have a roommate?" Maia asked.

Regan nodded. "Not here yet, I guess."

Finding the dining room, as they suspected, proved to be pretty easy. They followed the smell of food and the gentle clinking of dishware until they came to a huge room with a table the size of a yacht.

Holy shit ran through Regan's head for about the forty-seventh time that day, but she managed to keep the words locked in her head, thank God.

The table looked like it could seat about twenty people or more, but there were only three place settings on each side near one end, and then a place setting at the head of it.

"Welcome," May said as she appeared seemingly out of nowhere. "I hope you're hungry. Our chefs have prepared a virtual feast." She indicated the table. "There are place cards for each of you, so go ahead and find your seat."

As the three of them moved toward the table, two more women came into the room.

"Ah, welcome," May said again, then gave the newcomers the same instructions, and soon, the five women were seated at their places, roommates across the table from each other. Vienna sat on Regan's right, then a very petite woman named Paige sat on the other side of her. Across from Regan was an empty chair, then Maia, of the pink hair, then a woman with a super-friendly smile who'd introduced herself as Madison.

"So?" Madison asked. "Where are we all from? I live just outside of Chicago. Born and raised."

"New Orleans," Vienna said, using her fingers to give a little wiggle-wave.

"I'm from Portland, but live in San Diego now," said Paige.

"Denver," Maia said, raising her hand.

It was Regan's turn. "I was born in Cleveland and my family's still there, but I work in a bakery in New York City."

"Oh, very cool," Madison said.

"You're from all over the country." A new voice chimed in. It was firm and authoritative, and it belonged to Liza Bennett-Schmidt herself. A collective gasp went around the table at the sight of her, as if all five of them had been surprised. Regan certainly was.

She did her best not to gawk, but it was so hard. After all, this was a woman she'd idolized for most of her adult life and a good portion of her teenage years, when she'd started to realize she might want baking to be some kind of a career.

Liza was fifty-eight but barely looked out of her forties. Kind of shocking for somebody who worked with—and one could only assume sampled—sweets all day. There was probably a trainer involved, along with hair and makeup. Living in New York City, Regan had seen more than her share of celebrities on the street or even in her bakery, just going about their day like normal people, and for the first year or two, it always surprised her how normal they all looked without their styling entourage following them around. How regular.

That was not the case with Liza. Not tonight. She looked incredible. She wore a flowing jumpsuit in ivory that flattered her smooth, flawless skin. A minimal yet elegant gold hairpin softly pulled back her auburn hair, and her jewelry—dangling earrings and a thin bracelet—was simple and elegant. A uniformed gentleman appeared out of nowhere and pulled her chair out for her, and Regan marveled yet again over how the staff seemed to materialize out of thin air.

Regan remembered watching *Whisk Me Away* on the Food Network for years when she was just out of high school and then in college. She'd attended a community college and planned her classes around episodes of *Whisk Me Away* until she was able to find them online and watch at her leisure. She'd learned so much from that show, from basic desserts like cookies and cakes to fancier stuff like soufflés and crème brûlée. For a baker who never had any kind of pastry schooling, Liza's show was like a daily class, and Regan had soaked up as much as possible from the woman now standing right in front of her.

The five of them were mesmerized by Liza, that much was clear, and Regan felt better realizing she wasn't the only one trying not to stare. *I cannot believe I'm here* ran on a loop through her head.

Liza seemed to take a moment to look at each of them, and Regan had to work hard not to squirm when it was her turn. "Welcome to Black Forest Hills," Liza said. "It's been my home for about five years now, and I'm so glad you're here."

Murmured thank-yous went around the table, and Liza paused to receive them before she continued. Another member of the waitstaff appeared then with a bottle of wine and proceeded to fill each person's glass, emptying one bottle and uncorking another before he was finished.

"Tonight, we will dine and drink and get to know each other a bit. Tomorrow will be the beginning of your retreat. So don't drink too much." At that, she grinned. "I want you fresh as daisies in the morning." She held up her glass. "To this year's Bennett-Schmidt retreat and its participants. May it be memorable."

They had to stand up to reach across the table and touch glasses, but they did it, laughing the whole time as they stretched, then sat down and sipped. Regan hummed her approval, as did Vienna next to her, and then salads appeared in front of them.

"So." Liza picked up her fork and pointed it at them before stabbing a cherry tomato with it. "Let's get to know one another." The cherry went into her mouth, and her eyes landed on Regan. "You. Tell us about you."

"Oh. Okay." Regan felt a jolt of nervous adrenaline shoot through her veins as all eyes turned to focus on her. "Um, I'm from Cleveland." She gave a weak fist pump. "Go Browns." Then she closed her eyes. "Oh, God, I can't believe I said that. Ignore me. The Browns suck. Um…" She cleared her throat.

Liza gave a soft chuckle. "No need to be nervous. We're going to be spending the next two months together. These are going to be very close friends by the end of that time."

"Right. Right. Sorry. Well, I'm from Cleveland, but I've been in New York City for the past ten years. I started in a five-star restaurant, and now I am the head pastry chef at a pretty well-known bakery. I love being creative, coming up with new ideas and new flavor combinations. I'm self-taught, so I'm used to experimenting."

"And what are your goals?" Liza asked. "Let's say for the somewhat near future. The next five years or so."

"Oh, um…my boss is getting ready to retire, I think, and when he does, he'll want to sell. I'd really like to buy—"

Before she could finish, the giant sliding wooden doors to the dining room—which had been closed at some point Regan hadn't noticed—slid open with a rumble that she could feel in her feet. May and Charlie were both on the other side.

"Your sixth is here, Ms. Bennett-Schmidt," May said and stood back to let the last attendee enter the room.

Whatever Regan had been saying flew out of her head at the sight of the tall brunette standing in the doorway.

"I'm so sorry," she said, somewhat breathless, her cheeks flushed pink. "I missed my train because my boss had me working today, and I had to catch the next one, but it had some mechanical difficulties and…" The woman let her voice trail off, maybe realizing that her excuse meant very little. She glanced down at her feet as her cheeks flushed. "I'm very sorry."

Liza waited a beat, and Regan wondered if that was intentional to make her stew, and holy crap, how uncomfortable. A heartbeat later, she blinked and stood. "No worries at all. You can't control the trains, right?" She waved at the empty chair across the table from Regan. "Please. Sit. You must be famished." The woman murmured a thank-you and came into the room where the waiter pulled the chair out for her.

"Ladies," Liza said, "our last attendee. Ava Prescott."

Ava smiled uncertainly, clearly embarrassed. She got herself situated at her seat and looked up and around the table, giving a slight nod to each woman. When her eyes stopped on Regan, they went sightly wide in what looked like shocked surprise.

Regan looked back at her but didn't smile. She had no smiles for this woman. None. Three words kept playing themselves in a loop through her brain.

Ava Fucking Prescott.

❖

Excited.

Frustrated.

Furious.

Proud.

Embarrassed beyond belief.

Flabbergasted.

Ava had been feeling all of those emotions on a running loop for the whole of that day. She couldn't seem to make her brain understand how what should have been the most amazing day of her adult life could also be one of the absolute worst. How was that even possible?

Luckily, she'd only missed the salad portion of dinner. She wasn't happy that she hadn't had a chance to freshen up first. She was pretty sure she had hat hair left over from what was supposed to be her half day at work—Goldie had asked her to come in and work a day shift in place of the evening shift she was going to miss—that had turned into closer to a full day. Thank fucking God she'd had the smarts to bring her bags to work, just in case Goldie did exactly what she'd done. If nothing else, Ava knew her boss well.

She'd gotten through dinner with a minimum of additional embarrassment, and she'd even managed not to dwell too much on the fact that Regan Callahan was seated directly across from her. It had been years, but she'd never forget those blue eyes...or the way they could throw daggers. Very sharp, very slicey daggers.

Dinner finished, Liza suggested they all head up for an early night, being they'd all traveled and the retreat would begin in the morning.

"I trust you all will sleep well. Also, there are gifts in your rooms. Bring your recipes with you. Also, I have a full fitness room off the kitchen. Feel free to use it at any time. If there's something you're missing, don't hesitate to ask May." Liza gestured to the woman standing in the corner dressed in black and white. Ava hadn't even realized she was there. With that, Liza stood and exited the room through the door behind her seat where the waitstaff had come through.

May moved toward the table. "Breakfast will be right here at seven sharp. Sleep well."

Clearly dismissed, they all pushed their chairs back and stood, voices low. They filed out of the dining room and up the grand staircase that Ava had only had time to glance at when she'd arrived. Her bags were gone, Charlie having told her he'd take them to her room, but she had no idea where that was. At the top of the stairs, she watched as the girl with pink hair and the Black woman headed into the same room. Then the super-cheerful one and the tiny one headed into another. That only left Regan.

A sigh. "Yeah, you're in here with me, I guess." Regan didn't wait for a response, just opened the door to her room.

Ava stood in the doorway. Her bags were there next to the bed up against the right-hand wall. She stifled her own sigh.

Well, hell.

White chef's coats hung at each of their dressers, their names embroidered in red on the left pocket area. Ava crossed to hers and ran a hand over it, feeling a surge of pride well up in her. When she glanced over at Regan, she looked the same way—soft smile on her pretty face, puffed-up chest.

She stood there for a moment until Regan turned and collapsed onto the bed on the left, then reached for her phone.

Releasing a quiet breath, Ava shut the door behind her. They were in here together for the night, whether they liked it or not.

Regan continued to scroll on her phone, not looking up, so Ava took the opportunity to glance around. It was a sizable room—it had to be to fit two queen beds, two dressers, two nightstands, and two desks. She crossed the room to peer into the bathroom. Expensive and gorgeous, and Ava figured she could fit four, maybe five, of her own bathrooms inside this one. She looked longingly at the enormous soaking tub but reminded herself she was there to bake, and there likely wouldn't be any time to soak. But who knew? Maybe there would.

Hauling her suitcase up onto the bed, she said, "I'm gonna take a shower, if that's okay." Why? Why was she asking anybody—Regan Callahan, of all people—for permission to shower?

As if privy to her thoughts, Regan lifted one shoulder in a shrug and didn't look up from her phone.

Yeah. Taking her toiletries and pajamas into the bathroom with her, Ava shut the door tightly, locked it, and blew out a long, steady breath, one she felt like she'd been holding all day long.

What a fucking disaster today had been. She was spent. Exhausted. Frustrated. She had nothing left. If Goldie showed up in front of her right now, Ava would punch her in her stupid fucking face. As it stood in that moment, she was reasonably sure she wouldn't have a job when she returned, and she honestly didn't know how she felt about that.

A sure sign of her exhaustion.

She took the hottest shower she could stand, wanting nothing more than to wash the entire day off her skin, out of her hair. She soaped and scrubbed and shaved until her skin was red from the heat and she'd grown sleepy. Once out, she brushed her teeth, slathered lotion on what would end up being very dry skin after such hot water, and dried her hair. Then she put on her pajama pants and T-shirt and finally exited the bathroom, the wet heat following her out.

Regan, now in boxer shorts and a tank that Ava assumed were her pajamas, pushed off her bed with a muttered "About time" and went into the bathroom, clicking the lock behind her.

Oh, yeah, this is gonna be awesome.

Ava shook her head and took the moment of solitude to unpack and put her things into the dresser drawers. A glance across the room told her that Regan had not done the same. Her suitcase lay open on the floor, a mess of fabrics and colors spilling out of it like paint. Instantly, she had a flash of flour on the floor and trails and drips of chocolate ganache along the counters. Apparently, some things never changed.

By the time the bathroom door opened and Regan came out, Ava was tucked into bed, sitting up and reading. She watched over the rim of her glasses as Regan crawled across her own bed, pushed under the covers, and picked her phone back up. Then she grabbed a small white case from the nightstand, pushed AirPods into her ears, and lay down.

Okay. Good talk.

Which was fine. Ava didn't really know what to say to this woman, so she was perfectly fine letting it all go. For now. Because there was no way they could live like this for eight weeks. No way. It crossed her mind to ask Liza tomorrow if she could switch rooms with somebody, but she'd already shown up late for the retreat *and* been late for dinner on top of that. She'd pretty much used up any good graces Liza might've had for her. She'd have to earn some back.

And so she would. Simple as that.

Switching out her Kindle for her phone, she sent a quick text to Courtney.

You're never gonna believe this. Guess who my roommate is.

The gray dots bounced, telling her Courtney was typing back. *Cate Blanchett.*

Ava gave a quiet snort. "I wish." *No.*

I give. Who?

Ava looked over her glasses again, but Regan was all hunkered down, so all she could see was her golden brown hair. *Remember Regan Callahan, the one who worked with me a few years ago?*

Courtney typed back, *Aww, that cute one? The one you fired?*

Ava sighed. *Hey, *I* did not fire her.*

Except you did, tho...

Ava gave her head a shake, not wanting to debate semantics. *Whatever. But, HER. She's my roommate.*

Courtney sent a string of emoji, most with some kind of surprised face.

I know, right?

The dots bounced. *You can't really ask to switch. You're already on the shit list for being late.*

Ava nodded, even though Courtney couldn't see her, appreciating that she got it. *It'll be fine. I'll figure it out. But what a small world, huh?*

The tiniest. Just don't kill her in her sleep.

Ava grinned, typed, *No promises*, and sent a knife emoji, then said good night. Setting her phone back on the nightstand, she gazed across the room at Regan.

It would be fine. They were adults. This wasn't high school. She wasn't there to play games. She wasn't there to make friends. She was there to learn and become even better at her craft, so that was what she was going to do.

Regan Callahan be damned.

Chapter Four

The atmosphere in the dining room the next morning was filled less with nerves and trepidation than it had been the previous night and more with anxious anticipation and excitement. Regan could feel it in the air almost as clearly as if it had been tangible, like she could scoop it out of the emptiness in front of her.

Because of her usual business hours, she'd woken up very early and taken advantage of that. Making less noise than a character in the movie *A Quiet Place*, she managed to shower and dress without waking Ava and, glad she hadn't been forced into some kind of morning small talk with the woman, she left the dark room to find coffee.

Paige and Madison were on their way down the staircase, so Regan joined them and made a trio.

"Bakery?" Madison asked, and Regan nodded with a grin.

"You?"

"Yup. Both of us."

Paige grinned. "I'm usually up and headed to work by three thirty."

Liza Bennett-Schmidt must've understood that because the three found freshly brewed coffee on the buffet along a wall in the dining room. There was also a plate of scones that still had steam coming off them, a pile of fresh fruit, blueberry muffins that were also still warm, a tall, stainless steel pot marked Hot Water, and a selection of teas.

Regan went for the scones immediately, something she always sampled when given a chance. Scones could be difficult to get just right, and she'd met several bakers who didn't subscribe to her "everything must be cold" rule around them.

Madison took a bite of a muffin and began to hum her delight. Paige did the same, then they moved to the scones. They looked to Regan, who nodded. No words were spoken, but it was clear the three of them approved of the baked goods. Which only made sense, considering whose house they were currently standing in.

By the time the three of them had coffee and a second pastry, Maia, Vienna, and Ava wandered in.

"Ugh," Maia said with a groan as she stumbled toward the coffee. "How is life even allowed to happen this early?"

Madison, clearly taking on the role of social director, said, "We all work bakery hours. You guys?"

"The restaurant where I work is open from four until midnight," Vienna said, adding a disturbing amount of sugar to her coffee.

Ava poured a cup of her own and spoke quietly—one of the things Regan remembered very clearly about her. She was soft-spoken, but volume meant nothing. If you didn't live up to her standards, you'd know it. "Mine too. I'm usually there around three."

Maia added her two cents. "I work in the kitchen at a five-star hotel, and I don't start until five. I work until one in the morning."

There was a moment of quiet, when everybody was chewing or sipping or doing her best to wake up. Then Maia said, "You guys know a couple years ago, Liza gave away a shit ton of money at this retreat, right?"

Murmurs went around the room.

"It was a surprise, wasn't it?" Vienna asked.

Maia nodded. "The contestants showed up to learn and were told that one of them was gonna get a chunk of money, and she'd decide who."

"Just random like that?" Madison asked. "Why?"

Maia shrugged. "Girl's swimming in money. Gotta do something with it, right?"

"The whole thing is always kept all hush-hush," Vienna said. "Mysterious. I guess that's why there were NDAs in the packets."

"Yeah, that was odd," Madison said, wrinkling her nose. "Definitely mysterious."

"Nothing wrong with a little mystery," Maia said.

Before they could talk any more about the money or their lives or where they'd each come from, Liza breezed in, looking like she'd been up for hours, fresh and ready to go. Her pants were a champagne color, her top a rich ivory, and her auburn hair was loose and flowing today, hanging well past her shoulders in waves of fire and sunset. May entered behind her in her same black-and-white attire from the day before.

"Good morning, chefs," Liza said with cheer. "I'm glad to see you all bright-eyed and bushy-tailed. I'm afraid our bakery employees had a bit of an advantage over our evening restaurant workers, but that will even out in time." She clasped her hands together and let them hang in front of her. "Today, you will meet your assistants."

A slight hum of surprise rumbled through the six of them. Assistants? This was news to Regan.

"That's right," Liza went on. "Some of the things we'll learn and bake and create over these next two months will be complicated, so you'll each be assigned an assistant, a sous chef, to help. Trust this person with all your ideas and creativity; they're here for you, to make your life easier."

Regan glanced around the table, and each of the other attendees seemed both surprised and pleased, just as she was. Even Ava had a pleasant expression on her face.

"We have a busy first day ahead of us, so if you need something more substantial for breakfast, please let May know, and she'll have the chefs whip something up for you. Eggs. Oatmeal. Pancakes. Whatever. Just say the word." Liza looked at the sparkling gold watch on her slim wrist. "We'll meet at the bottom of the staircase at ten o'clock, and I'll take you to your workspaces." With a laser sharp look toward Ava, she added, "Don't be late. And wear your chef coats."

Ava nodded and said nothing, but her cheeks each blossomed a circle of pink.

She was still stupidly pretty. Regan had thought so the second she'd walked into the dining room last night. Even harried and nervous and frazzled, she was gorgeous. Dark hair, dark eyes, and a smile that could light up a room because it didn't happen often, so when it did, it seemed to have extra wattage. Those were other things Regan remembered about her. She wasn't tall, she was average, maybe five foot five or six, but she commanded attention when she walked in, so she felt taller. People turned to look. Regan always wondered if Ava knew that, knew that she literally turned heads.

Stop it, her brain said, and she gave her head a little shake. *Looks aren't everything.* She'd learned that a long time ago.

Back in the present, the six of them had some time, so they lingered.

"Well, I don't know about the rest of you," Vienna said, "but I could use some protein to get me through what I think is gonna be a long and possibly stressful day." She gestured to May and asked if the chef could maybe make her some scrambled eggs and bacon.

"Of course," May said. "Anybody else?"

They all exchanged glances around the table before adding their orders. Eggs and bacon for Maia and Paige as well. Oatmeal for Madison. Yogurt and fruit for both Regan and Ava, who glanced at each other when they asked for the same thing. Ava gave her an uncertain smile. Regan looked away.

❖

The combination of excitement and nerves was palpable. Ava had never quite understood that phrase until that very moment when May met the six of them, all dressed in white coats, at the stairs and led them down a long hall, past the kitchen, down some stairs, and out into a huge, sunlit room, floor-to-ceiling windows on both sides.

Murmurs of delight and awe tickled through the group as they took in the sight. Six workstations, three on either side, stood before them, pristine in their whiteness. At the front was a seventh workstation, and Ava could only assume that was where Liza would be. Several refrigerators in bright red lined the back wall, along with shelves that held various small appliances, spices, utensils, fruits and veggies. Name plaques affixed to the end of each counter indicated who would be working where.

"Feel free to check out your workspaces," May said. "Chef Bennett-Schmidt will be here momentarily."

The women wandered farther into the enormous room, each finding their place. On the left, Maia, Ava behind her, and Paige behind Ava. On the right, Vienna, Regan behind her, and Madison behind her. Regan's workstation was directly across from Ava. Not close, but not far.

Ava pulled out drawers to see what kinds of tools she had to work with. She opened the oven, checked the proofing drawer, and turned the red KitchenAid mixer on and off.

"Good morning, chefs." Liza Bennett-Schmidt floated into the workspace, the way she seemed to get anywhere, as if she entered every room on a hoverboard. She stood in front of the head workspace and held her arms out from her sides. "Well? What do we think?"

A little rumble of murmurs went through the chefs, everybody smiling.

"I thought about having this all built in tent form outside, like they have on *The Great British Baking Show*, but since we're starting on the very edges of spring, I thought it would be better for everybody—as well as the pastries—to be in a temperature-controlled environment." She seemed to give them a moment to absorb her words before she continued. "As I said last night, we're going to be making some complicated creations, and therefore, I want you all to have an extra set of hands, the way you would in a high-end restaurant or bakery." With that, she stood to the side and held one arm out like she was Vanna White presenting a grand prize. Six women in white chef's coats filed in and took their places next to each workstation.

The woman who stopped next to Ava was about the same height as her with red hair and freckles. She smiled and held out a hand.

"Hi. I'm Becca. It's great to meet you."

"Ava." They shook hands.

She glanced to her left to see Regan shaking hands with a tall and lean brunette.

Liza spoke again. "Take some time, get to know your assistants. And assistants, get to know your chefs. Understanding how they operate in the kitchen will be key to you helping or hurting them during projects. I will return in thirty minutes, and we will make our first dessert."

Finally!

Ava was psyched. "I wonder what we're gonna make first," she said, not really to Becca, but since she was standing right there, okay. To Becca.

"Me too. I have no idea." There was an awkward beat before Becca added, "So, where are you from? What do you do?" Then she snorted a laugh. "I mean, I know what you do, obviously, duh." She blushed and it was super clear on her pale skin.

Ava pulled out drawers and took a more thorough look at the tools provided. "Well, I'm from Northwood, upstate, but I work in New York City at a restaurant called Pomp."

"Oh! I've heard of Pomp!" Becca's enthusiasm was actually kind of sweet. If Ava had to guess, she wasn't a whole lot younger than Ava's own thirty-five years, but her excitement made her seem more in her twenties. "Never been there but would love to go sometime."

Ava didn't add that if Becca got to go, she probably wouldn't be the pastry chef there any longer. "So, how did you get here?"

"Oh, we all applied to the retreat." Becca waved an arm, and Ava realized it was meant to encompass the other sous chefs. "Liza picked us for this instead." She shrugged, as if she didn't quite get it either.

"Wow. I didn't even realize that was a thing."

Becca nodded. "Yup."

Conversation stalled momentarily, mostly because Ava was so painfully bad at small talk. "So, um, what about you? Where are you from and stuff?" *And stuff? Jesus, Ava, way to be creative.* She managed not to roll her eyes at herself. Instead, she leaned against the counter and forced herself to pay attention.

"I'm from North Carolina. Near Charlotte. I own a really nice restaurant there."

"You own it?"

"Mm-hmm."

"That's impressive."

"Thanks. Takes up about ninety-five percent of my life," she said with a soft laugh, "but yeah. I love it."

Ava loved her job. She loved working in a restaurant, loved the bustle and busyness of it, how it worked like a beehive, with the worker bees doing their individual jobs and the queen bee overseeing and the lot of them producing deliciously sweet and golden honey. But she could not imagine doing Goldie's job. Being the queen bee? It sounded good in theory, but managing all those people? No, thanks.

"So? What do you think Liza will have you make first?"

"That is an excellent question I wish I had the answer to." She'd been scanning all the ingredients on the back shelves, hoping for a clue, but it seemed like the inventory pretty much covered anything.

"What do you love to make?" Becca asked, her blue eyes twinkling with curiosity.

"That, my friend, is a very broad question." Ava grinned. "I mean, what *don't* I love to make?"

"Okay, then that."

"What?"

"What *don't* you love to make?"

"Pie crust," Ava answered without missing a beat.

Becca blinked, then kind of snort-laughed. "Pie crust? Random. Why?"

"Because I suck at it. I can't get it to be flaky without it also being dry. Mine always ends up dry."

Paige spoke up from behind her. "Oh God, me too," she said with a frown. "No matter what I do, I can't seem to get it right, and it messes with my head." She sighed.

"I get that. Pie crust is hard," Ava said. "Took me a long time, and I still struggle with it." She held out a fist for Paige to bump. "To the pie crust failures." Paige grinned at her and bumped.

As Becca mimicked Ava from earlier and began to pull out drawers and examine their tools, she said, "So, I'm here to help you in whatever way you need. Don't hesitate to give me something to do, okay?"

"I'll remember that," Ava said.

"Good." Becca went back to checking out all the gadgets.

Ava glanced across the way to see Regan chatting with her assistant. She said something and the assistant threw her head back and laughed heartily, and that's when Regan met Ava's eyes, held them for a beat before letting them go and returning her attention to the laughing assistant.

A weird flutter tickled low in her body.

"You know her?" Becca asked, clearly having seen the whole thing.

Ava forced her attention back to their own kitchen space. "Nope. Not at all."

❖

Regan's assistant's name was Hadley, and she had a great laugh. Loud and contagious, the best kind. An easy laugher was somebody Regan wanted to be around, and she and Hadley had meshed right away.

"What do you think Liza will have us make first?" Hadley asked, rubbing her hands together, clearly ready for their first bake. Then she rested her forearms on the counter.

"No idea," Regan said honestly, following suit so they were in twin positions. "I can't decide if she'll go easy first or dive right into the complicated stuff."

"I bet she goes in between."

"You think?"

Hadley lifted one shoulder and spoke very softly. "It would make sense. Can't go too easy, that's a waste of time 'cause she already knows you're good at your job. That's how you got here. But if she goes too difficult right out of the gate, she could destroy your confidence. Hmm." She pursed her lips.

The two of them stayed that way for several moments, each lost in her own thoughts. Finally, Hadley pushed herself to standing, and so did Regan. "So, ever heard of anybody here?" She scanned the room.

"Me?" Regan asked. "No. Not really."

"Not really? What does that mean?"

Regan used her eyes to point in Ava's direction. "I worked for her years ago. So I know her but don't really *know* her. You know?"

Hadley laughed that laugh. "You're funny."

"Well, looks aren't everything," Regan said, using a line her father used often. "What about you? Know anybody here?"

Hadley shook her head. "Nope. I don't think any of these people would even know where in Missouri my bakery is."

"You have your own?"

"Yup. Very small. Just me and three other people, but we do okay."

"Pretty impressive that you caught Liza's eye."

Hadley gave a modest shrug. "Thanks. What about you?"

"I work in a bakery, too. I don't own it, but I've been there for years, and my boss, the owner, is ready to retire. I'd love to buy the place from him, but…" She sighed and shook her head. "I'm not sure I have the financial capability to do that. Not in New York City." It was her turn to shrug.

Before they could delve more deeply into that—and Regan was thankful for the interruption—Liza was back, and the gentle murmur of conversation faded into silence. This time Liza, too, wore a chef's coat, and she took her place behind the front counter, her own assistant moving to stand next to her.

"Hello, chefs." She smiled as her gaze moved from person to person. "You may remember Corinna, my sous chef from *Whisk Me Away*." She gestured to the tall woman next to her. Corinna had piercing blue eyes and short, dark hair, slicked back and tucked behind her ears.

"I loved her on the show," Regan whispered to Hadley. "I always got the impression she didn't miss a thing, even though she never said much."

Next to her, Hadley nodded. "Same."

"So." Liza clapped her hands together. "I thought we'd start out with one of my favorite desserts." Behind her was one of the red refrigerators, and Corinna opened and pulled out a gorgeous cake of three clear layers, its white frosting only between the layers and on the top, leaving the golden brown cake visible. Regan whispered it as Liza said it. "Carrot cake."

"Oof," Hadley said next to her in a low voice. "Deceptive cake. Looks easy. Isn't."

"No problem," Regan whispered back. "I got this."

"Yeah?"

"Absolutely."

Liza was talking about the cake. "There's a fine line between carrot cake being perfectly moist and too soggy, so keep that in mind. I expect your cream cheese frosting to be tangy and sweet, just the right thickness. Not too much, but not too little. Corinna will work on mine while I wander and see how you're all doing. And remember this." She raised her voice here. "You're here to learn, so don't hesitate to ask questions. Now get started."

Each baker got to work. In front of her, Regan noticed, Vienna had a binder with her that was packed full of stuff. Everybody else used their phones, Regan included. When Vienna glanced over her shoulder and saw Regan looking, she grinned. "What can I say? I'm old school."

Regan grinned back. "Not a thing wrong with that."

"A bit messy," Liza said as she wandered, hands clasped behind her back. "Also makes it easier to steal your secrets, hacks, and ideas."

Regan couldn't see Vienna's face but noticed she kept her head down.

Across from Regan, Ava was already gathering ingredients and setting them on her counter, and Regan realized that if any of them had peeked into the refrigerators when they initially got there, they'd have likely seen all the carrots and figured out they were making carrot cake.

Ah, well. It's not a competition, she thought. *You're not on* Spring Baking Championship *or something.* She scrolled on her phone until she found her go-to carrot cake recipe, then set it on the counter so Hadley could see it too.

"Oh!" Liza's voice cut through the din of prep work. She stood centered between the rows of workstations and held up her hands as if she'd just remembered an important detail. "One more thing." The bakers all stopped and turned their attention to her. "I know this is a retreat and you're here to learn, that it's not a game or a competition. However..."

Oh, shit.

Regan braced because she'd read rumors, remembered what Maia had said, and she'd wondered.

"At the end of this retreat, I'll give a hundred thousand dollar check to the pastry chef who impresses me the most with their work." She waved a dismissive hand, as nonchalant as could be, as if she'd simply told them it was going to rain that day. "Okay. Back to carrot cake."

Just like that, the atmosphere in the room changed. The chefs exchanged glances, lots of mouths hanging open, frozen stances, disbelief clear on their faces.

"Holy shit," Hadley said quietly. "Did you see that coming?"

"I mean, I know she's done it before," Regan said, keeping her voice low. "But no. I thought she'd have said something last night. Holy shit is right."

The last time this had happened was three retreats ago. The pastry chef who'd won had used the money to open her own restaurant in Phoenix. It was now one of the top restaurants in the Southwest.

"What would you do with that kind of money?" Hadley asked.

Regan didn't even have to think about it. "I'd buy the bakery I work in when my boss retires next year."

Hadley nodded. "Very cool. Well," she glanced around, "let's make some kick-ass carrot cake, then." She held up her hand for a high five.

"I like the way you think," Regan said, slapping the hand. "Let's do this."

❖

Everything was suddenly different now.

Ava was so many things. Surprised. Excited. Nervous. Determined. A little bit annoyed. She tried hard not to think about what she could do with a hundred thousand dollars, but opening her own little boutique wine bar that served only wine and desserts—desserts she made herself—was first on the list. Of course, trying not to think about it only made her think about it, and she was interchanging different décor in her mind when Becca spoke.

"Should we get started? What can I do?"

Ava snapped back to the present. "Sorry. Yes. Absolutely. Let's get moving." They scanned the recipe Ava used most often, then split up to gather ingredients and bring them back to their workspace. She tried not to track where in the room Liza was at every second.

Carrot cake was well known and quite popular, in Ava's experience, but it could be tricky as well. You had to decide in the beginning just how dense you wanted it to be. If your flour-to-chunky-ingredients (carrots, raisins, nuts, etc.) ratio was too uneven one way, the baking soda and baking powder wouldn't be able to do their job, the batter wouldn't be able to rise as high, and you'd end up with a dense, heavy cake. Too much in the other direction and there wouldn't be enough texture for a traditional carrot cake. It would be boring and bland.

"How do you feel about getting started on the frosting?" Ava asked Becca.

"I'm here to help you. You tell me what you need."

"Awesome. I have a cream cheese frosting recipe that I use all the time. I'll send it to you." She did, and soon Becca was on her phone, scanning through the recipe. "When you get to the powdered sugar, let me know."

With a nod, Becca was off to grab ingredients.

A hundred thousand dollars.

Jesus Christ, she couldn't dwell on that, on what it could do for her. For her life, for her work. Her annoyance surged again. She'd come here to learn, not to compete. And now she felt compelled, like she had no choice but to run in this race she hadn't signed up for. She glanced across to Regan's station where she was weighing out flour while Liza watched. Yikes, that had to be nerve-racking. In front of her, Vienna was deep in conversation with her assistant, their heads almost touching. Things had definitely shifted. What had started as a group of women who'd been brought together to learn had become a group of women in competition with one another for a substantial prize, and that made the very air around them feel suddenly, weirdly charged.

Liza had said the winner would be the baker who impressed her the most. How the hell did she intend to measure that? How the hell were they supposed to figure out how to do that? She thought about actually asking these questions, but she'd read in several articles that Liza Bennett-Schmidt had a bit of an eccentric streak—and more money than God at this point—so it shouldn't have come as a surprise at all that things had taken an eccentric turn, right? Maybe asking her questions wasn't a smart move. She didn't want to piss off the giver of money, did she? Still, Ava found herself shaking her head in disappointment as she began grating carrots.

Carrot cake could be tricky for inexperienced bakers, but Ava could bake a carrot cake in her sleep. She'd dealt with all the pitfalls at some point in her career and knew now how to avoid them. She also had a flash of realization that Liza was testing them, trying to throw them off. For example, she noticed there were both whole carrots and pre-grated carrots in the fridge. Ava knew freshly grated carrots worked best in a carrot cake. They helped with the moisture level and had a sweeter taste. She saw that Madison had grabbed a bag of pre-grated carrots, probably thinking she'd save herself some time. And honestly, if this had remained a learning experience, maybe they'd have talked about that, as a group. Now that it was a competition, Ava kept her mouth shut as she grated whole carrots on her own. A glance to her left told her Regan was doing the same thing, and then Regan looked up.

Their eyes met, held for a beat, and was Ava the only one irritated by the little flutter she felt low in her belly?

Giving herself a mental shake, she forced herself to focus on what was in front of her, which were things she could control. The amount of carrot. The smoothness of the flour. The weight of the raisins. The type of nuts (pecans instead of walnuts) and oil (vegetable rather than coconut). She was the boss when she baked. She was in total control, and she liked it that way.

Ava had a sort of a zone when she worked, almost like a mental bubble she closed herself into. It likely came from working in a large kitchen with so much other activity around her, plus having a boss like Goldie who seemed to enjoy making her employees nervous simply from her presence. So Ava had learned to tune everything else out. Sometimes, she even put her AirPods in and *literally* tuned everybody out. She didn't have them today, thinking this was going to be a class of some sort, and now she was wishing she did.

But she could focus. She was good at it. Keeping Becca in her periphery so she could make sure the cream cheese frosting was done right, she got to work combining wet ingredients and then dry. No mixer for this cake, as the batter was thick and chunky. She poured the wet into the dry and used a rubber spatula to mix them together until she had a lumpy brown batter, which she then spooned into three round baking pans. Once she slid them into her oven, she glanced around.

Vienna and Regan both had their cakes in. Madison, Maia, and Paige were close. And Liza was watching her.

"Nice work," she said with a nod, and continued to the next workstation.

They all moved on to the frosting.

CHAPTER FIVE

"Well," Maia said, as she fell back onto her bed. "That was a day. Wow."

"Jesus, right?" Regan said, bringing her glass to her lips and sipping her wine.

The six of them had gathered in Maia and Vienna's room after dinner. They were all exhausted but also wired, so they asked May if they could take two bottles of wine and some glasses upstairs with them, and they convened in one room.

"Sure was." Ava sipped from her own glass as Madison laughed and said, "Says the woman who made the best carrot cake." She raised her glass. "Nicely done, by the way."

They all raised their glasses in toast.

Madison sat on the foot of Maia's bed, her feet dangling off and swinging slowly. Vienna and Ava sat on the other, while Regan and Paige were in the rolling chairs they'd pulled out from the desks.

"You guys." Paige shook her head. "A hundred grand. Like, what the actual fuck? Did anybody see that coming?"

Regan raised her hand. "I mean, I knew it was a possibility. She did the same thing three retreats ago, like Maia said."

"Yeah, but like, on a whim?" Maia asked. "'Cause that seemed like it was on a whim."

"I'm sure she wanted it to seem that way," Ava said. "But I don't care how much money you have, you don't just randomly give away a hundred grand without running it past some people first."

"Agreed," said Vienna, who had kicked off her shoes and was now rubbing her right foot. "There are tax implications. Things like that." Ava nodded her clear agreement. "So, likely not an actual whim."

Regan sat back and listened, sipping her glass of very good Merlot as she moved her gaze from one woman to the next, all of them unique in looks, personality, talent. Vienna was the only woman of color, which Regan found surprising, and it made her sad that Vienna seemed to not only accept this but expect it. Maia's hair and tattoos told Regan that she was her own woman, and she didn't give one tiny fuck what others thought of her. Paige was easily the most petite person there. She couldn't have been more than five-one, and if she weighed a hundred pounds soaking wet, Regan would've been shocked. Paige had kind eyes and a big smile, and it was only fitting that she roomed with Madison, who was probably the most cheerful person Regan had ever met. Her positivity was contagious.

And then there was Ava. Regan tried to study her without studying her. She was definitely the quietest of the group. The most reserved, and that was by design, Regan knew. Ava had told her once when they worked together that she thought people talked too much and didn't listen enough. So she made a habit of staying quiet in a group and listening carefully before she spoke. Now she sat next to Vienna, her gaze moving from woman to woman as they spoke, and that was another thing she remembered about Ava: You could always be sure she was listening to you because her eye contact was very direct. It never wandered. She didn't do other things while you spoke to her. She *looked* at you.

It could be unnerving.

"So, is anybody else disappointed?" Maia asked the question, then reached her empty glass out to Regan. The wine was on the desk behind her, so she refilled the glass and handed it back.

"What do you mean?" Vienna asked.

"I mean…" Maia sighed. "Maybe this sounds stupid, but I came here to learn. I applied to this retreat so I could hone my craft, you know? Not so I could battle the rest of you. Yeah, the money would be amazing, but now it all feels different." She gazed around the room at each of them, clearly looking to see if any of them agreed. "You know?"

"There's definitely been a shift," Ava said, her own glass dangling between her knees.

Murmurs and nods went around the room, and then a silence fell, as if each of them was lost in her own thoughts.

"I love your shirt, Regan," Maia said, pointing at her.

Regan grinned as she glanced down at the print on her navy T-shirt that said *Life Is About Taking Whisks* and had a picture of a baker holding a hand whisk. "Thank you. I have a ton of them. My last girlfriend gave me this one as a gift, and I found the website and bought a bunch of others." She shrugged as she looked up to find Ava's dark eyes on her. "They're corny, but they make me happy."

"Something to be said for happiness," Maia said.

"Definitely," Paige agreed.

There was another beat of silence and then Maia asked, "So? What do we do now?"

Ava slid off the bed and to her feet. "Well, I don't know about the rest of you, but I'm wiped. I'm headed to bed."

It was the nudge they needed, clearly, because they all started to stand and shift and pick things up. Good nights were bid and soon Regan found herself trailing behind Ava down the hall and into their room.

A strange situation, to put it lightly.

They didn't speak at first, each retreating to her own side of the room. Regan dug her pajamas out of her suitcase, kicking aside some of her clothes on the floor that were in her way.

"Mind if I use the bathroom first?" Ava asked.

"Be my guest."

The door of the bathroom clicked shut and then the lock slid into place, and Regan rolled her eyes. *Does she think I'm gonna bust in there while she's naked?* Not that she'd hate seeing that, but still. That wasn't the point.

She heard the shower running and realized she had some time, so she flopped onto her bed and grabbed her phone.

Hey, loser, she typed.

The bouncing dots were immediate, and soon Kiki typed back *How was Day 1?*

Regan had let her friends know she'd arrived last night but was too tired, her brain too packed full, to carry on any kind of conversation beyond that.

Crazy. Insane. You won't believe it.

Kiki sent a wide-eyed emoji, followed by *Tell me!*

Regan smiled. She could always count on Kiki to make her feel important. She typed.

A list:

1. We made carrot cake today.

2. Liza liked mine 3rd. 2 people ahead of me, 3 behind. Not great, but OK.

3. My roommate is Ava Prescott. She followed this with alternating grimacing emoji and wide-eyed emoji.

4. Liza is giving $100k to whichever of us "impresses her most."

5. Don't FT me. Cuz roommate.

Then she sat back and waited, a knowing grin on her face. Kiki's first instinct was going to be to FaceTime her, but there was no way she'd have any kind of out-loud conversation that Ava might possibly be able to hear. Shower or not, she had no idea how thin the walls were. Or how good Ava's hearing might be.

And then her brain reminded her that Ava being in the shower meant she was *naked*, and that sent her down an entirely different path for a moment...

Thank God her phone buzzed in her hand and Kiki had sent about a zillion wide-eyed emoji, followed by *The bitch who got you fired?* followed by a GIF of somebody falling out of their chair in disbelief.

Regan laughed and typed, *That very one.*

Srsly, Kiki typed. *What are the odds?*

I know, right?

The dots bounced, stopped, bounced again, and Regan noticed the shower had turned off just as Kiki's sweet message came through. *You gonna be OK?*

She smiled, and not for the first time, she thanked her lucky stars for her friends. *Totally. Kinda awkward, but it'll be fine. I'm a professional, ya know.*

Kiki sent back *You are! Just let me know if you need somebody to come shove her off her high horse.*

Regan grinned. *I'll keep it in mind.*

The bathroom door opened then, so she sent a good night and set her phone down.

"All yours," Ava said with—was that a tiny smile?

"Cool." Regan grabbed her stuff and scurried into the bathroom.

❖

Ava rubbed the towel against her damp hair as she watched Regan close the bathroom door behind her. She blew out a breath, only then realizing the underlying stress of sharing a room with somebody she'd had fired. Several years ago or not, warranted or not (it was), it was still ultra uncomfortable to share space with somebody who didn't like her.

It was really only because of the day's whirlwind of work and unexpected information that she'd been able to set it all aside and focus on why she was there.

That's what I need to keep doing, she said to herself as she rubbed lotion into her legs. *Remembering why I'm here. I earned this spot. I* deserve *to be here.*

And apparently, so did Regan.

While she found that hard to believe, she had to admit that it was possible for people to grow and change and learn, and it had been years since they'd worked together. And Liza Bennett-Schmidt was a well-known stickler for competence and creativity. She'd have never accepted Regan if she didn't have what it took.

Bit of a hard pill for Ava to swallow, but there it was.

With a sigh, she plugged in her blow-dryer and sat at the desk, which she'd arranged as a vanity instead, as there was a mirror on the wall above it. She was almost finished drying her hair when Regan exited the bathroom. Ava's back was to her, but she could see her in the reflection, boxer shorts leaving a lot of leg that Ava had to force herself not to stare at.

It would certainly be helpful if Regan wasn't a woman who was fun to look at.

Hair dry, she unplugged her dryer and wrapped the cord around it, then set it to one side. She moisturized her face, then arranged all her toiletries in a neat row before she stood up and pushed her chair in.

Regan was already under the covers, and Ava could feel her eyes on her. When she glanced over, Regan gave her a small smile.

"Hey, congratulations on your carrot cake. It was really good." Ava's shock must've been visible because Regan snorted a laugh and rolled her eyes. "Don't look so surprised." Then she turned off her bedside lamp and rolled over, and that was the end of that.

"Thank you," Ava said quietly.

Sleep was elusive. It always was when she slept in a new place, in a new bed. Plus, she was used to the constant soundtrack of the noise of New York City. Here in the Catskills, it was disturbingly quiet. She saw 1:00 a.m. on her phone. Then 2:17. She must have finally dropped off because the next thing she knew, Regan was shuffling around and headed into the bathroom.

It was 5:27.

Ava stared at the ceiling for a moment before accepting that there would be no more sleeping for her. Tossing off the covers, she got up, pulled her leggings and a hoodie from the drawer, and got dressed. She pulled her hair up into a messy bun, found her Nikes, and tucked her phone into the hoodie's front pocket, then headed out.

The mansion was surprisingly quiet, nobody in the dining room. She wasn't quite ready for coffee yet. What she wanted was fresh air, so she let herself out the front door. While the sun wasn't fully up—and wouldn't be for another twenty minutes, according to her weather app—it was light enough for her to wander without worrying about getting lost.

The grounds were huge. She'd noticed a large pond in the back when looking out one of the windows, so she headed in that direction, hoping to be able to walk around it. The quiet in the house extended to the outdoors, though she noticed the birdsong beginning to pick up as the sun crept toward the horizon.

Ava loved spring. The whole concept of it—clean slate, new beginnings—was something she could get behind. God knew she was ready for that kind of thing for herself. She was in a rut. Career-wise. Creatively. Emotionally. Relationship-wise. She was beyond ready to dig herself out of it. She just wasn't sure how and had hoped maybe learning from one of her baking idols could help. She hadn't expected the competition part. The financial possibilities. She'd felt fairly calm and confident upon her arrival, but now...?

Ignoring the dew on her sneakers, she kept walking toward the pond, then stopped when she saw deer. A mama and her two fawns were grazing on the fresh young grass that ran in a lush circle around the pond, and the sight was honestly almost surreal. The sun peeked over the horizon behind them as they munched...it was breathtaking. Ava stayed completely still and just watched until they moved along. She was no stranger to wildlife, having grown up in the suburbs in upstate New York, but she'd been in New York City for more than a decade now, so seeing deer in their natural habitat, just enjoying breakfast and not worrying about getting hit by a car or shot by a hunter, gave her a peace in her heart she hadn't felt in a while now.

As she did a couple laps around the small pond, she felt herself relax. She was good at carrying and handling stress. Too good, actually. She was so good at it that she didn't realize when it was too much. And she'd been dangerously close to "too much" when she'd been accepted to this retreat. She hadn't even realized it then, but she did now: These eight weeks were exactly what she needed. Despite the fact that they were ending up slightly different than she'd expected when she got there, they were still time away from her stressful job and an opportunity to learn from the best.

She'd take it.

On her way back around the mansion, she came upon a van pulling up the driveway. When it stopped, Ava recognized the assistants stepping out. They waved and shouted good mornings to her as they headed inside, and Ava hadn't realized they weren't staying on the property with the rest of them. Maybe there just wasn't enough room.

Whatever. The walk and fresh air had done their job. Ava felt awake, invigorated, and ready to face the day. And when she got back to her room, Regan was gone, which she didn't want to be relieved by but was.

"All right," she said quietly to the empty room as she gathered clean clothes for the day and headed toward the bathroom. "Let's kick this day in the ass."

CHAPTER SIX

The next week flew by in a whirlwind of flour and sugar and bread dough and icing with no breaks for even a weekend. Liza did a little teaching and a little observing and a whole lot of intimidating, but Regan felt pretty good about her work. Her scones came out a bit dry, but her cranberry orange bread was a thing of beauty. By the time they reached their first weekend off, Regan was more than ready for some downtime.

But before she could have that, there was a plan suggested for Saturday afternoon and into the evening. Liza was heading out of town for a long weekend for some kind of press thing, but she'd given them suggestions, things to do in town if they wanted to get out of the house for a while, one of which was an adult arcade and game room.

"Who's in?" Madison asked, as the six of them sat around the dining room table Saturday morning, sipping coffee and eating breakfast. "I don't know about you guys, but I hear Skee-Ball calling my name, and I will wipe the floor with you bitches."

Maia raised her hand and laughed as she spun her purple bandanna around her neck and said, "Awfully cocky for somebody who's going to get her ass kicked by *moi*."

"Oh, it is *on*," Vienna contributed. "'Cause I'm gonna slaughter both of you."

"I suck at Skee-Ball," Paige said, with a slight frown, but raised her hand anyway.

"No worries," Madison told her. "I googled this place last night, and there's tons of stuff to do. Are you good at video games? They've got some cool old-school ones like *Ms. PacMan* and *Frogger*."

"I was just gonna stay here and rest," Paige said, her voice shy, as if she was worried about some kind of judgment for not wanting to go to an arcade. She scrunched up her face in clear concern.

Regan reached over and gave her arm a squeeze. "I was, too, but then I thought maybe I'd go today and blow off some steam, then chill tomorrow and Monday, since we have that off, too. You know? What do you think?"

Paige's expression was grateful, and she gave a gentle nod. "That sounds like a good plan."

"Ava?" Madison prodded, looking at the only one who hadn't chimed in.

Ava looked around the table and must have realized how unsociable it would look for her to be the only one who opted out. She gave a nod and raised her hand. "Sure. Why not?" Madison clapped, and murmurs of approval ran around the table.

All right. So they were going to an arcade to play video games and act like kids that afternoon, and then they'd get dinner and drinks. Liza had graciously provided them with a driver and a van so they didn't have to worry about a DD, which was, honestly, pretty freaking cool of her.

"I'm off to shower," Maia said, draining her coffee cup and then grabbing a banana off the fruit tray. Then she pointed around the table. "You should probably prepare for defeat. Peace out, bitches."

Madison snorted and Paige and Vienna both laughed as they all pushed to their feet, as if Maia's departure was their cue.

"Meet in the foyer at noon?" Vienna asked, and they all agreed.

Regan had some ideas she wanted to research, bakes for upcoming days and weeks. She glanced at Ava to see if she was headed upstairs, too, because she wasn't sure if she wanted to be in the room with her. They were still sort of circling each other as roommates, and they didn't talk much, but they were civil. When Ava stood with the rest of them, Regan decided it was fine. The room was big enough for them to work on their own sides and not be in each other's way. Her mother had raised her to be polite. She could make it work. She should make it work. She *would* make it work.

She headed up.

When she got to her room, Ava was headed into the bathroom, a pile of clothing in her hands, and Regan wondered about that. Was it because Regan was gay, and Ava knew it and didn't want to undress in front of the gay chick? The idea annoyed her a little bit, but so did a lot of things about Ava Prescott.

Deciding she didn't care at all about Ava's weird little hangups, she whipped her own top off, then her bra. She was bent over and rooting through her suitcase for clothes for their outing when Ava came out of the bathroom, startling her.

Regan stood, breasts on full display.

Ava stared, eyes going immediately to them.

A beat passed.

Then three things happened in quick succession. Ava yanked her gaze away just as Regan's hands flew up to cover her nipples. Then Ava hurried to her side of the room and Regan hurried to the bathroom and shut the door.

Neither of them said a word.

In the bathroom, Regan leaned back against the door and blew out a breath. "What the fuck?" she whispered to the empty room.

So I'm a boob woman. So what? There's nothing wrong with that. The thought kept rolling through Ava's head as they bounced along in the van on their way to the arcade. The mood was jovial. There was laughing. Joking. Excitement.

All Ava could think about was boobs.

Specifically, Regan's boobs.

She was shaking her head, disgusted with her inability to control her thoughts, when Maia called her out.

"Ava. What are you shaking your head about? The fact that you're gonna lose to me?"

"Yes," Ava said. "Exactly that. It makes me question the entire point of my existence."

Maia barked a laugh as Madison broke out in a horrible rendition of Billie Eilish's song "What Was I Made For?" Then she pointed and laughed harder as the van slid into the parking lot of the arcade and she saw the name: Joysticks. "You know a guy owns this place," she said good-naturedly.

They piled out of the van. Their driver was named Jimmy, and he was big and quiet. "The strong, silent type," Vienna had said, trying to get a smile out of him. Spoiler alert: She did. Ava saw him touch Vienna's arm, then hand her his card. He turned to get back in the van and Vienna met Ava's gaze, then smiled. She lifted one shoulder in a half shrug as she walked up to Ava. "What can I say?"

Ava grinned and shook her head. "You don't have to say anything. He's cute."

"Right?" Vienna tucked her hand through Ava's arm, and they followed the others to the front door of the arcade. "He said he thought I looked responsible, so I should just call him when we're ready to go to dinner." She suddenly stopped walking and looked at Ava, stricken. "Wait. Ew. I look responsible? Not hot? Not fun? Just…like I could house-sit for him or do his taxes?"

Ava laughed and opened the door for her.

They caught up to the others, and Regan said, "Oh my God, this is like walking into my brother's room when we were kids. Dark and a little creepy, with lots of blinking lights."

"If I find any damp socks lying around, I'm outta here," Madison said, followed quickly by Paige's "Ew!"

Being an only child with a hardworking mother and a father who always had other things to do, video games and such had become Ava's babysitters. There had been a community center within walking distance from her house, and she spent many afternoons there during the summers, playing games with other lonely kids. Looking around Joysticks now, she saw new games and old—Ping-Pong, air hockey, pool tables, foosball—in addition to all the video games, Skee-Ball and claw machines. The clientele was of all ages. Small children jumped in the bounce house, older kids and teens played video games, as did some adults. The sounds of bouncing Ping-Pong balls, slapping air hockey pucks, and cracking billiard balls filled the air and mixed with the bings and bongs and ray guns and music from the video games to create a soundtrack that reminded Ava a lot of her youth.

"Holy crap, I love this place already," Regan said softly, seemingly to herself. When Ava glanced at her, Regan's eyes were wide, and she looked like a little kid on Christmas morning.

"What should we do?" Madison asked.

"Who's up for a tournament?" Maia asked, and Ava was beginning to understand that this was the person who liked taking on the role of organizer. Ava was fine with that, as she absolutely didn't want that job. "If anybody wants to do video games, go for it. I thought maybe we could do some tournaments on the tables. Like, air hockey, pool, Ping-Pong? I don't have the first clue how to play foosball, so I'm out on that one."

Murmurs and head nods went all around, everybody agreeing.

"Poor foosball," Regan said. "Ousted from the games before it even had a chance to get started."

Ava grinned and shook her head. "So sad."

"I see a free Ping-Pong table and an air hockey one," Maia said, almost to herself.

"I bet there's a way to reserve next play," Vienna suggested, then headed toward the pool tables to talk to the guys currently playing.

Maia headed to the front desk to get the equipment they needed, and within ten minutes, they were ready to go. "Who wants air hockey?"

"I'll play," Ava said, holding her hand out for the mallet.

"Who's taking on Ava?" Maia asked.

"I will," Vienna said, raising a hand.

They turned on the table.

"Wanna warm up?" Vienna offered.

"Sure."

They spent the next few minutes tapping the puck back and forth to each other. It floated effortlessly between them, bouncing off the sides of the tables until it slipped past Ava's mallet and into the goal. The table beeped and the little electronic scoreboard gave Vienna a point.

"Thanks, table, but that was just a warm-up," Vienna said, and reset the score to zeroes. "What do we play to? Ten?" She glanced at Regan and Madison, who were spectating between Ava and Vienna on the air hockey table and Maia and Paige playing Ping-Pong.

"Ten works for me," Ava said.

"Ready?" Vienna asked. At Ava's nod, the game began.

And ended less than ten minutes later. Ava: ten. Vienna: one.

"Holy shit, what the hell was that?" Vienna said, blinking.

"Luck?" Ava said with a wink.

Vienna tossed the mallet to Madison. "You're next."

Madison did a little bounce on the balls of her feet, comically preparing, giving herself a pep talk: "Okay, here we go. You got this.

You got this." Then she put her hands on her hips, lifted her chin, and stood there for several seconds without moving.

"Are you Superman now?" Regan asked with a laugh.

"I'll have you know there are studies," Madison informed her, still holding her pose. "Standing like this for a few moments before anything important—big meeting, conference call—"

"Air hockey game?" Regan asked.

"Air hockey game, yes. Standing like this helps you build up your confidence and feel better about taking on whatever you have before you."

That confidence lasted a full seven minutes, until Ava scored her tenth goal and Madison stood blinking in disbelief.

"Um, what just happened?"

"Pretty sure Ava just handed you your ass," Vienna said. "You can hang it up next to mine." She raised her voice so Maia and Paige, who were still playing Ping-Pong, could hear. "I think we have a ringer in our midst."

"Seriously?" Maia asked with a chuckle. "Ava, you been holding out on us? You an air hockey pro? You play on a national team?"

"I do not," Ava said. "But I may have played quite a bit when I was younger."

Madison handed her mallet to Regan. "Next lamb for the slaughter. Don't bother with the Superman pose. Waste of time."

Ava watched Regan approach her own end of the table. She moved her mallet from side to side, apparently getting a feel for it. Placing her left hand on the corner of the table, seemingly to brace, she finally met Ava's gaze. "Ready?"

Staying calm was a characteristic of Ava's. Always had been, because of her childhood. Freaking out and losing her mind over something never got her far. In fact, it only made things worse in her world. So she'd perfected remaining stoic. Unemotional.

That being said, Regan, at the other end of the table, ready to play her, did weird things to her composure. Regan's blond highlights were picking up all the neon in the place, so she looked almost like she was AI, different colors streaking her hair, bouncing off her smooth skin, seeming almost unreal. Her big blue eyes looked wider than usual, and Ava's gaze roamed down to her chest. Of course, her brain chose that moment to send her a snapshot image of Regan's bare breasts, exactly as she'd seen them that morning. Creamy white skin, pink nipples, a bit larger than she'd expected—a picture that was going to live rent-free in her head.

She swallowed hard, then cleared her throat.

Okay, yeah, enough of that.

"Ready."

Regan served.

The volley went for a good minute before Ava scored, and she instantly knew Regan was going to be a good match. "You've played before."

"My brother may have taught me."

Ava nodded and served, and she was going to have to work for this win. She loved a challenge, that was true. That the challenge came from Regan was going to make it even sweeter when she won. She tucked that in her back pocket and forced herself to focus. She bent her knees slightly so she stood lower, making it easier to predict the trajectory of the puck. The red disk flew over the white table, slamming off sidewalls and thwacking off mallets. It seemed like forever before she managed to score again.

Only then did she notice they'd amassed a bit of an audience.

❖

People were watching them.

Regan hadn't realized that until the puck had gone flying off the table, and she had to bend to grab it. When she'd stood and glanced up, there were a good six or eight spectators on top of their own fellow pastry chefs—who'd stopped their own Ping-Pong matches to watch.

Great. 'Cause that won't add to the pressure. She took a deep breath and served.

Ava was good at this game. Damn good, and Regan almost laughed at the sheer ridiculousness of the whole situation. Her past with Ava, ending up rooming with her at the retreat, and now playing a game as freaking obscure as air hockey against her. Who would have ever seen this coming?

Ava scored.

Damn it. She was losing. Time to focus. She bent a bit at the waist, concentrated on watching the puck while it was on Ava's side of the center line, rather than trying to track it all the way to her mallet. Her brother had taught her that method of defense and she employed it now, trusting her hand to move the mallet where it needed to be without her having to actually look down at it.

She focused, blocked several shots, then made one of her own.

Goal!

Ava's facial expression hardly changed at all. How the hell did she do that? No smile. No frown. Just...neutral. Whether she scored or Regan scored, Ava was neutral. It seemed to be her thing.

Except...it wasn't her thing that morning. Oh, no. When she'd seen Regan topless, her expression certainly had changed. It had been neutral, then had instantly cycled through surprise, shock, approval, desire, and embarrassment. All of them, in the space of about three seconds, and Regan had seen each one clearly.

Yes, she'd seen desire.

She was sure of it, and that put a whole new spin on things, because the rumors about Ava's sexuality she'd heard years ago while working with her seemed to have been confirmed with just that simple glance at her breasts.

Bam! She scored again.

The only proof it had registered on Ava's radar was the slight raising of her eyebrows.

That's right. I will see you looking at my boobs for the rest of this retreat. The thought made her grin as they volleyed, but then Ava came way too close to scoring again, and Regan hunkered down.

Eventually, her quads started to ache a bit, and she realized it was from standing with her legs slightly bent throughout the game...which had been going on for nearly half an hour. It was a tied score, and Ava was about to serve. When Regan glanced up at her face, she was smiling softly, and why the hell that disarmed her, she had no idea, but Ava served the puck directly into Regan's goal.

Game point.

Shit. Okay. Focus, Callahan, come on. Her brain was screaming at her, so she took a deep breath and served. Clearly, this was the forever volley because it went on and on and on until Regan was sure her arm was going to fall off or her eyes would drop out of her head from the exhaustion of following the damn puck.

She gave it a smack and it ricocheted just right and into Ava's goal.

"Tie score and game point," Maia reported to the crowd. "Whoever scores next wins."

In almost any other situation, Regan might've argued the "must win by two" rule, but she was too freaking tired and ready to be done. "Here we go," Maia said, apparently reverting to color commentary as the crowd hushed. "Ava's serve."

The puck whizzed at her hard and fast, but Regan blocked it, sent it back, though not as hard as she would've liked. Ava bounced it off the side, and Regan stopped it, shot it back.

Maia would probably say later that it was the longest volley in air hockey history—and it was pretty fucking long—but much to her own surprise, Regan eventually managed to score, and while she would've loved to jump around in celebration, she was exhausted, both mentally and physically. She went around the table to shake Ava's hand.

"Great game," she said, meeting those dark, dark eyes. Ava's hand was hot and infuriatingly not sweaty like Regan's.

"Back atcha. That was fun. I haven't played somebody as good as you in a long time." Her smile was tight, the only clue that she was annoyed at having lost. Regan recalled a time in her life when she was reasonably sure Ava was not human. She was an android or an alien or something, and this tight smile only added to that. Like Ava didn't quite know how to smile.

Of course, she just lost, so…

Regan decided to cut her a little slack.

"Well, so much for the rest of the tournament," Madison said with a laugh. "We're all starving and ready for food and drinks."

"*I* am certainly ready for a drink," Regan said.

"Vienna's calling our driver," Maia said. "That was epic, you guys. Wow. How did you get so good?"

Regan looked at Ava, whose cheeks were tinted a cute pink. Ava spoke softly as she said, "I didn't love being in my house when I was a kid. There was a youth center a couple blocks away, and I hung out there a lot. Played a lot of air hockey." She lifted one shoulder in a half shrug, and Regan was surprised to hear her speaking with such modesty. And then those dark eyes locked onto hers, and Regan cleared her throat.

"I have a brother, and my grandparents had an air hockey table in their basement. I think it was my dad and uncle's when they were growing up. We spent a lot of time messing around with it until we got good."

Vienna returned to the group then. "Jimmy's outside. You guys ready?"

Twenty minutes later, they were seated at a round table in a casual restaurant called Domingo's. Regan didn't realize how famished she was until the smell of sizzling burgers hit her nose, and her mouth filled with saliva.

"Holy crap, I'm suddenly starving."

"Me too," Ava said.

Despite Regan's hope that she might avoid it, she ended up seated right next to Ava, their thighs brushing every so often. Ava smelled nice, even after a nearly forty-five-minute, intense air hockey match. Her scent was soft, like lilacs or baby powder, subtle and inviting. Meanwhile, Regan was pretty sure she smelled like a locker room.

They ordered a round of drinks, and once they came, Maia asked, "Hey, why do you guys think the assistants don't stay at the house like us?"

Vienna shrugged, then took a sip of her beer, a trace of foam left on her upper lip. "Probably not enough room."

"Our room could've fit another couple of beds," Paige said with a snort. "It's huge."

"Ours too," Regan added.

"Does everybody like their assistant?" Madison asked. "Kitty seems very cool. Knows her stuff. She was a big help this week."

"I feel like Becca talks a lot," Ava said with a soft smile. "But that might just be because I don't."

"And she's gotta ask," Vienna said, as if she totally got it.

"Exactly." Ava scrunched her nose. "I should probably work on that."

"I'm the same way," Vienna said. "Just stay out of my way and let me do my thing."

Ava raised her glass in salute, and Vienna touched hers to it.

"You guys are funny," Madison said. "I want all the help I can get. What about you, Regan?"

"I like Hadley," she said. "She seems cool and knows what she's doing. And I'm not gonna turn away an extra set of hands, you know?" She wasn't surprised that Ava didn't really feel the need for anybody's help. It had been a while since she'd worked with Ava, but she remembered her being very solitary. Quiet and solitary, focusing on her work—which was good. But anybody assigned to help was out of luck, especially if they wanted to learn anything. Ava was a terrific pastry chef, and a shitty teacher. "She asks a lot of questions, which I appreciate. Feels like she's trying her best to learn."

Okay, yeah, that was passive-aggressive, and she knew it.

She didn't care.

Also, she'd beaten Ava in air hockey. She hid her grin with the rim of her glass as the waiter arrived to take their orders.

CHAPTER SEVEN

Having three days off felt weird after going full speed for more than a week. But it was also nice to wake up and be able to just chill, even though she was still on bakery time. A glance at her phone told her it was just approaching five a.m. Then she noticed the date.

How the hell was it June already?

Regan couldn't figure out how time was moving so quickly. She felt like she'd just gotten to Black Forest Hills, yet it had already been nearly two weeks. With a sigh, she tossed off her covers, deciding to go for a walk, get some fresh air.

She was surprised to see Ava sitting up in the dark, feet dangling over the side of her bed, still.

"You okay?" she whispered, not wanting to startle her.

"I thought I heard something," Ava whispered back, then reached for the bedside lamp and clicked it on.

On the floor near the door was an envelope that looked like it had been slid underneath.

"What's that?" Ava asked as Regan went and picked it up. It had both their names on it, and she held it up so Ava could see. Ava came to stand next to her, smelling faintly of laundry detergent and that soft, inviting scent that Regan had begun to think of as simply…Ava.

She tore open the envelope and read out loud.

As many of you may know, June is Pride month for the LGBTQ+ community. As such, I would like you to think about creating a tiered wedding cake for a same-sex couple.

Could be male, female, nonbinary, trans, whatever you wish. I expect creativity not only in the look of your cake, in its overall appearance, but also in the flavor. I know a lot of competition shows use premade cake, but we don't do that at the Bennett-Schmidt retreat. You will bake your own. Choose the flavors, the colors, the design. It's all up to you. Use today to hash out your design, and we will begin putting them all together first thing tomorrow morning.

One more thing...for this project, you will be partnered. This time, we'll go with roommates. Therefore, teams are as follows: Ava and Regan, Maia and Vienna, Madison and Paige. Assistants will not be on hand to help this time. It'll just be the two of you.

Impress me.

The two of them stood there staring at the paper in Regan's hand for a long moment. Then their eyes met, but they continued without words for another moment before Regan finally said, "Wow. Okay, I didn't really expect that."

"Which part?" Ava asked with a snort. "The Pride project, that it's a wedding cake, or the creation of teams?"

"Yes," Regan said. "All of it." She had mixed emotions around this project. Of course she did. She was pretty sure Ava did as well, considering how she couldn't seem to look her in the eye. Regan finally sighed. "Look, I know you'd rather not partner with me. To be honest, the feeling is mutual. So let's just get through it, okay?"

"I didn't say I didn't want to partner with you." Ava seemed to be going for insulted and added, "Don't assume you know what I'm thinking, okay?"

"Of course. Sorry. It's fine. We can manage this. We're grown-ups. And you can't get me fired from here, so we should be good."

Ava poked the inside of her cheek with her tongue but said nothing. Instead, she turned back to her own side of the room and pulled her covers up, making her bed.

Okay. Fine. That's how we'll play this.

Regan returned to her own space as well and dug out clothes for going outside. A long time ago, she was a runner, but getting up by three thirty in the morning just to get to work didn't leave much time for jogging. By the time she was out of work, she was exhausted, so she'd graduated from running to simply walking. She took her clothes into the bathroom, changed, brushed her teeth, pulled on a black hat with the Sweet Temptations logo embroidered in pink, and was done in mere moments.

In the bedroom, Ava was sitting at her desk with her laptop open. She didn't look up.

"I'm going for a walk," Regan said, then immediately wondered why she felt she needed to report her intentions to Ava. She sighed at herself, grabbed her phone, and headed out of the room.

❖

Ugh. That woman.

Ava had to consciously unclench her jaw so that she wouldn't get a headache. Stress did that to her, and Regan was giving her some stress, it was true.

She would never say anything, but losing to Regan in air hockey the night before was still niggling at her. She'd expected to win. She hadn't been prepared for Regan to be that good. Who the hell else under forty was good at air hockey? She stifled a groan of frustration because she didn't lose well. She knew this about herself, which was the only reason she was able to school her expression afterward and be gracious. Inside, she'd been seething that she'd lost. To Regan, of all people.

Before she could dwell any longer, there was a soft knock on the door. Who in the world was visiting before six in the morning? She crossed the room and opened the door to find Maia and Vienna standing there.

"You guys up?" Maia whispered, craning her neck to look around Ava.

Ava nodded. "Regan went for a walk."

Maia held up an envelope. It was identical to the one Ava and Regan had received, but with Maia and Vienna's names on it. "You see this?"

Another nod. "We got one, too."

"What are you guys gonna make?" Maia asked, and Vienna gave her a light smack.

"You can't ask them that."

"Why not?" Maia's voice held a slight whine. "They have an unfair advantage with Regan being gay."

"What?" Ava asked. "How?" She didn't add that she was gay, too, because she was far too curious about this so-called advantage it gave her. "Do you think she's better at rainbows?"

Vienna rolled her lips in behind Maia, clearly trying not to laugh at her pastry partner.

"What? No. That's silly. It's just..." She seemed to fumble for words, then tugged at the ever present purple bandanna. "I don't know. It just seems unfair."

"You're ridiculous," Vienna said, her tone good-natured.

"Hey, what's with the bandanna?" Ava asked. "I've wanted to ask since the third time I saw you wear it."

Maia looked down at it. "This? It's lucky. I actually have about eight of them, so they do go in the wash, for anybody who's wondering." She eyeballed Vienna, who held up her hands like she was being robbed.

"I didn't say a thing." But Vienna smiled.

"Ah, okay." Ava stifled a grin as she said, "'Cause it looks kinda gay."

Maia's eyes went wide. "What? Does it?" Again, she looked down at her bandanna, pulling it out as far as it would go while tied around her neck. "Seriously, does it?"

Vienna's laugh was throaty as she began to pull Maia away. "Let's go before you dig yourself a hole you can't get out of." Behind her Vienna met Ava's eyes and they both laughed, then she tugged her roommate away.

Ava grinned and shook her head as she closed the door. She returned to her desk where she'd been about to jot some notes on ideas when Regan returned. "Short walk," she commented.

"Rain."

"Bummer." Ava hadn't even glanced out the window, so she had no idea it was wet out. She watched Regan as she took off her sneakers, crawled onto her bed, and sat back against her headboard. "So, we had a couple visitors," she told her.

Regan furrowed her brow. "At six in the morning?"

Ava nodded with a grin. "Yup. Maia and Vienna came to see if we'd gotten an envelope, too."

"Ah."

"Also, Maia thinks we have an unfair advantage because you're gay."

Regan's snorted laugh somehow gave Ava whatever it was she needed to say the next words.

"I didn't have the heart to tell her I'm gay, too. I was afraid her head might explode."

Regan's bark of a laugh was so quick and loud, it made Ava jump in her seat, and she laughed along with her.

"I also questioned that purple bandanna she wears all the time. I may have told her it was a little gay."

"Oh my God." Regan laughed harder. "It *so* is, though."

The two of them laughed for a moment before Regan pushed to her feet and grabbed some clothes out of her wreck of a suitcase, still open on the floor. "The rain made me cold. Gonna shower and think about how we can use our gayness to make better gay cake." As she walked past Ava's desk, she pointed at her with a grin. "I knew it, by the way. I knew you were." Then she closed the bathroom door behind her with a click.

Ava kept smiling.

The rain that had arrived that morning slowly became angry and morphed into storms, complete with thunder and lightning, and while Ava couldn't speak for Regan, she was glad to be able to just stay in their room and work on design ideas. She'd never liked thunderstorms. They frightened her, which she knew was silly and childish, but she'd never been able to shake it.

As if to underline her thought, a loud crack of thunder shook the house, and Ava nearly jumped out of her skin.

"You okay?" Regan asked from where she sat on her bed across the room, laptop open, seemingly unaffected by the crashing of the clouds above them.

Ava nodded, and she needed a moment to swallow her heart back down out of her throat and into her chest. "Thunder's not my favorite." She grimaced as she glanced out the window, bracing for the next crack.

"You're welcome to come sit here with me. I promise I won't bite. Or say something assholish." Regan shot her a look that was half grin, half grimace. "Plus, we're both working on the same thing. Might make it easier…" She let the idea drift off, then made a show of scooting over on her bed.

Ava glanced around the room. Regan's bed *was* quite a ways farther from the window than Ava's desk. And they *were* working on the same thing, namely their idea for the Pride cake. With a quiet sigh and one nod, she picked up her laptop, pen, and notepad and moved to sit next to Regan on her bed.

As if making their anger about her move known, the clouds crashed together again, and this time, the lights flickered. Ava flinched, a quiet gasp escaping her lips.

And then Regan's warm hand was on her thigh. "It's okay," she said softly. "I'm right here. No worries."

The combination of embarrassment for being such a baby and arousal from Regan's hand on her body annoyed her. But she found herself giving Regan an explanation anyway. "When I was a kid—I was twelve, actually—there was a night when my dad didn't come home. This wasn't unusual. He was a drinker and a womanizer and verbally and emotionally abusive, but my mom always did her best to keep him out of trouble. So that night, the bar he normally frequented called my mom and told her to come get him because he was being 'unruly.'" She made the air quotes. "She left me home alone in case it got ugly, and it did. He apparently got in a fight and was arrested, and Mom had to follow him to the police station, and it was a whole thing. She ended up being gone for hours."

"During a thunderstorm," Regan guessed.

Ava nodded. "During a *raging* thunderstorm that knocked out the electricity and the phone. So, I was alone in the dark, expecting my parents home in a few minutes that became several hours, with no way to contact them."

"At twelve?" Regan's eyes were wide. "Yikes. I'm so sorry. You must've been really scared."

"I hid in my closet the whole time."

"You poor thing."

"And I wet my pants."

"Oh God, that's horrible. I'm so sorry."

Ava turned her head to meet Regan's gaze and saw nothing but sympathy there. At the same time, it was as if she'd been in some kind of trance and just been snapped back to reality. She covered her eyes. "Jesus, I don't know why I felt the need to tell you all that." She felt the red crawling up her neck and settling into her cheeks, the hot shame making itself known.

Regan squeezed her leg once, then pulled her hand back, as if sensing that the touch was no longer welcome. "Hey, like I said, no worries. I'm a vault." She turned an imaginary key in front of her closed lips and mimed tossing it over her shoulder. Then she pointed at her laptop screen. "Wanna focus on this instead?"

Grateful, Ava nodded, and they got to work. The next rumble of thunder was loud but didn't seem quite as nerve-racking, but she wouldn't let herself dwell on the fact that maybe it was because Regan was so close.

Nope.

Not dwelling. At all.

❖

When Regan glanced at her phone and saw that it was almost six in the evening, she did a double take. Holding up the phone, she nudged Ava with an elbow.

Ava looked up from her notes and gasped. "Oh my God, how did it get so late?" Her head snapped to the side so she could look out the window to see that though the storms had eased, it was still gray and gloomy out. "Maybe because it's been so dark all day."

"And we've had our noses stuck in our laptops for hours." She rolled her head around on her shoulders, and her neck gave a loud pop that had Ava's eyes going wide.

"Is that gonna fall off now?"

"What?" Regan asked.

"Your head. Should I brace to catch it?"

"I mean, feels like maybe…" And at that, her stomach gave a loud rumble. "God, I'm freaking starving."

"Same."

By unspoken agreement, they set their laptops and notes aside and worked their way off Regan's bed, stopping to stretch. More of Regan's joints made noise.

"I hate to tell you this," Ava said as she grabbed her hairbrush off her desk and ran it through her dark hair, "I think you might be falling apart."

Regan snorted a laugh as she walked around with one shoe on. "Story of my life." She bent to look under the bed for the other, found it, and put it on. "Ready?"

Down in the dining room, they met up with the other four women seated at the table, two bottles of wine open.

"There you are. We were about to send somebody up to get you two." Vienna was pouring and looked expectantly at each of them.

They both nodded, and Regan pulled out a chair, then collapsed into it. Ava sat next to her.

"We lost track of time," Regan said.

"Easy to do in this weather," Paige said.

Vienna set the filled wine glasses in front of them, then took her seat. "So? How does everybody feel about tomorrow?"

Murmurs went around the table, everybody nodding or shrugging. Regan couldn't resist teasing Maia, so she said, "I mean, I've had my idea done for hours, considering the massive advantage I have."

"And with both of us on the same team," Ava added. "We can't lose. All our big gay juju on one big gay project..." She shrugged, then took a sip of her wine, watching in delighted satisfaction as Maia's face turned very, very red.

"Okay, listen. I was dumb."

"Truth," Regan said, hiding a grin. "Despite the bandanna."

Maia covered her eyes as the others laughed. "I'm sorry. I don't know what I was thinking." To her credit, she did look apologetic. Contrite.

"I suppose we can forgive you," Ava said, and Regan was surprised by her playing along.

"Wait," Madison said, seemingly just catching up. "You're both gay?"

Regan glanced at Ava and they both nodded.

"And Maia thought that gave you an advantage in making a wedding cake for a same-sex couple?" Madison went on.

"Yup," Regan said.

"Okay, I'm caught up now," Madison said, shaking her head at Maia.

"What?" Maia whined. "I said I was sorry. I panicked."

"I mean…" Vienna said softly. Regan had noticed that she seemed to be nearly as quiet as Ava, silently taking in the people around her, actively listening to conversations but contributing very little. "It would really suck if you guys didn't win. Right?" Her expression was dead serious for about three seconds before she burst into laughter.

Soon, the entire table was cracking up, and it felt good to release the tension Regan thought they'd all been unknowingly shouldering.

Then Ava leaned her way and whispered, "It would, though."

Regan laughed harder and nodded. Because she was right. The gay team losing the battle of the gay wedding cakes would be kind of pathetic. She leaned back toward Ava. "We'd better win, then."

CHAPTER EIGHT

Their design was flawless, and Regan knew it. So did Ava, she was pretty sure. All they had to do was get each step exactly right, watch their time, and stay relaxed. The second one—or both—of them stressed out, they'd be sunk. They both knew this, as well, and there'd been a bit of a nervous silence that morning as they'd gotten dressed.

Regan was in charge of the cakes themselves, and she could make cake in her sleep. She was a baker, after all. Who worked in a bakery. This would be...well, not to be too ridiculously on the nose, a piece of cake. They were doing a two-tiered, seven-layer cake with four layers on the bottom tier and three on the top. The cakes were Meyer lemon, and each layer was a different color of the rainbow. They would put a raspberry compote between each one.

"Should we have done three tiers?" Ava said for about the fourth time, clearly worried. "I wonder if we should've done three tiers." She glanced across the workspace where Maia and Vienna were clearly doing more than two tiers, talking to Liza about their design with excitement. Liza said something low that Regan couldn't make out, and Vienna's face fell. "Oh God," Ava went on. "We should've."

Regan grabbed her forearm and forced her to make eye contact. She kept her voice just above a whisper, trying not to show her irritation as she said, "It doesn't matter. It's too late to change now. Let's just focus on making the best damn two-tier cake ever. Okay?"

Second-guessing annoyed Regan. When possible, she avoided doing it. If something got screwed up she'd fix it the next time, but it was rare for her to switch direction midstream, so to speak. They'd planned two tiers. That's what they were going to do.

• 95 •

Seven bowls filled with equal amounts of yellow batter were spread out on the counter in front of her, and she got to work adding color. It was hard to get the red to be *red* rather than a dark pink, but she worked at it until she was satisfied. The rest were easy, and once she had every color of the rainbow, they went into seven round cake pans and then into the oven to bake.

Wiping her hands on her apron, she glanced behind her where Ava was rinsing bowls.

"Did you do frosting yet?"

Ava shook her head. "No, I had to clean these. I can't work in a disaster of a space like this." It seemed like she was trying to sound a little less annoyed than she was, but Regan heard it.

"Yeah, sorry, I'm kind of a messy baker."

"No shit."

Okay, yeah, *that* was snarky. Regan chose to ignore it. They were both clearly nervous and stressed, and that could make people snappy. "How about the compote?"

Ava indicated the pot on the stove. "Cooling."

Regan glanced in the pot at the deep crimson sauce, filled with chunks of raspberries. It occurred to her that maybe they should've squeezed the raspberries through cheesecloth to filter out the seeds, but again, it was too late to do that now. Plus, she liked that there was some texture there.

She grabbed a spoon and dipped it into the pot, then tasted. "Oh my God."

Ava's head snapped around from the sink, an expression of panic in her eyes. "What? Did I forget something? Not enough sugar? Too much sugar? Should we have filtered out the seeds? What?"

Regan tipped her head with a grin. "How about you take a breath, Stressy McWorryson? It's fantastic. The perfect amount of sweetness, very smooth, I like the seeds. It's fantastic."

Ava's relief was almost comically apparent as she let out a huge breath. "Oh. Okay. Good. Whew."

Regan recalled the Ava Prescott she had worked with as calm, cool, and collected. Rarely stressed. Never raised her voice. Never seemed panicked about anything. So this version of her, this bundle of nerves, was new, and Regan wasn't sure what to make of it. Ava had also seemed very stoic and regulated during the past week of bakes. The only difference between then and now was…

Oooohhhh.

The difference was Regan.

Ava didn't have 100 percent control over her project. She had to share decisions and labor with Regan, something she hadn't had to do before, and it was stressing her out.

Well, wasn't that interesting?

She supposed it made sense that a control freak wouldn't enjoy having to share their control, so she was going to try not to take it personally, snippy comment about her being messy aside.

"And how's it going over here?" Liza Bennett-Schmidt was suddenly standing next to Regan, who gave a slight flinch of surprise. Before she could answer, Liza had grabbed a spoon and tasted the compote. She tipped her head one way, then the other. "You left the seeds in."

Regan couldn't tell if the statement was accusatory, amused, or neutral, so she simply nodded.

"Mm." Liza nodded, then headed to the ovens where she squatted down and peeked through the windows. "Mm," she said again.

Regan and Ava held a silent conversation over her head that essentially had one of them asking what "Mm" meant and the other shrugging, "I have no freaking idea."

Liza stood up and headed toward Madison and Paige.

Regan was pretty sure her own face matched Ava's wide-eyed expression. What the hell had Liza thought? It was a mystery.

There was a beat and then Ava returned to the sink and the dishes Regan had dirtied.

The cakes were going to need a good thirty minutes before Regan even risked opening the oven doors, so she looked around for ways to busy herself. Really, the only things left to do were make the frosting, put the cake together, and frost and decorate it. She went to the sink and gently hip-bumped Ava out of the way.

"Go. Make the frosting. I can clean up my own mess."

Ava nodded and reached for a dish towel to wipe her hands.

Regan was no cake decorator. She excelled at many things when it came to baking. Actually, no. She excelled at *most* things when it came to baking. Unfortunately, cake decorating was not one of them. She had no trouble envisioning what she wanted the finished product to look like, but getting from point A to point B always proved more difficult than she'd expected. And at Sweet Temptations, there was an official cake decorator, so she didn't have to worry about it. Today, she kind of did.

Decorating their two-tier wedding cake was in Ava's hands. Ava, who was also not a cake decorator.

As she washed the remaining dishes, she glanced around the workspace. Because there were six workstations but only three teams, each team had two stations at their disposal. Regan was at one station but using the ovens at both, and Ava was mixing frosting across the aisle at the other station, out of the way of Regan's mess, she figured. Vienna and Maia seemed to be working like the proverbial well-oiled machine, one of them whipping something in a bowl while the other measured sugar. Behind them Madison looked slightly ill while Paige held her arm and seemed to be quietly pep-talking her. Regan wondered what was going on there but didn't want to interrupt to ask. She hoped nothing bad had happened.

By the time she got all the dishes washed, badly missing the industrial-sized dishwasher at the bakery, she crossed the aisle and sidled up next to Ava.

"How can I help?"

Ava used her chin to point toward the bowl of lemons. "I need about three tablespoons of lemon juice. I also need zest. Couple of teaspoons'll do it."

"You got it."

Liza was wandering some more, and while Regan understood that was part of why she was here—to learn from Liza—this wasn't learning. This was scrutiny, and it made her nervous.

"Going with lemon buttercream?" she asked as she took in their counter and its ingredients.

Ava and Regan both nodded.

"Lofty." She observed for a few more seconds, then moved on, and the look of absolute panic on Ava's face when she turned to Regan almost made her burst out laughing.

"Listen." Regan moved close to Ava and spoke just above a

whisper. "I've seen you work. You're a badass. And you're not a woman to be trifled with or intimidated. Right?"

Ava grimaced.

"Right?" Regan asked again, and this time, Ava nodded. "Good. So, put on your game face and make the best damn lemon buttercream anybody's ever tasted. I have faith in you."

Their eyes met and held, and then Ava nodded. "Okay" was all she said, but the set of her body and the determination that suddenly appeared on her face told Regan she'd heard her.

Regan squeezed her arm. "You got this."

She went back to her lemons.

Lemon buttercream was tricky, and there was a big—very big—part of Ava that wished they'd chosen something much simpler and way less risky. If she couldn't get the balance of liquids just right, if she added too much confectioners' sugar, if it curdled, that was it. Their cake would be ruined.

Ava was not a woman who was easily intimidated. Regan had been 150 percent correct about that. She'd been doing this work for years now. She ran her own part of the kitchen. She was the head pastry chef at a five-star restaurant. Nobody could make her feel like she didn't know what she was doing. Nobody.

Except, apparently, Liza Bennett-Schmidt.

Ava wasn't sure what it was about her, but the second she got close, Ava felt like she was back in culinary school again and Chef Boccatini was criticizing every single thing she did, trying to break her down before he built her back up again. Her nerves jangled. Her hands shook ever so slightly. She felt a bead of sweat roll down between her breasts.

It was infuriating.

Liza had made the rounds, but because there were only three teams, she was back again pretty quickly, watching Ava work. "If your frosting comes out, this could be an amazing cake."

Yeah, no shit, Ava wanted to say, but simply smiled and nodded and continued to measure.

"Careful it doesn't curdle."

Ava clenched her jaw, and part of her was worried she might crack a tooth, but then Liza moved on to the next team, and she blew out a breath.

"You okay?" Regan asked very quietly, her eyes on Liza as she talked in low tones to Vienna and Maia.

"Yeah, that wasn't nerve-racking at all," Ava replied, but the relief at not being scrutinized while she worked was big, and she felt her shoulders descend from her ears. She heard Liza in front of them tell Vienna if she over-whipped her cream, she'd ruin the whole project. Vienna looked ill. "Is she trying to jinx us all? 'Careful it doesn't curdle.'" She said the last line in a whisper but made a snarling face along with it.

Regan snorted a quiet laugh. "You got this," she said for the second time. And for whatever reason, that totally clichéd line made Ava feel the tiniest bit better. "Here's the zest, and here's the lemon juice." Regan set two ramekins down near her.

"Excellent. Thanks." She worked carefully. She wanted creamy and tangy and just a little bit of sweet. Too much and the frosting would be cloying, taking away from the flavor of the cake itself.

"I think sticking with heavy cream and not using lemon extract were good calls," Regan commented. "It's gonna taste so much better."

Ava nodded, pleased at the comment. "Agreed. I've made it with extract, which is fine, but fresh lemon juice is so much better. I've also skipped the cream, but it curdled on me. Won't do that again."

She felt Regan nod more than saw it, and again, she appreciated the agreement. She increased the speed on the stand mixer, then set a timer on her phone for three minutes. Three minutes that seemed to take an hour. The two of them stood there, silently watching the paddle spin around, the frosting become smooth, and when the timer sounded, Ava turned off the mixer and looked at Regan.

"Moment of truth."

Regan nodded once.

Ava dipped her spoon in and tasted. She dipped a second spoon and gave it to Regan, then she watched as Regan tasted, rolled the frosting around on her tongue.

"God, you're so right about the fresh lemon juice and zest. Wow. It's got that fresh, bright flavor without being sour or too tangy." She seemed to be tasting further, then said, "How do you feel about adding just a touch more confectioners' sugar? Like, a tablespoon or two?"

Ava nodded, and she couldn't help but grin. "I was thinking exactly the same thing." She turned the mixer back on and added one tablespoon of sugar. They did the taste test again before adding one more.

"Perfect," Regan pronounced, just as the timer went off for her cakes.

Ava watched as Regan pulled one cake pan out and touched the cake with her fingertips, checking for doneness. When she turned to Ava and grinned, Ava couldn't help but grin back.

She took a moment to scan the room, something she hadn't done yet, and now she was curious what the other teams were doing.

Madison had several bowls of colored frosting spread out on her counter. *Ah, going for the rainbow*, Ava thought. Over at Vienna and Maia's station, it looked like they were shaping their cake into a curve. *And the* very literal *rainbow over there.*

She crossed the aisle to Regan and they stood looking at the cakes. Seven of them in seven different colors. Bright, vibrant colors, hard to do with cake.

"These look great," she said and meant it.

"Thanks." Regan stood with her hands on her hips, slightly shorter than Ava. They both scanned their cakes. "All right. We let 'em cool, and then we get to assembling." She looked at Ava. "You still good with frosting it?"

Ava nodded. "We can do this. I mean, I'm not a cake decorator, but I think between the two of us, we can make this work."

"Me too."

Ava knew they'd nailed the flavor portion of this contest. Hands down. She didn't even need to know what the others were making. Between their cakes, their compote, and their frosting, their cake was going to taste fucking orgasmic.

Putting it together and making it look pretty was going to be the harder part because, as they'd both mentioned multiple times, neither of them was a cake decorator. The other women were not to be trifled with. Or worse, underestimated. They all came from different back-grounds, and Ava had no idea who knew more or less than she did about cakes.

All they could do was their best.

That's what her mother would say.

Her father wouldn't be nearly as optimistic, telling her it should be simple and if she screwed this up, what the hell good was it for her to be a pastry chef. She could almost hear his gruff voice. "It's a goddamn cake. How hard can it be?"

Eventually, Regan pressed at the center of each cake and determined they were cooled enough for them to assemble.

"Ready?" she asked Ava, eyes bright with clear excitement. She was enjoying this, Ava realized. The spark of competition. The challenge of working with somebody new.

"As I'll ever be," Ava said, as Regan started tipping the cakes out of their pans and setting them on wire racks. She held each one with her palm on the bottom.

"They're all cooled. Let's do this."

For the next hour, they worked on trimming and stacking the cakes in order, a thin layer of raspberry compote in between each one. Just a bit. Too much would make the cake soggy and overpower the lemon. Regan trimmed up the top three cakes so they were smaller in diameter than the four on the bottom while Ava spun those bottom four on the turntable and frosted them. The frosting had come out nearly perfect, and it was going on the cakes as smoothly and easily as paint on a wall.

Thank God.

She smoothed it on and added a small dowel in the center to hold the next three layers. They made sure to do the colors in the order of the rainbow, and their frosting stayed white with just a hint of yellow.

Regan spoke in a low voice, close to her ear as they worked. "Looks like the other teams are being super obvious that it's a gay cake." She pursed her lips, and Ava knew just from her expression that she was wondering if they should've done the same thing.

"I think Liza appreciates subtlety and surprise," she said, keeping her voice just as low. Their initial design idea—to keep the cake elegant and classy—had been Regan's. "I think your instincts were right on the money."

"I guess we'll find out."

❖

The cakes were done and on display.

Each team sat quietly, their workstations all cleaned up, utensils and equipment put away. Regan felt very much like they were on an episode of *The Great British Baking Show*, waiting for Paul Hollywood and Pru Leith to come taste and judge their cakes.

They'd had some time to wander around and check out each other's work. The other two teams had definitely gone overt. Obvious. Vienna and Maia had made a cake in the actual shape of a rainbow—three tiers of it!—and they'd done a great job. Their edges were clean, their frosting piped smoothly in subtle, more pastel shades of the rainbow. Regan was curious to see what kind of cake it was. Paige and Madison also did three tiers, each one frosted in rainbow stripes. Their colors were bolder than Vienna and Maia's, louder, and their cake definitely screamed gay.

"Oh," Madison said, drawing the word out so it was long and breathy. "Your cake is *so pretty*." It was. She wasn't wrong. Despite her last-minute misgivings and near panic, Regan was proud of their work. True, the cake was only two tiers—a full tier smaller than the other two—but it was elegant. The ivory-colored frosting was smooth and had a slight shine to it. Ava had done a spectacular job piping the trim, which resembled the seams on a lacy wedding gown. They'd added two bride figurines at the top, which seemed a bit corny until Ava had created a path for them in the frosting. Now? Now it looked like they'd walked to the top of the cake and had taken their place there together.

It was gorgeous, she had to admit.

"I don't know why I'm so nervous," Ava whispered to her as she sat on the stool next to her and watched Liza walk in, followed, as always, by May.

"Well," Liza said from the front of the room. "You've had all day. Let's see what you came up with, shall we?" She wore black pants and her white chef's coat, her auburn hair pulled back in a low ponytail. Hands clasped behind her back, she began a slow stroll from station to station, scrutinizing each cake, turning them so she could see all sides.

She furrowed her brow at Vienna and Maia's cake, but only for a moment. Then she narrowed her eyes in a squint and gave her head a very subtle shake.

She tipped her head to one side when taking in Paige and Madison's cake, turning it with one hand while seemingly studying the frosting.

As she moved to Regan and Ava's cake, Regan caught a mere split second of her eyes going wide with surprise before Liza corrected herself and went back to her usual stoic expression. She bent at the waist to look at the bottom tier, then stood up and tipped her head again, examining the top. More nodding followed.

Hands once again clasped behind her back, she returned to the front of the room, turned to face them all, and clasped her hands in the front. It seemed almost choreographed to Regan, which was something she had always thought about the way Liza moved on her TV show. Slowly and deliberately. Stretching out the tension. Surely, she'd been coached to do so for the most dramatic effect.

"It's very interesting how different the cakes all are on the outside. Seems each team had their own unique view of what a same-sex wedding cake should look like. Your designs are...unique, that's for sure. Some are better than others, but as I said earlier, the taste of the cake is just as important, if not more so." Liza clapped her hands together once. "Let's cut."

Regan slid off her stool and grabbed the large knife. "I always hate this part," she said with a smile.

"Me too," Ava agreed. "While I do want people to taste the cake and see how great it is, it's always a bit of a shame to destroy something that took so much work."

"Exactly." They held one another's gaze for a beat before Regan shrugged. "Okay, moment of truth. Here we go." She sliced a piece off the top tier and laid it onto the plate Ava held up for her. Holy freaking shitballs, it was perfect. Each layer was distinct, its color prominent, the raspberry compote in evidence, but not too much. Regan had tasted the scraps of cake when she'd had to cut down the top tier, so she knew it was awesome.

Next to her, Ava said a very quiet "Ooohhh" under her breath, and Regan turned a grin to her.

"We did good," she whispered, and Ava nodded her agreement.

Vienna and Maia were up first. They looked confident as Vienna handed a slice of cake to Liza. It was white, so Regan assumed vanilla but was proven wrong when Liza said, "Nice coconut flavor. Could've used a bit more punch. Overall, not bad. Not great, but not bad." Vienna and Maia had twin expressions on their faces that seemed to be a mix of disappointment at her words and relief that they were done.

Liza moved on to Madison and Paige's cake. With an amused smile, she asked Paige, "Are you going to be sick?"

"I hope not," Paige said with a sheepish grin. "Nerves."

Liza nodded as Madison handed her a plate with a slice of their cake. Looked like red velvet to Regan, who thought it was a bit of an obvious choice for a wedding cake.

"Red velvet isn't terribly original," Liza commented, almost to herself, as if reading Regan's thoughts. And Paige's complexion went back to slightly green. Liza took a bite, seemed to think on it as she chewed. "It's moist, though. Dense without being too much so. Good depth of flavor. Quite tasty. Just boring." She set the plate down.

Paige felt behind her, clearly looking for her stool before dropping onto it.

And then it was their turn.

Regan wondered if Ava could hear her heart hammering in her chest. She did hear Ava swallow as she handed the plate to Liza.

"Well, first of all, it looks absolutely lovely," Liza commented. "You went with the internal rainbow, I see, and left the outside with more of a classy appearance. Subtlety. I like it. Creative." She put a bite in her mouth, slid the fork out slowly, and Regan was pretty sure her own head might explode in anticipation. Her brain went to people who baked in competitions on tv and her only thought was *Jesus, how do people do this?*

"Oh." Just that one word. That's all Liza said for a full minute. And then she did something completely unexpected…she took a second bite. "Oh, my." She turned to them with what seemed to be a completely bewildered expression on her face, as if she hadn't expected any of them to make a decent cake. "Good Lord, that's delicious." She pointed at the slice with her fork. "The lemon is tangy and tart, but not too much so, and it's evened out by the raspberry compote, which is absolutely perfect, by the way." She gave a nod to Ava on that. "God." She set the plate down and seemed almost a little irritated as she said, "That might be one of the best pieces of cake I've ever tasted." She turned and headed toward the front of the room.

When Regan turned to meet Ava's gaze, her dark eyes were wide with clear disbelief. She rolled her lips in and bit down on them to keep from bursting into delighted laughter. Because oh my God, Liza Bennett-Schmidt had just told them their cake rocked.

"I did not see that coming," Ava whispered when Liza was far enough away to not hear.

"Same," Regan whispered back, but she reached for Ava's hand and gave it a gentle squeeze, and she was surprised to feel Ava squeeze back before letting it go and turning her attention to Liza.

"I am impressed. I threw a last-minute challenge at you, made you work with somebody you're not terribly familiar with, and you all stepped up. Very nicely done." She gave them time to bask in that before she went on. "As for who impressed me the most, I have to go with Ava and Regan. Not only did they make a most delicious cake and then color it in deep, vibrant colors, they made it look elegant and beautiful, a cake any betrothed couple—same-sex or not—would be thrilled to have at their wedding reception. Good work, you two."

Liza began clapping, and the others joined in for a round of applause. Regan knew she was grinning like a big dork, and that was okay because so was Ava. Before she could stop herself, she wrapped Ava in a hug. Just a quick one. Ava looked slightly surprised but went with it. She let her go after only a second or two.

"You all have worked very hard today. Cocktails and appetizers have been set up in the dining room. We'll have the cakes brought up so you can try each other's. Feel free to go freshen up and then head that way. Again, nice work today, ladies. I'm proud of you."

And with that, she turned and left, May on her heels.

CHAPTER NINE

The rest of the week had flown by. Honestly, it was crazy how fast time seemed to be going. Ava felt like she'd only arrived a day or two ago, but the reality was, it had already been two and a half weeks.

It was Sunday, and Liza had given them the day off. Nothing had slowed down after the same-sex wedding cake bake-off. They'd gone right back to work the next day. Liza had helped them perfect their scones for the second time on one day and pizza dough the next. Friday had been soufflé day, which Ava didn't really need any help with, but she'd picked up pointers anyway. Then yesterday they'd worked on macarons, the most deceptively difficult cookie, in her opinion. It had taken her four batches before she got the feet just right on hers. Liza seemed to grow slightly impatient with her, and her scrutiny only made for more nerves for Ava, which didn't help her to focus. Vienna had had the same issue—not able to get the feet right—and it was clear Liza's continual criticism was flustering her. Ava felt bad for her.

Now she sat at her desk with her laptop open, initially reading an article on commercial mixers, but found herself gazing out the window more often than not.

Behind her, and on the other side of the room, Regan sat on her unmade bed, phone in hand. If Ava had to guess, she was texting with somebody, judging by how often her thumbs flew as she typed.

"I'm gonna go for a walk." Ava blurted the statement out as if she was reporting to somebody, though she wasn't sure why.

Regan looked up, clearly surprised. "Now?"

"Yeah." She pointed out the window as she took off her glasses.

"There's a pond in the back with a path around it. It's nice out. I thought some fresh air might be good. I'm tired of sitting around."

Regan seemed to think about it for a moment, then gave a nod. "Can I go?"

Surprised, Ava turned to meet her gaze. *Honestly, some company might be nice.* "Sure."

"Awesome. Lemme just send this text." Her thumbs flew some more, and then she stood up and slid the phone into the back pocket of her joggers.

A few minutes later, they both had sneakers on and were headed out the front door of the mansion.

She'd been right about the day. It was gorgeous. Not too hot. Bright sunshine in an electric blue sky. She inhaled deeply and let it out.

"There's something to be said for being surrounded by trees and grass and green after living in the city for a few years, isn't there?" She didn't really expect an answer. The question was kind of rhetorical, just thoughts she'd spoken out loud. But Regan answered.

"God, yes." She mimicked Ava's deep breath. "Can you smell that? Leaves and woods and *earth*. It's intoxicating." They started walking along the mansion, then around the side, Ava leading the way. "So, you've been out here before?"

"A couple times, yeah. I'm not usually up until after ten in my normal life, but for some reason, I wake up early here."

"I'm sure it has nothing to do with the number of us that work bakery hours and are awake before the ass crack of dawn."

Ava gave a soft laugh.

"Or maybe it's the quiet." Regan's sneakers whooshed through the blades of grass as they walked. "I had a really hard time sleeping the first week because there's no sound. No traffic, no sirens, no arguments on the street at midnight..."

"No garbage trucks emptying dumpsters at four a.m. or street cleaners buzzing by before dawn..."

They looked at each other, and Ava felt a solidarity with Regan she hadn't before. City girls in the country.

They reached the back of the mansion where the pond became visible. "Oh," Regan said quietly. "That's so pretty."

"Isn't it? My watch says it's not quite a mile around, so I've just been walking it until I feel like being done." She shrugged and set her watch, then looked at Regan.

"Sounds good to me."

They began the first lap.

They seemed to have an unspoken agreement to start off quietly, to simply enjoy the sounds of nature they didn't get to listen to in the city. Birds singing. A light breeze rustling the leaves in the trees. The faraway sound of a jet high above them. They made it more than halfway around before Regan sighed, then spoke.

"I miss my cat," she said, a wistful tone in her voice.

"Oh my God, me too," Ava said in surprise. "So much. It's just me and him. I hope he doesn't think I left him for good." It was a thought she'd had since the first week at the retreat, and it had only tugged harder at her heart as time went on.

"Who's watching him?"

"My neighbor. She's a sweet elderly woman who just loves him, so I know he's being spoiled rotten." She had a flash of Jiminy all curled up in Mrs. Carter's lap, watching *Wheel of Fortune* or *Jeopardy*, and she was both happy and sad. "Still..."

"You want to be the one spoiling him."

"Exactly." They walked. "Who's got yours?"

"I have two roommates," Regan said. "So they're taking care of him. But I think the same thing you do: What if he thinks I'm never coming back? That I've left him for good? Eight weeks is a long time."

"It really is." Ava sighed. "What's yours named?"

"King Arthur." Regan shot her a look.

"For the flour?" Ava asked with a grin.

"I found him behind the bakery, near the dumpster with his head in an empty bag of flour, so it seemed perfect. I call him Artie." Regan's entire face lit up when she talked about her cat. Her blue eyes got brighter, and her smile grew wider.

"Okay, that's officially adorable."

"And yours?"

"Jiminy Cricket."

Regan laughed. "Oh my God, that's so freaking cute. Why?"

"Because when I got him as a kitten, he used to jump around and he'd sort of...pop straight into the air like a cricket." She mimicked the action with her hand, curving it and then popping it straight up, the way he used to. "He doesn't do it anymore because I'm sure he was just trying to figure out his body and how to move it, but it was stupidly cute."

"Jiminy. I love it."

Silence fell again for several moments before Ava ventured to ask a question she'd been thinking about for a while. "So...what do you think of Liza?"

Regan glanced at her quickly, then looked down at her feet, then gazed out over the pond.

Ava released a small chuckle. "I get it."

"I mean, I'm enjoying learning from her."

"Same."

"This place is amazing." Regan swooped her arm out to encompass the pond, grounds, and mansion.

"Agreed."

"She kind of..." Regan seemed to struggle with finding the right words, but Ava waited her out until she finally said, "She kinda seems to enjoy when one of us fucks up."

"Thank you." Ava's relief was palpable. "I was worried I was the only one who saw that."

"You're not. I think she's determined to get Paige to throw up at some point during this retreat."

Ava snort-laughed, but caught herself. "I shouldn't laugh. Paige is a sweetheart. So is Vienna, and Liza seems extra rough on her."

"She does, right? I actually like everybody here. All the attendees." Regan started to say more but seemed to think better of it.

"What?"

Regan shook her head. "Nothing."

Ava avoided rolling her eyes in annoyance. Regan clearly had something to say, but she wasn't about to pry it out of her.

They kept walking.

❖

Apparently, the walk hadn't been enough because Ava decided to go hit Liza's little gym and "get in a workout," as she'd put it.

Now Regan was alone in their room, and she was kind of happy about that. She knew she'd ticked Ava off by not sharing something she'd thought better about sharing, but so the fuck what? She didn't owe her anything, right? Plus, what she'd been about to say was that she almost wished Liza hadn't put the money into play. Regan wasn't there to compete, but thinking about that money and what she could do with it, how she could use it to give Billy a fair offer for Sweet Temptations and what that would do to her life, had changed the way she thought about the others. People who had started off as potential friends were now competition to be eliminated. Or at least defeated. The change was unnerving, kind of sad, and she didn't want Ava to know she felt that way about it. She wasn't cutthroat and she didn't like that she now felt forced to be exactly that.

Ava was pretty cutthroat, she suspected, judging from their history. Ava seemed to want the best and seemed to want to *be* the best, so this kind of thing was probably right up her alley, which was a big part of why Regan hadn't wanted to talk to her about it.

With a resigned sigh, she picked up her phone and FaceTimed Kiki, who picked up before the second ring.

"Hey, bitch," her roommate said with a grin. "I was just going to call you. How's it going up there in the Land of Baked Goods? Have you voted all the others off the island—er, out of the mansion yet?"

Just hearing Kiki's voice made her muscles relax a bit, and she started to feel better almost instantly. "Not exactly how it works. Which is…strange."

"No? What do you mean?" Kiki set the phone against something on their counter, and Regan watched as she poured herself a cup of coffee.

"I don't even really know. Apparently, Liza decides at the end of the eight weeks who she thinks deserves the money. She didn't really give us rules or details other than that."

"I have read more than once that she's an egomaniac, you know."

Regan grinned. Kiki loved celebrity gossip. She read all the sites that reported on bad behaviors, the lists of *worst celebrity tippers*, that kind of thing. Regan wasn't at all surprised that she had dirt on Liza Bennett-Schmidt. "I know. You've told me many times."

"Are you alone in your room?"

"Yes." Regan drew the word out, not understanding why Kiki would ask that until she continued.

"How's the roommate situation? You haven't killed her in her sleep yet, have you?"

"Not yet." Regan's brain decided right then to show her an image of Ava at her desk, black-rimmed glasses on her face, looking studious and, yes, damn gorgeous. "It's been fine. But listen, I want to see my cat. Where is he? You're not letting him go to parties, are you?"

Kiki bent out of the frame, then stood up with Artie in her arms. "Nope. Only strip clubs. I hope that's okay."

Regan's voice devolved into baby talk, as it often did when she spoke with her cat, and her heart clenched in her chest as she was filled with a sense of longing. Damn, she missed her boy.

She had just hung up from Kiki when there was a soft rap on her door. When she called for the visitor to come in, she was surprised to see both Madison and Paige.

"Hey, you guys," she said, hopping to her feet. She noticed Madison look from Ava's very tidy side of the room to her own disheveled side and, for a moment, wished she'd at least made her bed that morning. "What's up?"

"We're bored," Paige said. "We're gonna go into town for lunch. Wanna join?"

Well, she'd already talked to her cat, and her plan for the rest of the day had been to look over some of her recipes for upcoming bakes, but she certainly didn't need the entire afternoon to do that. "That sounds excellent. I'm in."

❖

When Ava returned to the room from her workout, she was relieved to see a pile of freshly laundered towels on each of their beds—courtesy of Liza's household staff—but no sign of Regan, and she blew out a breath. Man, that woman could push her buttons, and what was worse, she didn't understand why.

The workout had helped. Liza had a state-of-the-art treadmill—no surprise there—and Ava had lifted some weights, then done a three-mile run before walking for another two. She felt invigorated now, realizing how much she'd missed regular exercise being away from home. She vowed to use the gym more often as she headed into the shower.

Once she was all refreshed and had decided to let her hair air-dry, she combed it back from her face, then got comfy on her bed and sent a text to Mrs. Carter, checking on Jiminy. A surprisingly tech-savvy senior, Mrs. Carter texted back immediately and even sent a photo of Jiminy looking right into the camera with his bright green eyes. Ava smiled and felt a pang of sadness hit her right in the chest. "I miss you, buddy," she whispered softly, running her fingertips over the photo. A quick check of the calendar told her there were five and a half more weeks left in the retreat, and in that moment, they felt like a lifetime.

Shoving down her homesickness, she pulled out her laptop. She'd intended to do some surfing and check out some of the bakers she followed on TikTok and YouTube, but suddenly, she just felt sad and low-energy. The exercise had invigorated her, but missing her cat had pulled her down off that high. She clicked on to Netflix and had just settled in to watch a movie when the door opened and Regan came in. Or stumbled in, which was more accurate.

"Hey," Ava said, looking up from the screen.

Regan blinked at her several times before waving.

Ava studied her for a moment before venturing a question. "Are you drunk?"

Regan held her thumb and forefinger close together as she dropped her butt onto the end of her bed. "I'm not drunk, but I am most definitely a little tipsy." Except she said the word *little* like *l'il*.

"And how did that happen?"

"I had some drinks, that's how."

Ava nodded, gave her head a quick shake, and turned back to her movie. When a few moments went by and it stayed quiet, she glanced back up to see Regan still sitting on her bed, staring at her. "Something I can help you with?" she asked. She hadn't meant it to come out snarky, but it kind of did, and she grimaced slightly at her own tone.

"Yes. Why did you fire me?"

Here we go. Ava paused the movie and said simply, "I didn't fire you."

"Okay." Regan drew the word out, clearly annoyed by the semantics. "Why did you get me fired?"

Ava cleared her throat. From the moment she'd realized she was rooming with Regan, she knew this subject would likely come up. She just didn't think it would happen while Regan was clearly inebriated. "For what it's worth, I didn't mean to get you fired. That wasn't my intention."

"Well, it's *worth* nothing because I *did* get fired."

"I know. I'm sorry about that." She played with a small hangnail on her thumb.

"Are you?"

Ava looked up and squinted at Regan. "Yes."

"I loved that job. And I would've gotten better. I learn fast. I just needed a chance and somebody to guide me. I'd hoped that would be you. Instead, you complained."

A deep breath and a slow exhale. "Look. I didn't complain. I was concerned. You weren't keeping up. You were causing others to fall behind because they had to pick up your slack. I know you wanted to learn, and I know you're good. Now. But then? You were a detriment."

"A detriment?" Regan's eyes went wide. "Wow. Harsh."

"You asked."

"I did. And certainly, don't sugarcoat it for me or anything." She stood and walked around the side of her bed.

"I'm sorry." Ava didn't know what else Regan expected her to say. But she still felt bad. She wasn't lying; she hadn't expected her boss to fire Regan on the spot. She'd been as shocked as Regan had by that.

"So you said." Regan stepped out of her pants, then peeled off her shirt. "I need a shower," she said softly, seemingly to nobody—or maybe just to herself—and Ava couldn't pull her eyes away as the bra and then the underwear followed the pants and top, and then Regan was standing there naked. And there were her glorious breasts. Again.

This time, Ava didn't look away.

CHAPTER TEN

R egan was not a person who was often annoyed with herself. Sure, she made mistakes, just like every other human being on the planet. She fucked up on occasion. But she rarely held on to such things. Normally, she picked herself up, dusted herself off, and moved on. Mistakes happened. They were part of life.

But yesterday? Holy crap, had she fucked up. *And this is exactly why I should not be allowed to do shots.*

She shook her head in self-deprecation as she rolled out the dough for her pie crust. Why she'd let Madison and Paige talk her into doing shots when they were out, she wasn't sure. No, that was a lie. She knew exactly why: because she was frustrated with Ava and the state of things. She knew one shot would relax her, take away some of the stress she'd been feeling. Of course, then one shot became two, and then there was pressure because Madison wanted to do one more. And then Paige got teary because she was missing her husband, and so they did another shot.

It was all downhill after that.

She picked up the dough and flipped it over, then floured it and rolled some more as she stifled a groan and tightened her jaw.

So far downhill and so fast.

She'd stripped. *In front of Ava.* Just...took her damn clothes off. All of them. Paraded around naked! Okay, she didn't actually *parade*, but she'd walked from her bed all the way across the room to the bathroom. Naked. And to make matters worse, she'd forgotten to bring a clean towel in with her. Liza's household staff had collected towels that morning, laundered them, and brought them back, and as Regan had stood in the shower being absolutely mortified that she'd done what she'd done, she'd suddenly remembered the pile of towels she'd vaguely noticed on the end of her bed and realized she had nothing in the bathroom to cover herself with. There was no way in hell she'd ask Ava for her help, so she'd had no choice but to waltz back out into the room—this time not only naked but dripping wet—to grab a towel, wrap it around herself, and go back into the bathroom. She'd managed to avoid looking at Ava, though she did pass a mirror on her way back and was pretty sure she was being watched with an amused grin.

Goddamn, she was embarrassed.

"A little less flour." Liza's voice was close enough to startle her. She hadn't realized she'd made her way to Regan's station. "Don't dry it out."

"Right," Regan said with a nod. "Right." She knew that. About the flour. But her mind was elsewhere. Thankfully, Liza moved on.

Across the aisle, Ava was working on her own crust and was clearly frustrated with it—as evidenced by the fact that she picked it up off her counter, crumpled it into a ball in her hands, and threw it in the trash with some force, her assistant looking on in obvious surprise. Ava's lips were pressed tightly together as she pulled her mixer forward and, from what Regan could tell, started over again, just as Liza approached.

"Yikes, isn't this your third go-round?" she asked Ava, who nodded as a pink circle blossomed on each cheek. "Do they never serve pie in your five-star restaurant?"

Ouch. Regan watched Ava's throat move as she swallowed and said something Regan couldn't quite make out.

"Maybe the third time's the charm." Liza grinned, then moved on to Maia's workstation, Ava watching her go.

Regan followed Liza with her eyes, noticing her smug smile as she thought how unhelpful she'd been to Ava. She didn't want to have sympathy for her, but she couldn't help herself. Wasn't this a retreat? Weren't they there to learn from Liza? From what Regan had seen, Liza had been wholly unhelpful, and when she glanced over at Ava, her eyes were wet. In front of her, Vienna cleared her throat to get Regan's attention. She'd been watching, too, and her expression said she was as angered as Regan about what she'd just seen. She met Regan's gaze, shook her head, and turned back to her own pie.

Madison's workstation was behind Regan's, and she heard her

cough. When she glanced back, Madison was looking at her with wide eyes. "That was *cold*," she whispered, and Regan nodded her agreement. At the stove, Hadley was stirring the rhubarb, cooking it down so they could add it to the strawberries, and her eyes also followed Liza as she moved from station to station. Her expression was hard to read, but Regan was glad she wasn't the only one who'd noticed the whole exchange.

Over the next couple hours, Regan and Hadley put together three pies. Vienna did four. Madison and Paige each had two, though Paige had also struggled and had to restart one of hers. Maia did four. While Regan was pulling her triple berry out of the oven, Ava was just flopping her raw pie crust onto a pie plate, heart-wrenchingly behind the others. Her face was still red, and her forehead glistened with what was likely nervous perspiration. Becca, her assistant, had spent some time trying to get conversation flowing but had given up nearly an hour ago and instead was running all over the place, clearly doing her best to be helpful. Ava's was the most silent station in the space.

She made two pies. Becca must have been in charge of fillings, as every time Regan had hazarded a glance, Ava was working on crust. Becca filled the two pie crusts, and Ava slid them into the oven, looking so relieved, Regan wouldn't have been at all surprised to see her fall right down on the floor, a heap of exhausted muscle and bone.

Liza had spent the time wandering, offering pointers (to some), and judging. Regan had hoped she would make pies along with them so she could see her technique up close, but that didn't happen this time. She merely wandered, watched, snarked.

"I think these are gonna be delicious," Hadley said to her, clearly keeping her voice down a bit, probably to keep Ava from feeling bad.

"Triple berry has always been my favorite," Regan said, scrutinizing the surface of theirs. She'd used a crumble topping to give it more texture, and the oats had browned nicely. "I can't wait to have a piece."

"Same," Hadley said with a grin. "And have the others taste it. It's one of the things I like most about baking: the sharing."

"Yeah? Me too. It's a big part of why I started baking in the first place. I grew up in a pretty busy household." She smiled as she thought about her family. "I have a little brother and a little sister, plus my parents and my grandpa, all in the same house. So every time I baked something, I had lots of people to taste-test. And then when I got good at it, they would fight over who got to taste-test."

"Aw, that's so sweet," Hadley said.

Across the aisle, Ava was finally pulling her pies out. Regan hadn't been able to see what kinds they were going in, but coming out, at least one was cherry. She could tell by the latticework on top—and she found herself surprised that after all the redos and stress, Ava had taken the time to do a latticework on top of one of them. Good for her.

Liza had left them while their pies baked, but now was back, standing at the front of the room in front of her own station. "I trust all pies are now out of the oven?" Her eyes were laser-focused on Ava, who simply nodded and kept her chin up.

Jesus, Liza was all over her today. What the hell was that about?

❖

Ava felt sick.

Like, she seriously might throw up. Her stomach churned, and she had a sour taste in her throat, and if Liza singled her and her failure out one more time, she was going to hurl. There was not a doubt in her mind.

She wasn't sure why she was surprised at the intensity. She'd watched Liza Bennett-Schmidt on television for years, and whether Liza was cooking herself for an audience or had someone to teach on her show, she pulled no punches. She was rarely gentle. She was often critical. She tended to zero in on one person and they became her focus. Today, it was obviously Ava. A little bit of Paige, who also struggled with her crust, but mostly Ava. But this was a *retreat*. The point was to learn from her, right? Maybe she missed torturing folks on TV.

Of course it would be pie. Ava never could make a decent pie crust, as she'd told Becca. And Paige. There was some kind of disconnect in her brain or something, because she had never been able to get it right. And to answer Liza's snarky question: No, they did not serve pie in her five-star restaurant. Because Ava was the one who made the dessert menu. So there.

Painfully aware of the subtle peeks and quick looks sent her way by her fellow retreat attendees, she kept her head up and did her best to stay busy, washing dishes, putting things away, wiping down the counter. Five times. Possibly six. Becca had already done so. In fact, she'd been a godsend, doing any little thing Ava asked of her. Thank God she'd been there.

The rest of the day went as expected. Liza tasted everybody's pie, left Ava's for last, and was less than impressed. Then the remaining pies were taken up to be served after dinner.

Funnily enough, people seemed to like her pies. At first, she assumed their compliments were out of pity, but when she tasted her own cherry pie, she was surprised to find it was damn good. Even the crust. Huh.

Of course, after dinner and conversation—during which she listened more than participated—everybody was exhausted from the day and headed up to their rooms.

That meant alone time with Regan. In any other circumstance, there would be more dread, but she was so flat out *done* with the day that she didn't even have the energy to care. She headed upstairs, into their room, and flopped face-first onto her bed.

"Rough day," Regan commented as she came in behind her and shut the door.

Ava groaned into the blankets without lifting her head.

"Listen, Liza was a bitch to you. That was totally uncalled for."

Ava turned her head to look at her roommate.

"We couldn't say anything during dinner because, you know, May's and other sets of ears were around. But we did some texting and whispering when you were baking your pies. She was awful to you. Unnecessarily awful. Everybody thought it was totally not cool." Regan held her gaze for a moment before lifting one shoulder and adding, "I'm sorry you had to deal with that today."

"Thank you," Ava mumbled, her voice not as muffled by bedsheets.

With a nod, Regan grabbed some clothes off the floor, went into the bathroom, and shut the door, leaving Ava wallowing on her bed, with no desire to move.

She felt like a wrung-out dishcloth, damp and shapeless, and she lay there, doing nothing but breathing.

And thinking.

Because that was the curse of the person whose brain never stopped, wasn't it? Of course Regan would have everybody's number so they could text. Ava had nobody's number, and that had been by choice.

But now she kind of wished she had at least one. Maybe Vienna's? She seemed serious and professional, on the same page as Ava, right? And she probably still had Regan's number in her phone from way back, unless she'd changed it.

With Regan still in the bathroom, Ava sat up and grabbed her phone. She scrolled through her contacts and there it was: Regan Callahan. And now she was curious. With a sigh, she typed out a text. *Hey, thanks for being nice to me on an epically shitty day.* She followed it up with a smiling emoji. No hearts or funny faces. Just something simple. She hit send before she could talk herself out of it. She reached to set her phone on the nightstand when it buzzed in her hand.

Welcome. And the same smiling emoji.

Same number, apparently. Ava smiled and set the phone down, then pulled out her laptop just as the bathroom door opened. Regan's face was pink and freshly scrubbed, and Ava could smell the mint of her toothpaste. She was wearing thin boxer shorts and a tank top, her nipples making it clear that there was no bra because these were her pajamas. Ava forced her eyes back to her laptop screen and tried hard to ignore the sense memory from seeing Regan's bare breasts not once but twice.

After clearing her throat, she spoke. "Hey, what haven't we done yet? I'm looking some stuff up so I'm ready for the rest of the week."

"Good question," Regan said as she tossed the clothes she'd been wearing onto the floor next to her still-open suitcase. "Let's see." She gazed off into the middle of the room and counted on her fingers. "We did scones."

"Twice," Ava pointed out.

"Twice. Right. And I still suck at them."

"Same," Ava said with a snort.

"We did sweet bread."

"Not to be confused with sweetbreads."

Regan grimaced. "Valid. We did soufflé."

"Which I rocked."

"You did. That was dreamy. And we did layer cake. Which we rocked."

"True story."

Regan squinted, then added, "And macarons."

With a sigh, Ava said, "I wish we'd do those again. I struggled."

"Same."

"That leaves a lot." Ava typed into her laptop. "There are a million cookies. We've done no chocolate."

"Danishes. Muffins. Bagels."

Ava glanced up. "Have you made bagels?"

"I have. They're complicated, but delicious when you get 'em right."

Ava nodded and typed some more. "Streusel. Custard. Tarts. Holy crap, there's a ton left. I have no idea where to even start."

"I have an idea," Regan said as she padded in her bare feet to stand next to Ava's bed. "What if we just watch some episodes of *Whisk Me Away?* That would at least give us a refresher on Liza herself, what she likes and doesn't, her favorite stuff. That could help." Then she shrugged, as if trying to say it was no big deal whether Ava thought it was a good idea or a shitty one.

"I think that sounds like a fantastic idea." And it did. Ava felt a renewed sense of energy. "Let me get comfy like you and we'll sit and watch?"

"Perfect."

Ava pulled herself up, grabbed her pajamas, and headed toward the bathroom. For the first time all day, she didn't feel beaten up, embarrassed, or wiped out. As she closed the door, she glanced at Regan and felt a surprising emotion.

Gratitude.

❖

If somebody would've told Regan six months ago that she would eventually be sitting in her jammies on a bed next to Ava Prescott while they watched *Whisk Me Away* together, she'd have told that person they were off their rocker. She would have laughed and laughed and laughed.

And yet.

There she sat, on Ava's bed, under the duvet 'cause the house felt a little drafty tonight. She was in her boxers—and might've dressed differently if she'd known that was where she'd be, because her thigh was pressed up against Ava's. At least it wasn't skin on skin. Ava had been smart enough to wear pajama pants, thank God.

"Snickerdoodles," Ava said, yanking Regan out of her zoning.

"Huh?" She gave her head a subtle shake, trying to get back to the present.

Ava turned those dark eyes to her. She'd put on her glasses, and whether Regan loved her or hated her guts mattered not at all, because Ava was fucking stunning. No makeup, hair down, glasses on, and fucking stunning. There was no question. "They're a stupidly simple cookie, but Liza seems to love them." She returned her gaze to the laptop screen balanced between them on their thighs. "I wonder why."

"'Cause they're freaking awesome?"

Ava grinned. "Maybe that."

God, she smelled good, too. Regan tried to be subtle with her inhales, but Ava smelled like summer, and as she sat there, she tried to put her finger on each distinct scent. Sunshine, suntan lotion, sand, salt, grass...none of it made sense. How does a person smell like sunshine, for fuck's sake? But Ava did. Somehow, she did, and it was wonderful and warm and comforting.

"Oh!" Regan pointed at the screen. "Those lemon tarts. This is the third show where they were featured somehow."

"Third?"

"I've seen them twice on older episodes, and now they're on this one."

"Good catch." Ava was keeping a list on her Notes app, so she jotted down lemon tarts.

They watched quietly for a while, going from episode to episode and doing their best to mix up the seasons so they could see what things Liza repeated. Soon, they had a list of half a dozen items.

"I'm sorry," Ava said, breaking their quiet.

Regan turned to her, but Ava stayed watching the screen. "You're sorry? For what?"

There was a beat, and it seemed to Regan as if Ava was gathering something—courage, words, breath? She turned to Regan, and the eye contact was intense. "For causing you to get fired."

Regan knew she looked surprised because she felt it, like a little zap of electricity had been shot through her. "You are?"

Ava nodded. "I was young and out to make a name for myself. And I didn't yet understand that a kitchen is a team, that instead of simply excising a piece that isn't fitting, we need to help shape it so that it does. I didn't learn that until a couple years later, but you took the hit for my ignorance. I'm really sorry about that."

Regan sat there blinking at her, stunned into silence.

Ava laughed softly. "I can see by your wide eyes that this wasn't exactly something you thought I might say."

"Not in a million years," Regan said with a grin. "Wow." She had to clear her throat of the unexpected lump that had lodged there. "Thank you. That—thank you." There was more she could've said. She could've told Ava that it was fine because she found a much better place in Sweet Temptations, that it was someplace she did fit, and that her boss had helped to mentor her instead of getting angry, that he was retiring and she wanted so badly to buy the place but wasn't sure if she could. But she didn't. She stayed with the simple words of gratitude, along with a gentle smile.

"One more episode?" Ava asked, and her relief was almost tangible, like it hung in the air around them a bit before it floated away, leaving a clearly lighter Ava sitting on the bed. It made Regan happy for some reason.

She glanced at her watch. "I'm up for one more if you are."

With one nod, Ava found another episode and hit play.

Regan had no idea when she'd actually dozed off, but when she opened her eyes, she had a moment of confusion. What time was it? Where was she? Who was sleeping on her? Slowly, it all came back to her, and when she glanced at Ava, she saw that she, too, had fallen asleep. They'd both apparently slumped down as time went on, and Ava's head was pillowed on Regan's shoulder, her breathing deep and even. The laptop still balanced on their thighs, and the episode playing was not the one they'd chosen. In fact, it was several episodes into the season, Regan knew because she'd watched the show dozens upon dozens of times. When she looked at her watch, she flinched in surprise.

It was after three in the morning.

Her brain told her she needed to get up. To wake up Ava, to close the laptop, to move to her own—probably really cold—bed. Her body, on the other hand, did not want to move at all. *Why?* it reasoned. It was warm. Cozy. Not alone. Clearly, Ava felt the same way. Why move?

An internal battle raged. Her brain versus her body, and she felt like she herself had little say in the matter. She reached down and closed the laptop, completing the darkness of the room. Ava shifted in her sleep, burrowed a bit closer, and didn't wake up.

Regan's eyes grew heavy while she debated what to do, and somewhere deep in her mind, she knew the decision before it was even made.

She drifted back to sleep.

CHAPTER ELEVEN

A va loved the feeling of having gotten a great night's sleep. It didn't happen often, if she was honest. A lot of the time, work left her wired, and she had a hard time turning her brain off enough to fall asleep. Sometimes, she got less than five hours a night for several nights in a row. Not a healthy way to live. She'd tried sleep aids, but they left her too groggy to function the next day, so she made do as best she could during her shifts and tried to catch up on sleep on her days off.

She'd struggled at the retreat as well, mostly because the timing was all off. She was used to going to sleep in the early morning hours and staying in bed until ten or eleven. But here, things down in the work kitchen started by nine, so she needed to be up by seven thirty or so. Plus, some of the other girls kept bakery hours, which meant they were up before the sun, Regan included.

As she lay in bed now and slowly let herself swim up to the surface from her very deep, very restful sleep, she recalled the previous night. Regan had been good company, which surprised her—though it probably shouldn't have. People seemed to like Regan. She was a nice person. And it was really thoughtful of her to sit and watch episodes of *Whisk Me Away* with her, knowing how shitty Ava's day had been. She was grateful for that.

She was on her back and stretched her leg.

It hit another leg.

A leg that was not hers.

Oh God.

She stilled. Afraid to open her eyes, she replayed the previous night once more and realized she had no recollection of it ending. No memory of finishing an episode, closing the laptop, saying good night to Regan, watching her walk back to her own bed.

Oh God.

A weight suddenly settled in her chest over the realization, but weirdly, also *on* her chest. Still afraid to move, she forced herself to open her eyes, and there it was: a head of brown hair highlighted with gold streaks pillowed on her chest just below her chin. She could smell the watermelon scent of it, feel the warmth of the rest of Regan's body, specifically the arm that was thrown across Ava's midsection. Regan shifted just slightly in her sleep, and that arm slid along her skin where her shirt had ridden up a bit, causing a throbbing to begin low in her body.

Could she get out of this? Could she slip out of the bed without waking Regan? Because then, maybe she'd never know.

She was also being ridiculous. So they fell asleep. Together. Practically on top of each other. That happened all the time, didn't it? Totally normal. It was all totally normal. Right?

A snort escaped before she could catch it, and Regan stirred. Ava held herself still and waited.

Regan inhaled deeply through her nose—that sound of just waking up—and Ava could feel her giving her body a gentle stretch. And then she froze. Did she stop breathing altogether? Kinda felt like she did. Ava didn't move. She waited.

Slowly, Regan lifted her head from Ava's chest and turned it until their eyes met.

Ava swallowed at the sight of tousled, sleepy Regan, whose blue eyes went wide. "Morning," Ava said, and her voice was hoarse. She cleared her throat.

"Hey," Regan responded. "Um…" She pushed herself off Ava until she was in a sitting position. She seemed to notice Ava's laptop at the foot of the bed and reached for it. "Don't want this to fall," she said with a shrug and handed it to Ava while avoiding her eyes.

"Thanks." Without Regan's arm pinning her down, Ava sat up, too. She heard Regan swallow, and part of her was glad to know that even though she hadn't said as much, Regan was clearly as freaked as she was by their situation that morning. She said quickly, "Um, I'm gonna take a shower. Do you wanna—" She indicated the bathroom with her chin.

"Oh. Yeah. Yes. Thanks." And Regan jumped off the bed like Ava had used a cattle prod on her and hurried to the bathroom so fast, Ava wondered if her feet even touched the floor. The door clicked closed.

"Not awkward at all," she muttered as she slid out of bed and grabbed her clothes for the day. Regan was out of the bathroom in record time, didn't look at her, and they scurried past one another. Once Ava was safely ensconced and the door was locked, she leaned on it with both hands and let out a long, slow breath, absently wondering if she'd been breathing at all since she'd opened her eyes.

When the water was as hot as she could stand it, she stepped under the spray, turned her face to it, and stood there. Just stood there for a long moment. What she wanted to do was scream, but as there were no pillows available in the bathtub, she settled for nearly scalding herself as she did some quiet pep talking.

"So you fell asleep," she whispered to herself. "So what? It's not like you had drunken sex or something."

Wait, what? What was her brain trying to do to her? *No. No way. That is a visual I do not need, thank you very much. Nope, we are shutting that line of thinking right down. Now. Right now.*

She turned her attention to scrubbing. She scrubbed her skin hard. Too hard, really. She just wanted to keep her mind on something other than how nice it had felt to have Regan curled up against her while she slept. How she'd been warm and comfortable and content.

Yeah, she didn't want to deal with that last bit, so she gave her head a shake and finished up her shower. When she was dressed and finally worked up the courage to open the door, Regan was gone.

She wasn't proud of the relief she felt.

On her bed was a scrap of paper with a handwritten note.

Went for a walk. Sorry about last night.
~R

She held the paper for several moments, her eyes following the surprisingly flowery handwriting, the swoops of the *W*s and the drop-down curly curve of the *Y*. She felt bad that Regan was sorry, that she'd felt the need to apologize for something that was, pretty obviously, innocent.

They'd have to talk about it.

She groaned as she plugged in her blow-dryer.

Not long after, and half expecting to see Regan in the dining room, having breakfast and avoiding her, she was surprised to find she wasn't there. The others mingled around the room, pouring coffee and nibbling on pastries.

"Morning," Maia said on a yawn, and Ava noticed that her dark roots were starting to show at her part, slowly pushing away the bright pink.

"Rough night?" she asked with a laugh as she poured herself coffee.

Maia sighed, then took a sip of her coffee before she spoke. "Just up late. Doing research, trying to refresh my memory on everything I learned in culinary school, and jotting notes on what I'd love Liza to help me on."

"Same," Ava said.

Maia gazed into her mug and gave the contents a stern look. "Come on, caffeine, kick in." She took another sip.

Vienna sat at the table, looking not as tired as Maia but still slightly bleary-eyed. Ava took the chair next to her. "Morning."

Vienna held up her cup in salute but said nothing. In the two and a half weeks they'd been there, Ava had learned that words and Vienna were not friends in the morning.

Madison and Paige wandered in then, Madison with a soft grin, as usual. "Good morning, beauties," she said and headed straight for the coffee as greetings were murmured back to her. Once she had her cup in hand, she sat at the table and smiled at each of them. "It's fun to learn you all, to observe you and pick up on things," she said, apropos of nothing.

Paige grinned and Maia asked, "Yeah? Like what?"

"Here we go," Paige said, but her tone held affection.

Madison sat up, as if she'd been waiting for somebody to ask. Ava grinned and sipped her coffee, finding Madison to be very interesting. "Well, Vienna says nothing in the morning. She grunts or nods but avoids eye contact until halfway through her second cup." She glanced at Vienna, who raised her cup in confirmation and grunted but didn't look up. The others laughed.

"Now, my roommate here," she indicated Paige, who sat next to her stirring her coffee, "she's cheerful as fuck in the morning. She hums." Madison's eyes went comically wide. "*She hums*, people."

Paige nodded happily.

"Maia," Madison went on, "falls somewhere in the middle of these two." She waved her finger from Vienna to Paige. "She's not super cheerful in the morning, but she talks. It's also possible she's slightly addicted to the chocolate chip muffins because she's had one every single morning."

Maia looked down at the muffin on her plate. "Have I?"

"Every single morning, my pink-haired friend." Madison smiled.

"Huh," Maia said and took a large bite of the muffin.

Madison's gaze shifted to Ava, who tipped her head to the side and waited. "Now, you," Madison pointed a finger at her, "you're a tough nut to crack because you pay attention to everything—I don't think you miss a trick—but you don't say a lot. You're not removed, you're very much here, but you watch and listen more than you participate. It's mysterious." She widened her eyes on that last word, which made Ava smile and the others chuckle in agreement.

"And what about me?" Regan asked as she entered the room carrying a travel mug. Crossing to the sideboard, she refilled it. "What have you learned?"

Madison grinned. "That with the exception of my roomie here," she indicated Paige, "you are the most cheerful and sweetest of the bunch."

"Wait. After Paige, though." Regan sat down across the table from Ava.

"After Paige, yes. Sorry, but nobody's as cheerful as she is." Madison shrugged.

Regan gave one nod. "Gotta agree with that. I mean, she hums, for Christ's sake." With that, everybody laughed, Regan having not been in the room when that comment was initially made about Paige.

During the laughter, Regan met Ava's eyes across the table and gave her a soft smile, then glanced back down at her coffee.

Ava pretended not to notice the warmth that rushed through her.

❖

I fell asleep on her. She followed the text to Kiki with a wide-eyed emoji. She watched as Kiki's dots bounced and then her text came through.

So? You were tired. Big whoop.

Regan blew out a breath and typed, *No, you don't understand. I fell asleep ON her. Like, all night. I woke up this morning with my head on her chest.*

What followed was a string of laughing emoji. A seemingly endless string that went on for rows and rows.

This is not funny! she sent back.

Kiki typed, *Kinda is, tho.*

Shut up. It was all she could think of to say in the moment, and the dots kept on bouncing, so apparently, Kiki was having better luck with words. Finally, the text arrived.

Babe. Chill out. Just chill, okay? You worry about stupid things. If you fell asleep on this woman ALL NIGHT, you must be at least a little bit comfortable with her. Regan was rolling that around in her head when Kiki's next line came. *She didn't fire you from the bed, did she?* And then more laughing emoji.

Oh, ur hilarious. But she found herself grinning and couldn't help it. *She did not. In fact, she apologized for getting me fired in the first place. Seemed to actually feel bad about it. I was surprised, to put it mildly.*

The door of the room opened and Ava came in, having gone for a quick walk before they had to head down to the kitchen. Regan tried not to stare, but last night had opened something. Had cracked a seal or loosened a lid or something like that because now she found herself wanting to look. She'd hated Ava for a long time, but the combination of her apology and having let Regan sleep on her the night before had recalibrated some things in Regan's head. She could almost feel them moving around in her brain, opinions shifting and changing.

Ava was gorgeous. There was no denying it. Even in the deepest midst of her hatred for the woman, Regan would never say she wasn't. That would be an enormous lie. Even now, as she sat on her bed and slid her glasses onto her face, she was beautiful. Her dark hair was down and wavy—and Regan knew from experience that it would go up into either a clip or a ponytail before they headed down to work. She had great skin, smooth and creamy-looking. And after last night, Regan now knew that Ava's breasts were a bit larger than she'd expected, and very, very comfortable to sleep on.

A small sound escaped her, and she gave her head a quick shake. When Ava looked up at her in question, she recovered with "How was the walk?"

"Humid," Ava said. "Can't you tell?" She indicated her hair. "I become all frizzy at the first sign of humidity."

"Your hair looks perfect," Regan said before she could catch herself.

Ava glanced up and met her gaze, and they held for a beat or two before Ava said a very soft thank-you. "Ready to head down? I wonder what Liza has us making today. Any bets?"

Grateful for the subject change, Regan said, "I'm gonna go with…" She tapped her forefinger against her chin, making a show of thinking. "Tarts."

"Oh, good one," Ava said, crossing to her desk. Using the mirror above it, she twisted her hair up and clipped it at the back of her head. "I'm gonna say turnovers. Or popovers. Something with over."

Regan laughed. "Fair enough." She opened the door to their room. "Shall we?"

With a nod, Ava went through, and they headed down to the kitchen.

Turned out, they were both right and wrong. Liza was at her kitchen when the group arrived, the first time she'd been there before them. Already in her apron, with ingredients and equipment spread out on her workstation, she was in the midst of baking something when they got there. Their assistants were already standing at their individual stations waiting for them.

"Good morning, chefs," she said to their surprised faces. Regan moved behind her own station, stood next to Hadley, and shot a look across to Ava, who gave a subtle shrug back. "Today, we are going to work on our puff pastry." A very subtle groan went around the room, and Liza chuckled. "I see by the sounds you're making that you're not thrilled. And that is exactly why we're focusing on it today. And tomorrow, if we have to. It is one of the most important elements a baker can master, and too many give up and simply avoid making things that require it."

Regan glanced down at her hands, feeling guilty, as if Liza had singled her out. She did not enjoy making puff pastry because she struggled to get it right. The layering of the dough and the butter, the folding, the rolling, it just never came out the way it should. Puff pastry was her kryptonite. "Shit," she muttered.

Out of the corner of her eye, she saw Hadley glance at her with a grin, and behind her, she heard Madison murmur, "Same."

She clenched her teeth and shot a quick look across to Ava, who nibbled on her bottom lip. She didn't seem quite as worried, but she also didn't look super confident. She gave Regan a thumbs-up and then mouthed *you got this* and smiled. Next to her, Becca watched.

Regan's heart gave a happy skip, and that was the first moment the thought crossed her mind. *I like her.*

Well, who'da seen that one coming?

For the next few hours, they worked on puff pastry. Flour, salt, butter all went into stand mixers. A little vinegar with the water to help inhibit the gluten development. Billy had taught her that. Mix, mix, mix, and once a dough was formed, Regan took hers out of the bowl to finish by hand. Then she wrapped it in plastic to chill for about a half hour and started on a new batch. Liza's orders. She wanted each of them to do at least four batches, since a lot of time in the fridge had to happen.

While her dough was chilling, she measured out a square of parchment paper to ensure her butter was always exactly the right size. She was folding it using a ruler when a loud banging sounded. Across the aisle, Ava had a rolling pin in her hand and was beating the hell out of a few sticks of butter.

"That's one way to do it, I guess," Hadley said, her voice amused.

"It works. I'm gonna do it, too," Regan told her and pulled out her own rolling pin. Soon both she and Ava were beating sticks of butter into flat pancakes, glancing at each other with big grins on their faces.

Liza had apparently been watching them for a while and then strolled down the aisle between stations just as they finished with their butter. "Interesting way of doing it," she commented.

"My teacher in culinary school taught me," Ava said, her voice quiet. Liza looked to Regan, who held up her rolling pin.

"It was this or a meat tenderizer," she said with a shrug. Over Liza's shoulder, she could see Ava's shoulders move in silent laughter. She glanced at her butter, then Ava's, each in flattened squares, ready to be rolled into the chilled pastry.

"Looks like you both did a good job." Liza laid a hand on Regan's flattened butter, then went across to Ava's and did the same thing. "Still cold. Nice work." She waved a hand. "Continue."

Regan's first batch of chilled dough didn't roll well. It cracked and broke and frustrated her, and she ended up tossing it, hoping her second batch was better. Ava seemed to have a bit better luck, covering her butter in her dough, though she didn't look happy about it, so Regan wondered. Over and over, they made dough, flattened butter, chilled dough, put the butter in the dough, rolled, laminated, chilled, repeated. By the time they'd done six folds on four batches each and were ready to let it rest in the fridge overnight, Regan's feet were killing her, and her hands and wrists ached from rolling.

"You did well today," Liza said from the front of the room once more. She'd rolled out almost as much dough as they had. "Tomorrow, we'll make tarts and turnovers with our puff pastry." She took her apron off and gave them a wave. "See you bright and early." And with that, she was gone.

"I can't figure her out." Regan had meant to say it to herself but forgot Hadley was standing behind her.

"Who? Liza?"

A nod. "Yeah, it's weird, right? Like, we're here to learn from her. And I have, don't get me wrong. Today was good because puff pastry is hard, and I screw it up all the time, so I'm glad she was helping today instead of just watching and judging like she does other times. 'Cause that doesn't really help me when I've fucked something up, you know? Plus, it makes me nervous."

Hadley nodded as she wiped the counter with a wet cloth. "I get that. Hundred percent."

"Hey," Maia said from across the aisle. "We're gonna go out for drinks, bring the assistants this time. You in?"

"I'm in" was Ava's answer. She glanced over at Regan, and the expression on her face was hard to read. Of course, that was how it usually was with Ava, wasn't it? She was the epitome of stoic. Did she want Regan to come? Did she not want Regan to come? Who knew?

Regan couldn't hide her grin as she met Maia's gaze across the aisle. "I could definitely use a drink."

Next to her, Hadley nodded. "Same."

❖

The bar scene really wasn't Ava's thing, but as she sat at the large booth they'd secured—and had dragged a table up against so they could all fit—she found herself loosening up a bit, having more fun than she usually would in such a setting. It was loud. They'd broken into different groups, some at the bar, some playing darts, some at the booth where Ava was. People were talking over each other and laughing. Even Vienna, the person in the group that Ava thought was most like her, was laughing heartily and making jokes.

Puff pastry will do that to you, I guess.

"What are you grinning at?" Regan asked, sliding into the booth next to her.

She turned to meet those blue eyes, that nearly ever-present kind smile, and gave a half shrug. "Just observing how relaxed everybody seems to be tonight."

Regan looked around, as if gauging Ava's assessment for herself. "It was a rough day. I guess people are shaking it off, yeah?"

"So rough," Ava agreed, and took a sip of her rum and diet. "I hate puff pastry. No. Lies. I love puff pastry. I hate *making* puff pastry."

Regan held up her glass of beer so Ava could "cheers" her. "Same, same, same, my friend."

They touched glasses and sipped. Ava was on her second cocktail, courtesy of Becca, feeling that pleasant looseness in her limbs, and that was likely why she said what she said. "I never thought I'd hear you call me that. Like, ever."

"What?"

"Friend."

Regan held her gaze for a moment before saying, "Yeah, well, life is too fucking short, isn't it?"

"Very true."

Hadley came over from a trip to the bar. "Scooch," she said, then slid into the booth next to Regan, forcing her closer to Ava until their thighs touched. Ava felt Regan's warmth almost immediately, thought briefly of shifting away a bit, then couldn't seem to make herself.

Stupid rum.

"Whatcha doin' over here?" Hadley asked, her words just the tiniest bit slurred as she propped her elbow on the table and her head in her hand. She blinked her big eyes at Regan, then at Ava, looking almost comically interested.

"We're just chatting," Regan said.

"I didn't think you two did that," Hadley said, smiling into her drink.

Ava squinted at her. "What do you mean? Did what?"

Hadley lifted a shoulder. "I mean, don't you hate each other? That's the rumor."

"There's a rumor?" Regan's eyebrows shot up and she glanced at Ava before asking, "According to who?"

Another half shrug. "Lots of folks. What happened anyway? Didn't she," she pointed at Ava, "fire you?" She pointed at Regan, and something about the smirk on her face irritated the crap out of Ava.

Regan must've felt her tense up because she put a hand on her leg under the table, silently telling her to chill, and said to Hadley, "She didn't fire me. We worked together, and I wasn't holding up my part of the job, so my bosses let me go. It was the right call at the time. I've grown a lot since then."

To say Ava was too stunned to speak was a colossal understatement. She sat there in shocked silence, hoping her eyes weren't as wide as she felt they might be.

Meanwhile, Hadley looked a little bit like the wind had been taken out of her sails. "Oh. Well. Rumors can be wrong sometimes."

"Yes, they can," Regan said as Hadley slid back out of the booth, obviously disappointed, and headed back to the bar where three of the other assistants were hanging. Regan turned back to Ava. "That was odd."

"Alcohol, man," Ava said, then held up her own drink.

Regan laughed. "There was definitely some tipsiness happening there."

"Definitely." They sat in silence for a moment before Ava spoke again. "Thanks."

"For?"

"For dismantling the rumor." She said it with a grin.

"Nobody likes being fodder."

"Nobody."

"Anyway. You're welcome." Regan gave Ava's leg a squeeze, and they both looked down, suddenly seeming to realize that Regan's hand had been on Ava's thigh the entire time. Regan smiled softly, met Ava's gaze, and withdrew her hand. "Sorry about that."

"Don't be." Ava sipped her cocktail, watching over the rim as a blush crept up Regan's neck and settled into her cheeks. "You're cute when you blush."

Regan picked up her own drink and said before sipping, "Well, you're hot when you flirt."

Wow. Okay. We're doing this now, are we? Ava wanted to be horrified, thought she probably should be—both by her own behavior as well as by Regan's comment. But she wasn't. At all. In fact, it made her feel warm. Unexpectedly. She was enjoying it and decided to keep playing. "Been a long time since I did it."

"Flirted?"

Ava nodded.

"That's a shame."

"Yeah?"

"Oh, most definitely. I mean, it's fun, first of all." Regan's grin had chased away the blush, and now it was clear she was enjoying herself as well. Ava studied her, holding her glass in both hands in front of her mouth as she did so. Regan was strong and athletically built, and she was also very pretty. She had an oval face, her cheekbones not sharp but clear, and her chin strong. The dark lashes and eyebrows only served to accentuate the blue of her eyes. Her skin was smooth, a few freckles sprinkled across the bridge of her nose that only added to the appeal. Ava's gaze crawled slowly down along Regan's throat to the peek of cleavage at the spot where her shirt buttoned. Regan made a *pfft* sound and said, "Old news. You've already seen these."

"Twice," Ava reminded her, and the blush came rushing back as Regan pressed her lips together, making her laugh.

"God, I forgot about the second time." Regan shook her head but kept smiling.

"I did not." Ava held up her glass in salute as she said quietly, "To your boobs, which are pretty spectacular, by the way."

The blush deepened and oh, yes, Ava was having fun with this, so much fun despite the fact that it was so *not her*. She didn't do this. She didn't flirt openly and shamelessly. Nope. Not Ava.

And yet...

Regan looked at her nearly empty glass. "After that comment, I am in desperate need of a refill," she said, then reached for Ava's glass. "Be right back."

And yes, Ava watched her go, watched the gentle sway of her hips as she walked toward the bar, the way she sort of stuck her ass out as she leaned on the bar top and spoke to the bartender. After a moment or two, she managed to pull her gaze away and focus on the others around her, one of whom was Maia, and she was looking directly at Ava with a knowing grin.

It was Ava's turn to blush. She could feel it, feel the heat crawling up her neck. But instead of teasing her, Maia simply held up her drink in salute, gave her a wink, and went back to the conversation Vienna and Paige were having around her.

"Here you go." Regan slid a fresh drink in front of her and reclaimed her seat. "Now. Where were we?"

There was a pause, something between a split second and a quick moment, where Ava considered calling it a night. Putting an end to everything that had been happening, thanks to the rum in her system, and signing off for the day. But there was something about looking Regan in the eye, the openness of her expression, the smile on her face, and Ava wanted exactly the opposite of throwing in the towel on the evening. She wanted to stay. She wanted to flirt with Regan. She wanted to do more than that. She wanted to do so much more than that, and the realization hit her like a slap.

Stupid rum.

She picked up her glass and sipped.

❖

The fact that Ava Prescott was super good-looking was nothing Regan didn't already know. There was no denying it. It was a fact.

Even when they had worked in the same restaurant and Ava had seemed cold and distant and determined not to like her, even when she was making Regan's work life miserable, it was still a fact that she was crazy fucking hot.

And now? Now that she wasn't any of those other things, now that they were almost friends—*a moment to think about how outrageous that is, please*—the only thing that had changed was that Ava might be even hotter, something Regan didn't think was possible.

"Did you ever think we'd be sitting at a bar doing this?" she finally asked.

"Doing what? Drinking?" Everything about Ava was so damn sexy right now, so hot, Regan was a little concerned she might get scorched, that she'd leave with visibly scarred skin.

She laughed softly. "Yes. Drinking. That and...the other stuff."

"Oh, talking about your boobs and how you keep showing them to me?"

Regan tried to smother her smile but couldn't, so she covered it with her hand instead. "*Accidentally*. I *accidentally* showed them to you."

"Twice. You *accidentally* showed them to me *twice*." Ava was enjoying this. It was so clearly written on her face, the sexy smile, the crinkled eyes, the pink cheeks. Oh, yes, she was having fun. And if Regan was being honest, it was nice to see. Ava seemed like a supremely serious human, stoic, not prone to emotion...or even fun. At least, that was the Ava she remembered.

But now? Tonight? In this little town in this little bar, sitting next to her? Ava was different. Relaxed. Smiling.

It could be the alcohol. Regan had to admit that. A good cocktail could loosen up even the most sober person. She stifled a chuckle and thought, *See what I did there?*

"What's funny?" Ava asked, leaning closer. God, she smelled good, like all the best baking ingredients rolled into one, warm and inviting. A little bit of vanilla, a little bit of cinnamon, and a whole lot of comfort, along with that subtle, inviting scent that she couldn't quite identify.

Regan smiled and shook her head. "Nothing."

"Liar." Ava grinned but didn't push.

She continued to grin even as she sipped her drink some more and glanced out over the table at the others. They ended up staying for another half hour or so, but they were all exhausted from the day, and when Vienna commented that she was ready to head back to Liza's mansion, nobody argued against that.

Did their room get smaller while they were out?

A ridiculous thought, yes, but that's how it felt to Regan. Like Ava's side was closer, her desk, all her things. Her bed. It all seemed to suddenly be much more within reach, and she was smart enough to understand the psychological aspect of what her train of thought meant, but that didn't make it stop. She cleared her throat as Ava closed the door behind her, and then it was just the two of them. In their bedroom. Alone.

She stood at the foot of her bed as Ava leaned back against the door with her hands behind her and leveled a look at her that was heavy and hot. Regan felt her heart rate kick up. She swallowed.

Ava inhaled audibly, a large breath, and let it go slowly, continuing to hold her gaze.

Regan knew she'd look for things to blame later. The stress of the day. The drinks. Ava's goddamn sexy flirting. Whatever it was going to be didn't matter in that moment. All that mattered was Ava's eyes, Ava's mouth, Ava's body standing there waiting for her to make a move.

So she did.

Not allowing herself to debate for one second, she crossed the room, took Ava's face in both hands, and kissed her.

Her first thought was of relief, and that told her she'd actually been waiting to kiss Ava for longer than she'd realized. No. That was a lie. For longer than she was ready to admit.

Her second thought was of softness. Everything about Ava was so soft: her lips, her skin, her body as Regan pressed against it, hips pushing into hips.

Ava tasted sweet, remnants of rum and cola still clinging to her tongue, which Regan now touched with her own, just a hint, just a tease, before she felt Ava's hands on her waist, pulling her closer, before she felt Ava's tongue push into her mouth, before she let go of an erotic moan that she didn't recognize as a sound she'd ever made before.

A slight pull back, because she needed to look, needed to see where Ava's thoughts were, how she was doing with all of this. Her lips still lingered mere millimeters from Ava's, but she could see her, the hooded sensuality of her dark, dark eyes, the slightly swollen lips, the flushed cheeks. Ava's fingers dug into her sides, as if she was afraid of what would happen if she let go.

So Regan kissed her some more.

Time seemed to stop. It was so horrendously clichéd, that phrase, Regan almost laughed out loud when the thought hit. Except it was true. She had no idea how long they'd been kissing, what time it was, what day it was, which planet she was on. All she knew was Ava. Her hands. Her mouth. And the soft sounds of ragged breathing and lips as they kissed.

The next time they came up for air, Ava took her hand and led her to her bed, and when she turned to face Regan, she raised her brows in question.

As a response, Regan leaned in for another kiss and pushed until Ava sat, then lay back on the mattress. Regan balanced above her on her hands and knees and took a moment to take her in, to just look, to memorize the moment, to capture the look on Ava's gorgeous face.

"You're so beautiful," she whispered.

Ava's smile had a bashful quality to it—not a word she'd ever thought of using in relation to Ava—as if she didn't hear those words often, and she reached up to run her fingertips across Regan's bottom lip. Then she grabbed the back of her neck and pulled her back to her mouth.

The kissing.

God, the kissing!

It was something she could do with Ava forever, of that she was certain. They kissed and kissed, jockeyed for position. Ava rolled them so she was on top—which was a whole new level of erotic for Regan—until Regan rolled them again and reclaimed control.

Did time stop again? Had it screeched to a halt? It sure seemed like it. She pulled herself up so she could look at Ava once more. Both of them were breathless. Ava's eyes were still hooded, her eyes nearly black, her cheeks a lovely pink. She wet her lips before she spoke.

"Are you okay if we stop?" Ava asked on a whisper.

"Oh, of course." Regan nodded and rolled to her side.

Ava grasped her arm. "It's not that I want to stop—I kinda don't. But I think we should."

Regan didn't want to stop either but had to agree. She nodded again. "No, I get it."

They were quiet for a moment before Ava pointed to the pillows. "Do you want to, um, stay here? With me?"

"I mean, it's a pretty long commute," Regan said, glancing across the room at her own bed as she propped up on an elbow.

Ava laughed, and it transformed her entire face—hell, it transformed the entire *room*—making Regan realize how rare it was to hear that sound. She tipped her head, wanting to ask why Ava laughed so rarely but also not wanting to spoil what was a pretty amazing moment with something that might be taken as critical.

"Oh, she's a comedian now," Ava said, giving her a playful shove. Then she pushed to her feet.

"Always have been," Regan said. "Just ask my parents."

Ava kicked off her shoes and then pulled her shirt over her head and off, causing Regan's voice to stick in her throat. Ava stood there in jeans, bare feet, a navy-blue bra, and nothing else. The expression on her face said she knew exactly what the view was doing to Regan. "I'm gonna get changed. Be right back." Then she grabbed her pajamas out of a drawer and went into the bathroom, and the door clicked shut behind her.

Regan blew out a loud breath and fell face-first onto the pillow.

This woman just might be the death of her.

And what a way to go.

CHAPTER TWELVE

T hings took a turn after that night, and for the better.
Ava didn't know how that was possible. She didn't understand any of it, but it was so much more than what things around Regan had always been in her mind—so *beyond*—and she wasn't willing to overanalyze. Ava was not a "just go with it" kind of person, but it's exactly what she did. She just went with it.

It had been two weeks since their initial make-out session, and there had been more. Many more. Like, every night. Making out. Every single night. Then they'd stop and fall asleep together, in one bed or the other, snuggled close, entwined like vines. When was the last time Ava had felt so relaxed sleeping with someone else? Just sleeping? She couldn't remember. She'd woken up practically lying on top of Regan. And she'd woken up with Regan practically lying on top of her. And neither had been bad. Both had been awesome.

The atmosphere in the kitchen had changed, too. It had relaxed. Ava and Regan joked and played and laughed. Even the other chefs seemed to feel the shift, lightening up, their amusement clear, their own laughter seeming to come easier. When Ava had made a smart-ass comment to Regan on cupcake day and been rewarded by a handful of flour thrown at her, the entire kitchen had broken out into an impromptu food fight. Flour, brown sugar, chocolate chips, and cupcake cups had been launched across the aisles from workstation to workstation, shrieks of laughter filling the air, until Ava noticed Liza standing at the front of the room, hands clasped behind her back, looking not terribly pleased with the behavior of her retreaters. Ava cleared her throat loudly and shot a look Regan's way.

Regan was laughing but noticed Ava's expression and sobered quickly, also clearing her throat so that Vienna in front of her caught on and the rest of the room ceased their antics and smothered their grins.

"Well," Liza said, her voice stern, unimpressed. "I'm glad to see none of you care about the messes you make or the seriousness of this retreat."

Maia raised her hand before saying, "We're sorry, Chef. Just blowing off a little steam."

"Hmm," Liza said. She stood in silence for a moment, then waved a dismissive hand. "Clean it up. We're done for today. Hopefully, you'll come back tomorrow ready to be serious." She turned on her heel and stormed off while the rest of them stood in silence for a moment. For two. Finally, Vienna turned to look back at them and mouthed *yikes*, which broke the tension and allowed for quiet chuckles.

"Sorry, guys," Regan said, scrunching up her nose with guilt. "That was my fault for starting things." She glanced over at Ava and then flushed a pretty pink. Ava smiled at her but said nothing.

"I don't care what Chef says," Maia said softly. "I needed that. *We* needed that."

"Yeah, but now we won't finish cupcakes." Paige seemed bothered by this, and Ava glanced at Regan, who looked like she felt worse.

"I know. I'm sorry. I shouldn't have done that." Regan grimaced, and Ava wanted to wrap her up in her arms and reassure her.

"Listen," she finally said. "It's been tense here. Chef has put us under a lot of pressure, and sometimes…" She shrugged as she let the sentence taper off.

"Sometimes, a little fun is warranted," Madison said, shaking her head. "I mean, does she expect us to just be super serious all the damn time?"

"I think she probably does," Vienna pointed out, and Ava had to agree with her.

"Doesn't matter," Ava said. "It's done. Let's clean up and come back tomorrow ready to work."

Just as nods were going around the kitchen, May appeared in her usual black pants and white shirt. The retreaters all gave her their attention.

"Chefs, hello. Dinner will be served in the dining room at the usual six p.m. Assistants, Chef Bennett-Schmidt would like to see you all before you leave for the day. Please meet her in the conference room on the third floor in twenty minutes." And with that, she glided out the same way she always did—silently and seemingly not touching the ground.

"Man, she is so weird," Ava heard Maia mutter, and had to smother her own grin because Maia was not wrong. She went to find a broom to take care of all the flour that had ended up on the floor, and they all got to work on the cleanup.

Later that night, after dinner, the chefs split up. Vienna wanted to chill on her own for a while. "I need some introvert downtime" were her exact words. Maia, Madison, and Paige decided to go back to the arcade because, according to Maia, all her steam hadn't been blown off yet. She asked Regan and Ava if they wanted to join.

"Oh, um, I think I'm just gonna chill." Regan glanced at Ava, and Ava rolled her lips in to keep from shooting her a sexy grin. "You wanna go?"

Ava worked hard at her nonchalance, no easy feat. "Nah. I think I'm gonna read or something. But you guys have fun."

Maia glanced from one to the other and back. "Okay. Cool. Well, we'll catch you tomorrow, then." And when Madison and Paige had gone out the front door ahead of her, she turned back to them and winked. Then the door shut behind them, leaving Ava and Regan standing there.

"Did she seriously just wink at us?" Regan asked, her disbelief clear.

Ava laughed softly. "I believe she did, yes."

Regan shook her head. "I didn't think people younger than my grandpa even did that anymore."

"You're clearly mistaken," Ava said, then winked at her and headed up the stairs to their room.

It was strange now. Every time they ended up alone in their room together, the air felt suddenly charged, electrified. Regan's presence felt arousingly close, and Ava's underwear got instantly damp. She let Regan enter first, then shut the door behind them. No sooner had the latch clicked than Regan was on her, pushing her back against the door and pulling a soft *oof* from her.

Regan's mouth crashed into hers.

There was nothing gentle about this kiss, oh no. Regan was taking from her, demanding from her, telling her silently that Ava was not in charge right now, Regan was. This was a side of Regan that had been unexpected when she first showed it. Ava had been surprised. She'd never thought of Regan as anything close to assertive. Certainly not pleasantly aggressive. Not the tiniest bit sure of herself. But it turned out Regan was all of those things and more. And they made her unbelievably sexy.

Of course, Ava kissed her back with all she had, giving as good as she got, and before long, they were shuffling their way toward the bed, their mouths still fused together.

Goddamn, Regan was a spectacular kisser. Like, easily the best kisser she'd ever kissed. Not that she'd kissed tons of people, but she'd had her fair share. She and Regan were incendiary when they kissed, it was true, but something was different tonight. She felt it deeply. Something ignited in her, started with a steady heat low in her body and began consuming her from the inside. She didn't even think about it before she rolled them so she was on all fours above Regan, and she pulled away from the kiss. Regan's eyes were dark and hooded, and her chest rose and fell with her excited breaths.

Ava sat up on her knees and pulled her shirt over her head. Then she met Regan's gaze and, without breaking eye contact, reached behind herself to unfasten her bra and slip it off.

Regan's eyes went wide.

They hadn't gone this far yet, but Ava was ready. All she had to do was look at Regan's face to know she was, too, so she leaned forward onto her hands again so her bare breasts dangled just above Regan's mouth.

Regan looked at them, then shifted her gaze to Ava's. "Are you sure?" she asked on a whisper.

In response, Ava lowered a breast until her hardened nipple brushed against Regan's lips.

That was all it took.

Regan closed her mouth over the nipple and sucked hard. Ava thought she might pass out from the electric current of pleasure that shot through her. Regan's hands entered the game, one of them toying with Ava's other nipple so that both were being stimulated at the same time, and the moan that rumbled up from Ava's throat was a new sound for her. Sensual. Erotic. Regan drew them out of her somehow, all these new sounds. Moans and whimpers and cries, all new to her, all foreign, but incredible.

Regan's mouth was hot and talented. Ava had no idea how there could be more than one way to suck on a nipple, but Regan seemed to have an entire bag of tricks. Whatever she was doing, it was like magic. X-rated magic. And Ava didn't want to know the secrets, she only wanted to be the recipient of that magic.

Then Regan's mouth was back on hers while her hands kneaded Ava's breasts, but Ava wrenched away and pushed herself up on her knees. "You are alarmingly overdressed," she said, her voice hoarse as she waved a finger in front of Regan's torso. Regan's hands in hers, she pulled her to sitting, then tugged her shirt over her head. Regan's bra was next, and then there they were. Ava sat back on her haunches so their height was similar. Her nipples were hard, and she moved forward the tiniest bit until they were brushing Regan's, coaxing them to their own hardness. "That's better," Ava whispered, and with Regan's face in both her hands, she lowered her mouth to Regan's and kissed the bejesus out of her.

It had been some time since Ava'd had sex. The last time had been nearly a year ago, and it had been with someone she didn't really connect with. She'd had the itch—at that point, it had been nearly two years since she'd felt the touch of another woman, and she was drowning—and a friend encouraged her not to be so strict with her prerequisites. She'd met a very attractive woman in a bar, they'd talked, and she'd gone home with her. The sex had been fine but had left her feeling empty somehow, emptier than she'd felt before they'd met. After that, she'd vowed not to give herself to somebody she didn't know ever again. No judgment to people who could manage casual sex without issues, but it wasn't for her.

Nothing about things with Regan was casual anymore.

It was something she'd been realizing as time went on, as they'd gotten to know each other better and better. Things had shifted. Not only did she feel comfortable with Regan, not only was she starting to understand that she really liked her, but she also trusted her, and that was a big fucking deal, because Ava did not trust many people. But as they rolled and their positions reversed and Regan was now above her, looking down at her with such desire in her eyes, Ava trusted her. When Regan ran her tongue along the side of Ava's neck and down over her nipple, Ava trusted her. When she unfastened Ava's jeans and peeled them down her legs, Ava trusted her. Lying there on the bed, wearing nothing but her underwear, Regan braced above her, she trusted her. And when Regan's fingertips danced up her leg and along the inside of her thigh, when Regan slipped one finger beneath the elastic and skimmed through her hot wetness, pulling a gasp from Ava's lips, Ava trusted her.

"You," Regan began, then stopped and cleared her throat, as if overcome by...something. She shook her head with a smile. "I can't believe I'm here, touching you like this." Her finger was still in Ava's panties, and she moved it again. Ava gasped again. "And that I get to hear these sounds you make." Again. "God, you're so fucking sexy." Her eyes never leaving Ava's, she slowly slid the underwear down her legs and tossed it to the floor.

Ava was completely naked. Totally vulnerable. Not something she normally enjoyed, but Regan made her feel beautiful, and that gave her confidence, the confidence to lie there, open, while Regan's gaze raked over her with such an intense desire, she could almost feel it move along her skin. She was so turned on, she worried she might combust. Or that the second Regan touched her, she'd explode.

Regan's eye contact was impressive. Ava had always thought so. Even when she'd been criticizing her back in the restaurant all those years ago, Regan always took it standing tall and looking her in the eye. Now they were horizontal, but the eye contact remained. Regan held her gaze while she slowly moved Ava's legs so she could kneel between them. Regan held her gaze when she put a hand on each of Ava's thighs and pushed them further apart, exposing her—to the air, to Regan's hands, to her eyes, to her mouth. And Regan held her gaze as she lowered herself between Ava's legs and kissed her inner thighs, working her way almost to Ava's center before switching over to the other thigh. She got so close more than once, but she'd lift her tongue mere millimeters before the spot where Ava needed her to be, and it wasn't long before Ave was soaked and writhing.

Regan continued to go from thigh to thigh, her hands bracing Ava's hips and preventing her from shifting them so her center would meet Regan's tongue.

"Oh God" seemed to be the only phrase left in her vocabulary now, so she said it over and over as she gripped the sheets. When she finally managed to venture a glance down, Regan was grinning at her. "You're enjoying this," she accused.

"You better believe I am," Regan said, her voice low and husky. "You're the most beautiful thing I've ever seen."

At her words, Ava felt a rush of wetness and a lump in her throat, and she groaned as she dropped her head back to the pillow and ground her hips into the mattress.

"What do you want?" Regan asked softly. "Tell me what you want."

Ava wasn't a talker in bed. She never had been. Hell, she wasn't even much of a talker in life. But she was going to burst into flames and end up nothing but a pile of ashes in this very comfortable bed in Chef Liza Bennett-Schmidt's mansion if she didn't get release. Like, now. And if she was being honest, telling Regan what she wanted, verbalizing it, felt sexy somehow. She lifted her head.

Regan was smiling at her from between her legs, and Ava could feel her thumbs rubbing slowly up and down on either side of her center, keeping her arousal high—God, so high. She swallowed and her voice was hoarse, gravelly as she said, "I want your mouth on me. I want your mouth. Please."

"Ask and you shall receive," Regan said back, then lowered her head.

The first touch of her tongue was like heaven. Like angels singing. Like sunshine bursting through clouds. And Ava groaned, good Lord did she groan. Loud and long, as pure unadulterated pleasure began in her center and blossomed out into the rest of her body. It was like a switch had been flipped, heating her from the inside, letting loose that glorious wave of physical joy that slowly spread and then rushed through her entire body, from the middle of her chest and out to her fingertips and the tips of her toes, and she pushed her hips up off the bed as the orgasm ripped through her.

And the sounds she made!

Who knew she had it in her to make them? Not her. She had no idea that the cries and moans Regan pulled from her were even possible. How did she even know how to make these noises? And then she didn't care because another wave hit and there was only color exploding behind her eyelids, like fireworks in her mind.

How long did it take her to come down? For her hips to settle back onto the mattress? For her breathing to decrease to something that wasn't near hyperventilation? For her to be able to swallow and move her fingers and feel her legs?

"Did I black out?" she finally asked, and she could feel Regan chuckling, her head resting against Ava's thigh.

"I don't think so? But maybe."

She covered her eyes with a hand and shook her head, embarrassed. Regan moved, she could feel her weight shift, and then her hand was tugged away from her eyes and Regan's beautiful blue ones gazed at her.

"Don't do that," she whispered. "You were gorgeous, and the fact that I played a part in making you feel that good is the highest of honors. Trust me."

Ava swallowed, the lump in her throat appearing out of nowhere, and to her horror, she felt her eyes well up. She squeezed them shut and turned her head away. Oh God, was she now *that* girl? The one who cried after an orgasm?

"An honor," Regan said again, stressing the word. She settled in next to her, propped her head on an elbow, and stroked Ava's collarbone with her fingers.

Ava opened her eyes again and met Regan's gaze, the fingers still stroking her skin. She searched Regan's eyes, looking for anything— off. Anything that said her words weren't genuine, that *she* wasn't genuine. She found nothing but openness.

"Hi," she said.

"Hey, sexy," Regan said back, and her smile lit up the room.

❖

It had been a long time since Regan felt comfortable sleeping with somebody. She wasn't talking sex, she was talking actual sleeping. She'd gotten used to sleeping alone, so when somebody else was in the bed with her, she tended not to sleep very well, her brain absently wondering at this other presence, extra limbs, too much body heat.

That wasn't the case with Ava, and she didn't really understand why. But there was something comforting about being wrapped up in her, about being wrapped around her. She felt warm and safe and content lying next to Ava—and what a weird thing *that* was to say. You know what else was totally weird—but also totally awesome—to say? She'd made love to Ava Prescott.

She'd had Ava's naked, writhing body underneath hers. Ava had begged her for release, then asked if she'd passed out, it was that good. Was Regan pretty pleased with herself? Absolutely. But also, Ava wasn't a conquest. No, Regan would never—could never—think of her that way. No, Ava was something more. She was something special. Regan just wasn't sure how special yet.

She had drifted off to sleep, she was pretty sure. And how did she know this? Maybe because she was pulled back up from that gentle slumber by a soft, tingling feeling of pleasure, a slight pulling, a slight tugging, and when she opened her eyes, Ava was propped up next to her with a nipple in her mouth, gently sucking on it.

She had to swallow down the surge of pleasure that threatened to pop out of her throat before whispering, "Well, that's probably the best way to wake up ever."

"Yeah?" Ava asked, then moved her hand to the other nipple. "How about this?" And she worked both nipples simultaneously. The rush of wetness to Regan's center was not subtle, and she pressed her head back into the pillow, because holy shit, it all felt so good.

She sighed out a quiet groan. "That's…yeah, that's awesome…"

Ava shifted so her weight was a bit more on Regan and slid a knee between Regan's legs. "I feel bad that I fell asleep on you, so I thought it was time to make it up to you." Ava's voice was low and gravelly, and so fucking sexy that it sent another surge of wet to Regan's throbbing center.

"I am perfectly okay with that."

"Yeah?" Ava pushed her knee up into all that wetness, and Regan's groan was louder. "Oh my. You clearly *are* okay with that."

"Uh-huh" was all Regan could manage through her ragged breathing. Her hips began to pick up a rhythm as if they had a mind of their own, and Ava rocked with them, slowly and sensually. Then she shifted from Regan's nipple to her mouth and kissed her, hard and with intent. It was very clear who was driving this train, and it was not Regan.

She was perfectly okay with that, too.

Ava's fingers slid between her legs and into the hot wetness there, and oh my God, Regan was shocked the top of her head didn't blow clean off, the sensation was so intense. Even the simple mental image of Ava's long fingers stroking her ratcheted her arousal up about a hundred levels. She was enjoying that when Ava pushed her tongue into Regan's mouth and her fingers into Regan's center at the same time, and Regan's entire body felt like it had burst into flames. She grabbed at the back of Ava's head, trying to pull her in closer, harder, deeper, as she lifted her hips and grabbed Ava's wrist, trying for the exact same things. She rocked hard, fast, keeping with the rhythm of Ava's hand, and when Ava added another finger, filling her to capacity, she tumbled over the edge, wrenching her mouth away from Ava's so she could release the cry that had been building in her chest for what felt like hours but had actually been only minutes. The climax tore through her, tensing all her muscles and filling her with pleasure.

"Holy shit," she whispered, as her blood stopped racing and she was able to breathe again. "Holy shit." When she opened her eyes, Ava was smiling down at her, fingers still tucked snugly inside Regan. She wiggled them, and Regan gasped, then laughed softly, reached down, and eased them out. "Holy shit," she said once more, just to say it again.

"Three holy shits," Ava said. "I will take that. I will take all of them."

"Well, you should, because holy shit." Ava shifted her weight and Regan lifted an arm. Ava tucked herself in so her head was pillowed on Regan's chest and sighed with what sounded like absolute contentment, and it warmed Regan's heart. "That was amazing," she said with quiet awe.

Ava looked up at her. "Agreed. Sorry it took me so long to return the favor."

Regan shook her head. "No, no. None of that. I didn't do what I did so I'd get something in return. I did it because you're gorgeous and I'm stupidly attracted to you. Always have been."

Ava pushed up onto one arm so she could look down at Regan's face. "You have?"

Regan laughed softly at the shock clearly etched on Ava's face. "Um, yeah. Have you seen yourself?"

At that, Ava flushed a pretty pink that Regan could see even in the dim lighting that shone through their open window. "Thank you," she said softly.

"You seem...surprised. How come? Do you really not understand how beautiful you are?"

Ava's swallow was audible, and she looked away for a beat before saying, "It's not really something I was ever focused on. My childhood was...hard. I did my best to keep my head down, get good grades, and keep quiet." Her gaze met Regan's. "My dad. He was...hard."

"I'm sorry," Regan said, as she tried to imagine her sweet, kind, jovial dad making life hard for her. She couldn't do it. "That sounds rough."

Ava lay back down, and Regan got the impression it was so she could speak without Regan's eyes on hers. "He had some issues. He'd get mad"—Ava snapped her fingers—"like that, so my mom and I just did our best not to piss him off. We weren't always successful."

"Did he...hit you?" Regan shook her head then. "You don't have to tell me that." She really wanted to know, but because she wanted to know everything about Ava. Everything. She also knew it was none of her business.

"No, he was never physical. But he could be mean." Ava's voice had gone very quiet. "My mom was too fat or too skinny or she wore too much makeup or she never wore enough or she didn't make enough money or she made too much and he felt emasculated. He was never satisfied." She cleared her throat. "It was the same with me. I dressed like a spinster and nobody would ever look at me or I showed too much skin and how did he raise such a slut. I didn't get involved in enough extracurricular stuff at school, but then I tried out for softball and got on the team and suddenly I was too masculine and I'd end up a bull dyke. His words, not mine." She sighed. "I walked on a lot of eggshells growing up."

"God, it sounds like it. I'm so sorry." Regan pulled her closer, slightly alarmed by how badly she wanted to protect this woman, to wrap her up and keep her away from all harm. Unrealistic, and also *way* too soon for that, but she couldn't help it. She felt it.

She felt Ava's shrug under her hand. "He's gone now, so..."

"Gone as in...?"

"He died a few years ago. Heart attack. Not a surprise given how much anxiety he had around everybody and everything in his life." Her tone was interesting to Regan, like she was trying to shrug it off and act like it was no big deal, but also like that wasn't the case at all.

"I'm sorry."

"No need." Ava blew out a breath and glanced up at her. "The past is the past, right?" And before Regan could answer, Ava kissed her, hard and with purpose, and that was the end of conversation.

Regan was all right with that.

CHAPTER THIRTEEN

For the next week, the two of them couldn't wait until the day was over and they could get back to their room. Ava was trying hard to be super conscious of appearances. Would she rather go to happy hour with the other attendees and assistants or go back to their room and rip Regan's clothes off with her teeth?

I mean, it's no contest. Teeth-ripping of clothes will win every time.

But they couldn't just not go to stuff with the others. They were there for a baking retreat, not to fuck every chance they got. Much as she wanted to.

That thought sent a rush of heat through her body as she patiently added a tablespoon of sugar at a time to the egg whites being beaten in her mixer. They were making meringues today, and Liza Bennett-Schmidt was walking around observing. Across the aisle, she was at Regan's station.

"You look tired," Chef said to Regan. "Not enough sleep?"

"Probably not," Regan said with a smile that, when Ava glanced over, seemed slightly guilty and a lot sexy.

"Maybe you need to tell Chef Prescott over there to let you up for air every now and then." Without missing a beat or seeming to notice Regan's wide eyes or the horror on Ava's face, she pointed to Regan's mixer. "Don't overbeat that. You'll ruin the cookies."

She walked on back to Madison's station.

Ava met Regan's eyes across the aisle and watched as she rolled her lips in and bit down on them, then refocused on her mixer.

What? How did she know? How could Liza possibly know what

was going on? And judging by the soft chuckles and smiles around the kitchen, others knew as well.

She reined in the panic she felt suddenly building and clenched her teeth hard until it eased up. It wasn't like they weren't grown-ass women and consenting adults. They weren't doing anything wrong. That being said, Ava really didn't love the idea of everybody there knowing her business, especially when it came to sex. With a shake of her head, she turned her concentration to her mixer and tried her best to put the rest out of her mind.

It was a drawback she hadn't considered when she'd decided to add "sex with her roommate" to her list of things she worked on at the Bennett-Schmidt Baking Retreat: a slight lapse in focus. She was there to learn everything she could from a world-renowned pastry chef. But when she looked down at the fluffy meringue in her mixing bowl, with its glossy finish and stiff peaks, all she could think about were Regan's breasts, how they felt in her hands, in her mouth. She felt a surge of dampness in her underwear, a lump in her throat, and a steady throbbing between her legs. The same thing had happened yesterday when she was kneading dough and the day before that when she was filling cream puffs. Everything reminded her of Regan's body. Everything took her back to their room, to her bed or to Regan's bed—'cause they'd mixed it up and used both beds, as well as the floor and the shower, both desks, and also the vanity in the bathroom. There really wasn't anyplace left in their enormous room that they hadn't christened. Ava was sore in muscles she didn't know she had. She was drinking so much water because she was dehydrated. She wondered if she'd lost any weight due to all the calories they were burning. It made her smile. She couldn't help it.

Sex with Regan was... She didn't even have the proper words to describe it. It was beyond. Beyond surprising. Beyond exhilarating. Beyond fantastic. It was simply *beyond*.

She'd had no idea.

When she hazarded another glance across the aisle, Regan met her gaze and grinned, and just like that, all Ava's stress dissipated, floated away like vapor in the air.

How did she do that?

"What seems to be the problem, Chef?" Liza was saying now, and when Ava glanced up in front of her, Maia looked slightly frantic.

"My lucky bandanna," she said, patting her chef's coat, opening drawers and cupboards. "It's gone."

"And is that a big deal?" Liza asked, clearly not sharing Maia's obvious worry.

"It is to me. I can't bake without it." Maia turned in a circle. "I have to go to my room and look." And without waiting for permission of any kind, she skedaddled right out of the workstation, frantic.

Liza inhaled and let it out slowly as she shook her head, then moved on to Vienna's station.

Ava and Regan exchanged glances.

Later that evening, while Regan was in the shower, Ava was lying on her bed and asked Courtney the same question about Regan being able to calm her as they FaceTimed.

"What do you mean?" Courtney asked. It was her day off from the restaurant, and she was sitting on her couch with her knitting in her lap, her phone propped up so she could talk to Ava without needing to hold the phone.

"I mean...I don't know." She sighed, long and low. "She just— makes me feel better. Even today when Chef said something."

"Which was not cool, just so we're clear." Courtney had her readers on, as she always did when she knit, and she looked over the rim of them at the screen.

"Yeah, I know."

"It's nobody's business. You're adults. Fucking Liza Bennett-Schmidt doesn't get to tell you who you can or cannot sleep with, you know."

Ava grinned into the phone, her affection for her friend surging. Courtney had never liked Liza Bennett-Schmidt. She'd always thought of her as an egomaniac, somebody enamored with herself. Maybe she was right. "Whatcha makin'?" she asked.

"Booties for my cousin's kid." She held up a tiny shoe-shaped creation in light blue. "And I'm not ignoring your other question. I just needed to put in my two cents about that bitch."

"I mean, it was more like two dollars, but I accept it." Ava smiled and glanced at the bathroom door. She could still hear the shower running.

"The answer is simple," Courtney said, not looking up from the bootie. "She makes you feel better because you let her."

Ava scrunched up her nose. "What do you mean?"

This time, Courtney put down the knitting and looked at her. "Listen, I love you. You're my best friend. But you're not exactly warm and fuzzy. You're not easy. Getting to know you isn't simple. You have walls and barriers and fucking guards on duty. Guards in chain mail. With clubs. Spiked clubs. On horses. You're kind of a hard person."

Ava flinched. "Um, ouch."

"Please. Suck it up. I'm not telling you anything you don't already know."

Ava pouted but had to agree, because Courtney knew her well. And she was right. "Fine."

"But it sounds like, with her, maybe you let the walls down a bit? Give the guards the day off?"

The imagery was enough to make her grin. "I mean, maybe? Everybody needs a vacation day or two."

"Exactly." Courtney laughed softly. "See? You're a good boss."

"Why, thank you."

"Just be careful, okay?" Courtney's expression turned slightly more serious. "Don't make me worry."

"Nothing to worry about. Promise."

"It's just…" Courtney seemed to stop and search for the right words. "Where you are right now isn't reality, you know? It's like you're on *The Bachelorette* or something and you've been thrown together in this isolated, ideal situation where you work together during the day and share a room—and a bed—at night. But you're gonna come home at some point. And things will be different."

"Wow. Somebody took her Debbie Downer pills this morning." And then Courtney gave her a look, and even over the screen of the phone, Ava knew she was being called out for pretending not to understand something that she actually got, fully. As if, in her mind, Courtney had grabbed her by the hand and hauled her out of the mansion and back to Pomp. Back to her tiny apartment. Back to her very solitary life.

She wasn't sure how she felt about that.

Before she could analyze any further, she realized the shower had stopped. "She's done," she whispered. "I gotta bounce. Talk to you later." She blew a kiss into the phone.

"Wait!" Courtney hissed, then moved her face comically close to the screen. "How's the sex?"

"It's *spectacular*. Bye!" She was hitting the red button just as the bathroom door opened and steam wafted into the room. Regan exited wearing pin-striped boxer shorts and a red tank top. Her hair was combed and still wet.

She looked good enough to fucking eat.

When Regan glanced up and met her gaze, she quirked an eyebrow. "I know that look by now."

"Yeah? What look is that exactly?"

"That's the *why do you have so many clothes on* look." She picked up her little jar of moisturizer. "And I could give it right back to you."

Ava glanced down at her own clothes, marked with flour and various particles of food. She'd been waiting, as she had let Regan shower the day off first. "Well, allow me to shower and I'll be right out so we can address the question of who's wearing too many clothes, okay?"

Regan held an arm out toward the bathroom. "All yours." God, her smile, the way it lit up the room. Corny as that sounded, it was also true. Ava smiled back at her, then pushed off the bed, and toward her. Taking her face in both hands, she kissed Regan soundly on the mouth—thoroughly, with just the tiniest touch of her tongue—then pulled away. Regan almost fell forward as she tried to follow with her mouth, a tiny whimper escaping her.

"Be right out," Ava said, and it took everything she had to force herself to walk into the bathroom and close the door, because holy crap, had that backfired. Her intention had been to wind Regan up a little, get her worked up so she'd look forward to the end of Ava's shower. Instead, she'd worked herself up. She shook her head as she pulled off her underwear and noted how wet it already was. Jesus. How was this possible? How was the simple act of kissing a woman—a woman she'd kissed dozens of times at this point—enough to make her want to throw her clothes off and have sex, like, immediately? She'd never been so physically in tune with somebody, and it was mind-boggling to her.

She turned the water on and let it warm up, which didn't take long. An impressive feature of Chef Liza's mansion was that it never seemed to run out of hot water, no matter how many of them showered. She stepped into the enormous terrazzo-lined stall and stepped face-first into the spray, letting the water rain down on her head. Then she leaned her head forward and let it beat on the back of her neck—a spot that always ached after she worked all day, looking down at her counter.

And then there was a small rush of cool air, and Ava grinned, knowing Regan had stepped into the shower behind her. Hands ran down her wet back and around her waist, pulling her back against Regan's naked body, her nipples hard already, making themselves known against Ava's back.

She turned in Regan's arms. "Excuse me, ma'am, didn't you already have a turn?"

Regan's hand ran up her side and cupped a breast, kneaded it, zeroed in on Ava's nipple, and tugged lightly. "Yes, but my shower didn't have a beautiful woman in it."

"Mine does. You should call customer service and complain."

And that was it for words. Regan's mouth crushed hers and they were kissing as if starved for it, as if they hadn't kissed in months. Years. Water poured over them, and Regan spun her in her arms so they were back-to-front again, and Regan's hands were everywhere. Her stomach, her ass, her breasts—she felt them all over. One grasped her chin and pulled her head back, leaving her neck vulnerable to a full-on oral assault as Regan practically devoured her. The other hand was suddenly sliding between her legs. Ava was throbbing and soaked, and it had nothing to do with the shower. Regan's fingers moved and stroked and pressed, while Ava's hands braced against the terrazzo. And then Regan's mouth was at her ear.

"God, you're so wet," she said, then a flick of her tongue sent a jolt of arousal straight down to Ava's center. "Are you close?"

Ava swallowed hard. "Yes."

"Yeah? Should I stop?" And Regan's fingers ceased all movement.

Ava gasped. She couldn't help it. "*No.* Please. Keep going. Don't stop." God, who was she? Who was this person whose entire existence seemed dependent on the fingers working between her legs? "Please."

Regan's fingers started up again. Thank God. And Ava pushed her ass back into Regan's body, her arousal climbing once again. "Come on." Regan's voice was a whisper, barely audible above the sound of the shower spray, but Ava heard it loud and clear, as if it had been an order given over a bullhorn. "Come on, baby."

The sounds Ava made. Again, who was she? Who was this person who whimpered and gasped and nearly cried with the pleasure Regan created?

"Come for me, Ava. Come for me."

And she did. Hard. Long. A husky moan she hadn't known she was capable of making issued from deep in her throat as she arched in Regan's arms, her head against Regan's shoulder, her muscles spasming so strongly, she wasn't sure she could stay on her feet.

Regan held her tightly, kept her upright. "Jesus Christ, you are the sexiest thing I've ever seen," she said softly, her mouth still next to Ava's ear, her voice and her words only serving to prolong the orgasm. "Do you know that?"

Ava reached behind her and gripped the back of Regan's neck, still catching her breath, still feeling tiny aftershocks pulsing through her body. "God" was all she could manage to say.

Later, they lay in Regan's bed together, wrapped up in each other, legs entwined under the sheets, Ava's head pillowed on Regan's chest while Regan searched Netflix on her laptop for a movie for them to watch.

"What would you do with the money if Liza picked you?" Ava asked. She hadn't even really thought about the question. It just sort of left her mouth before she realized it.

Regan didn't miss a beat. In fact, she kept searching Netflix as she said, "Buy the bakery I work at."

"Yeah?"

A nod. "My boss is retiring. He's an awesome guy, and I know he'd love me to have the place, but I'm not exactly rolling in money. I don't think I could offer him a fair price. But with that kind of a down payment..." She let the sentence dangle because Ava knew exactly what she meant. "What about you? What would you do?"

Ava knew exactly what she'd do, but for some reason, she pretended to think about it for a moment. Finally, she answered. "I've always dreamed of opening my own little wine bar. Small and intimate, serving only wine and desserts that I'd make myself."

"Well, I would totally go hang out there," Regan said, then pointed to the screen at a rom-com from a couple years back. "What about this?"

"Perfect." And it was. That was the thing Ava had such a hard time accepting—how very little effort it took to enjoy herself with Regan. A full day of hard work, a hot shower, an orgasm that rocked her world, and now a comfortable position in bed to watch a romantic movie. Seriously, how much better could it get?

She drifted off to sleep as her brain was playing her various scenarios of better, and all the while, a little voice somewhere in the background kept whispering something about things being too good to be true.

CHAPTER FOURTEEN

"N ice work today, chefs." Liza Bennett-Schmidt clasped her hands in front of her and smiled, like she hadn't browbeaten Vienna into the ground earlier or called Maia's scones *what they would taste like if a four-year-old made them on the beach. I hope you find your lucky bandanna soon.* Harsh. Jesus. And Regan had been noticing lately that the smile was somewhat...cool. Almost a little icy. She'd been noticing a lot of things about Liza lately. She'd thought about saying something to some of the others, but if she was the only who felt that way, she didn't want her opinion getting back to Liza.

If you don't have something nice to say, don't say anything. A lesson from her mother, and it had served her well for the most part. She should probably stick to it. The last thing she wanted was to be singled out. Again. It was bad enough Liza somehow knew about her and Ava. God, that was mortifying.

"Seeing that tomorrow is a holiday, I'm going to give you some time away from the kitchen." Liza continued with the icy smile as she strolled down the aisle, and murmurs ran through the workstations. They'd been working nonstop for over a week. Liza held up a finger. "But...there's a catch."

"Of course there fucking is," Hadley whispered standing next to her, and Regan had to bite back a grin. She liked this girl more and more, that was for sure. She'd gotten lucky in the assistant draw.

"I'm going to set you loose," Liza went on, turning on her heel and heading slowly back toward the front of the room. "I want you to create your own project. Something representing..." She reached the front and turned to face the six retreats. "What July Fourth means to you."

Well, this'll be interesting.

Regan glanced across to Ava, who gave a subtle shrug.

"I suggest you keep your ideas to yourself rather than brainstorm, and those of you in the same rooms, don't share your notes with anyone but your assistants." Did she look specifically at Regan and Ava? Sure seemed like it. "I'm going to judge this project by originality, creativity, and flavor. You'll have all day tomorrow to come up with your ideas, and then on Saturday, you'll bake."

Nods all around, a few excited faces and murmurs of anticipation.

Liza held up her hands, and the room went quiet again. "Also, I almost forgot. There will be a fireworks display tomorrow night when it gets fully dark. One of my staff will set them off down over the pond, and we'll have cocktails and appetizers on the back patio. You are all invited." She clapped her hands together once, then turned and left the kitchen.

As had become the habit of the attendees, there was a moment of quiet, as if they were schoolkids waiting to make sure the teacher had actually gone before they cut loose. The moment passed and a collective breath was exhaled.

"Fireworks sound fun," Madison, ever the positive one, said with a smile.

"They do," Ava added, then glanced over to Regan and raised her brows in expectation.

"I love a good fireworks display," she said and got a little thrill in her tummy when Ava grinned her approval.

"Not exactly a unique topic for the Fourth of July," Vienna said, untying her apron. "What July Fourth means to me?" She sighed and shook her head as she pulled the apron over her head and folded it neatly.

Bethany, her assistant, seemed to want to make it better. "Well, maybe she kept it broad so we could come up with more ideas?"

"Maybe," Vienna said. "I'll meet you all at dinner." And without another word, she was the first to exit the kitchen. Bethany stood for a moment, clearly unsure of what to do, then opted to follow Vienna.

The others followed, one by one, until Ava, Becca, Hadley, and

Regan were left. They finished cleaning up their stations, left their chef's coats on the counter for the staff to launder, and headed out.

Hadley turned to Regan. "Text me when you want to meet tomorrow. I've got some ideas, so maybe we can brainstorm."

"Perfect."

"Same," Becca said, pointing to Ava. Then she turned to Hadley. "I think our ride's here."

They said their goodbyes and hurried to the front door where the van could be seen out front.

In the dining room to their left, a couple of the attendees were sitting around the table. Snacks had been left out, as well as sodas, bottled water, beer and wine. Madison and Paige were picking at cheese and crackers. Maia was peeling a banana. She had dark circles under her eyes, and Regan knew her missing lucky bandanna was weighing on her. Vienna was sitting at the table with a beer, which surprised Regan. She looked tired, and Regan wondered if all the stress and snark from Liza was taking a toll.

Vienna raised her bottle, not even bothering to use the pilsner glasses provided, and took a long pull. Regan sat down next to her.

"You okay?" she asked.

Vienna gave one nod, then took another slug. "Just ready to get the hell out of here and go home."

"Eight weeks is a long time," she agreed. "I feel you."

Ava sat down across from them, popped open a can of Diet Coke, and poured it into a glass of ice. "She was rough on you," she commented.

"They say not to meet your heroes, don't they?" Vienna said with a bitter laugh.

"We have less than two weeks left," Regan reminded her. "That's it."

Vienna nodded. She didn't look like she felt much better, but she nodded. "Yeah." She sighed and took another swig of her beer before adding, "I miss my kid."

"You have a kid?" Regan asked. "I had no idea."

"I do." A tender smile.

"Boy? Girl? How old?" Regan could see that talking about her child seemed to ease Vienna's stress at least a little bit.

Vienna turned her bottle in her fingers as she said, "James. He's seven. FaceTime has been great. I talk to him every day. But man...it's not the same, you know?"

Regan nodded. "I do know."

"He misses me, but he was all about my coming here. He knows that I watch *Whisk Me Away* constantly. He knows what an opportunity this is for me." Vienna looked up at Regan, then across at Ava. "He's really wise for his age."

Ava smiled at her, the soft smile that Regan loved. "He sounds like a super-cool kid."

"Are you guys talking about James?" Maia asked, joining them. "I see them FaceTime all the time. He's fucking adorable."

Vienna's smile grew, and Regan could tell they were slowly cheering her up, pulling her back from the dark corner in which she'd tried to isolate herself.

"I can't believe we didn't know you have a son," Ava said.

Vienna lifted one shoulder. "I guess I've been trying to keep my private life separate from"—she waved a hand around—"all this. You know?"

"Privacy is important," Ava said with a nod of agreement.

Maia obviously took the cue. "Speaking of privacy, what's going on here?" She waved a finger between Ava and Regan. "How are things?" Regan immediately blushed. She felt it shoot up her neck and settle into her cheeks, confirmed when Maia laughed and said, "Oh, okay. I see. That good, huh?"

Risking a glance at Ava only made her blush more. Ava sat with her elbows on the table, her glass of soda held in both hands, and she grinned over the rim as she took a sip.

"Uh-huh. Uh-huh. And is this just a retreat thing? Back to reality in thirteen days?" Maia's gaze went back and forth between the two of them, and Regan watched as Ava's grin tempered and then was gone. Maia was clearly looking for gossip, and being the subject of it didn't sit well with Ava. That was painfully obvious.

"Um...we haven't really gotten that far," Regan said, shocked by her honesty in this room of four other people she really didn't know—and one she wanted to know every single thing about.

"And it's nobody's business," Madison said, stepping in. She kept a smile on her face as she touched Maia's arm, as if wanting to rein her in. It seemed to work, if the quick flash of realization and embarrassment that zipped across Maia's face was any indication.

"Right. Right. Sorry." She sort of bowed her head quickly at the two of them. "I just think you guys make the cutest couple, and I'm invested is all." She waved a dismissive hand. "Anyway. Apologies. Never mind. You do you." She felt bad, Regan could see that, but she was also grateful to Madison for putting a stop to the direction of the conversation, given how uncomfortable it was making Ava. "But just know that I ship you guys."

That made Regan grin. She couldn't help it.

An hour later, the two of them were in their room, Regan sitting against her headboard, laptop in her lap, researching ideas for her Fourth of July bake. When Ava came out of the bathroom, she was wearing jeans and a black tank top. Her hair was down and loose, and was that eyeliner?

"I was going to ask if you wanted to watch a movie," Regan said, "but it looks like you've got other plans."

"Yeah, I'm gonna go grab dinner with Vienna."

"Oh. Okay." She watched as Ava opened her small bag and checked for her credit card, then stepped into her sandals. She looked fucking hot, there was no denying that. "You all right?"

Ava nodded and finally looked at her. She smiled, but it didn't seem to reach her eyes. "Yup. Fine. You?"

No, I'm not fine I want you to stay here with me I want you to only want to spend time with me I want to undress you and have my way with you and I want you to touch me and I want to talk about how we can keep seeing each other after this retreat is over because I really, really like you probably way more than you like me which terrifies me and there's so much I want to say to you... It all flew through her head in one giant run-on sentence, begging to be said out loud.

Instead, she smiled, gave Ava a nod, and said, "I'm good."

"Great. See you later." And she left the room, closing the door behind her with a click that sounded much louder in Regan's head than it actually was.

❖

Ava and Vienna took an Uber to a small, out-of-the-way Italian restaurant that Vienna had read about online.

"I'm tired of sports bars and mixed drinks," she'd said to Ava earlier. "I want a nice dinner and a glass of red wine. What do you think? You in?"

If Maia hadn't sidled up to them in the dining room and said what she'd said, if she hadn't shined a spotlight on Ava and Regan, Ava might have declined. Or she might have accepted but asked if Vienna would mind Regan tagging along. But that spotlight had illuminated other things as well, mainly the uncertainty and trepidation Ava felt around everything that had to do with Regan.

She was confused and floundering, and she didn't like it. Not one bit. Because Ava wasn't a person who let her feelings rule her. No way. She was practical. Logical. She followed lists. And rules. And being swamped by emotion was bullshit, as far as she was concerned. Having her brain be clouded by feelings? Bullshit.

The look on Regan's face when she'd told her she was going to dinner with Vienna—and didn't invite her to go along—was like something sharp poking her in the heart. And that was also bullshit, thank you very much.

They were seated at a small table for two in the corner, which was perfect because they could see the entirety of the small restaurant. There were maybe fifteen tables total and a small bar to one side. About half the tables were occupied, and the waitstaff bustled around, delivering drinks and baskets of bread—fresh bread, Ava noted, detecting the scent of it in the air, along with those of tomato sauce, basil, oregano, and parmesan. Damn, Italians knew what they were doing when it came to food.

Vienna seemed to melt into her chair, and the breath she released was huge enough to make Ava grin.

"All good now?" she asked.

"I will be once I have a glass of the Montepulciano in my hand." She shook her head. "I'm ready to be done with this thing."

"Really? Don't you want to see if you get the money?"

Their waiter arrived at their table, told them the specials, and took their wine order. They decided to split a bottle.

Forearms on the white tablecloth, Vienna leaned forward. "I

don't even care about the money. I just want to go home. I've learned everything I'm gonna learn from her, and I miss my family."

Ava understood. "I get it. I don't blame you. It's been a long six weeks."

The waiter came, uncorked, and poured their wine. Once they each had a glass, Vienna held hers over the table. "But you...here's to finding"—she tipped her head to the side, as if unsure of the right words—"a date? Extracurricular activity? Love? What are you two exactly?"

It was Ava's turn to sigh heavily, and she felt it in the very depths of her lungs. Touching her glass to Vienna's, she said, "I wish I knew."

Vienna sipped. "Haven't talked it out yet?"

"I mean, no?" It was kind of embarrassing to say, and she didn't realize just how embarrassing until she said it. She grimaced and took a gulp of her wine.

"How come?" Vienna then waved a hand like she was erasing an invisible board in front of her. "You know what? That was nosy of me. You don't have to answer that. It's none of my damn business."

"No. No. It's okay." And it was somehow. "I actually kind of want to talk about it 'cause..." She shook her head, and the smile that came to her face was one she actually felt blossoming. She couldn't help it.

"Oh, I see," Vienna said with a soft laugh. "There's some things happening there."

"Some things. That's a good way of putting it."

"And, what? You're on board? In doubt? On the fence? What?"

"I'm terrified."

There. There it was. She'd blurted the words quickly, said them out loud, and the walls hadn't come crumbling down. The roof was still intact. Nobody in the restaurant gasped and whipped their head around in horrified wonder.

Then the waiter was back, so Ava had to sit with those words hanging in the air over their table while he took their orders, refilled their glasses, and went on his way. She grabbed her wine and took a long sip, part of her irritated she'd said anything to somebody who was essentially a complete stranger, another part relieved that now she had no choice but to talk about it.

"What's terrifying you?" Vienna asked, her face open and

welcoming as she sipped. "Regan seems pretty awesome. I heard you two have some history. Did you date before?"

Ava shook her head. "No. Oh, no. That was never even an option. I don't date people I work with. Did that once. Disaster."

Vienna's laugh was hefty. "Oh, I hear that. I hear that. You do not shit where you eat, as my daddy would say."

"Exactly. No, we worked together at the same restaurant I'm at now. Years ago. She was new. I'd been there for a year or two and thought I was all high and mighty." She shook her head as she remembered the attitude she'd had back then, somebody at her young age a success in such a high-end place. "A little full of myself, that's what I was. I was given a lot of leeway by my boss back then, when I first came on, but I did *not* pay that forward to the people who came after me." She sipped her wine. "Not proud of that."

"We are stupid when we're young." Vienna's soft laugh rolled around the table as she broke off a piece of the warm bread the waiter had left and dipped it in the little saucer of olive oil. "We all have things we're not proud of."

"True." Ava followed suit with the bread, and oh my God, it was delicious. Yeasty and crusty and soft on the inside, the olive oil's flavor warm and subtle. "Damn, that's good," she said, and Vienna nodded her agreement. "So." She pointed her bread at Vienna as she continued her story. "Regan was younger than me. And so, so nervous. It would've been cute if it hadn't affected everything she did." A shrug. "She couldn't cut it. Couldn't keep up. That being said, I didn't cut her one single millimeter of slack. I was an asshole. Horrible to work with. Again, not proud of it."

"You get her fired?"

"I pretty much got her fired. Yeah." She glanced down at her bread plate, then back up. "I had no guilt around it then, but I do now. I was such an asshole."

"She forgave you?"

"Then? No. She was devastated."

"Yeah, but you're sleeping with her, so I'd say you're forgiven, wouldn't you?"

The waiter arrived with their meals, giving Ava time to absorb what Vienna had said. He gave them each cracked black pepper and parmesan cheese, then left them to their dinners.

"I think I am most definitely forgiven," Ava said with a grin as she spun her linguine on her fork.

"I would agree with that." Vienna had ordered the lasagna, and the piece on her fork stretched some fresh mozzarella for miles. "Wow. Look at this." They spent several moments eating and humming their approval of their meals before Vienna asked, "So, what's terrifying you? You haven't answered that yet."

No. She hadn't. And it was time to face that demon.

"My feelings. That's what's terrifying. The feelings I'm starting to have for her. They scare me to death."

Vienna set her fork down and dabbed at her mouth with her linen napkin and nodded. Then she took a moment, seeming to collect her thoughts. "I think we all figured you guys were just...having fun, you know? Like summer camp or something."

Ava had thought something similar, so the comparison made her smile. "Yeah. That's how it started. But now..." She took a bite, chewed, and swallowed before adding, "I don't love how we've been called out, though. Especially by Liza. God, so embarrassing."

"That bitch." Vienna shook her head. "They say never meet your heroes, and I finally get it. She's horrible. That was so not cool, what she did to you guys."

"Or you. Or Maia. Or any of us."

"Right? I came here to learn, not to be browbeaten by somebody I admired. I went through that in culinary school, thank you very much. I didn't need to go through it again." Vienna was worked up, and she took a sip of her wine, which seemed to calm her. She waved a hand. "Sorry about that."

"No need."

"So, these feelings. You gonna tell her about them?"

"God, I don't know. In less than two weeks, we go back to our own lives."

"You live in the same city, though."

"We do." Another bite of the stunningly good linguini. Perfectly al dente. Definitely homemade. She could tell by the taste, the bite. She forced her attention back to the topic at hand. "You know, I'm looking for a reason for things to not work. Like, searching for one. What *is* that?"

Vienna pointed at her with her fork as she chewed, then said, "You know, I have a theory about that, because I did the same thing with my husband."

"Tell me. Please. I will take any and all theories if they'll help me understand."

"Well, I don't know anything about your childhood, but mine was…difficult. Absentee father, mom who worked two jobs, so was hardly around. I took care of myself and my little brother and sister. Not a lot of time to focus on me, you know?"

Ava nodded, eating and listening, struck by the similarities, minus the siblings.

"When I was in culinary school, I met Jay. He was amazing. Handsome. Smart. Empathetic." She lowered her voice. "Sexy as hell, my God." They both laughed. "He was everything I had ever dreamed of in a guy, and he wanted me. Oh, how he wanted me. He tells the story to this day of how he knew he was gonna marry me from the moment our eyes met." She waved a hand. "Anyway. We started dating, and the closer he got, the more scared I got. See, I wasn't used to somebody else looking out for me. And I certainly didn't know how to *let* somebody else look out for me, since nobody ever had. So the easier thing to do was to run the other way. And I did."

"You broke up with him?"

Vienna nodded, gesturing with her wine glass. "Ripped his heart out, threw it on the floor, and stomped on it." She blew out a breath that was clearly filled with regret. "I am so incredibly lucky that he refused to give up." When her eyes met Ava's, they were wet with unshed tears. "He's an incredible man, and I know how blessed I am. But my God, I did everything I could to sabotage us." She shook her head, clearly disgusted with herself. "Sound like a boat you might be sitting in?"

CHAPTER FIFTEEN

R egan wasn't really into the movie she'd chosen to watch, probably because she was barely paying attention. Between checking her phone for messages from Ava to letting her mind wander off in wonder of what Ava might be doing/saying/thinking at any given moment, she was useless.

She closed the laptop with a sigh, put it away, and went into the bathroom to take care of her nightly routine. Face freshly scrubbed and teeth brushed, she climbed into her bed and turned off the light. It was earlier than she usually went to sleep here at the retreat, but she was sad and stressed and just wanted the day to be over. Clearly, Ava was having a blast out with Vienna if she wasn't yet home, three hours later.

Lying on her back in her bed in the dark, she thought about Ava coming home and being unable to see a thing. With an irritated groan, she threw off the covers, crossed the room, and clicked on the small lamp on Ava's nightstand, cursing herself for giving a shit whether Ava tripped over her shoes or ran into the bed. She yanked the covers up and turned onto her side to face away from the door.

Unsure how much time had passed once she'd started to drift off, she was startled awake by the click of the door opening. She heard the rustling of clothing and figured Ava was changing into her pajamas. Closing her eyes again, she focused on slowing her mind and going back to sleep.

That's when she felt weight on her mattress. Ava slid under the covers and nestled close to Regan's back, spooning her.

She was naked.

It didn't make Regan proud to know that the simple touch of

Ava's skin was enough to wake up her entire nervous system, but that's exactly what happened. Ava's hips pushed against her ass, Ava's breasts pressed into her back, and Ava's hand slid from her outer thigh, over her hip, across her stomach, and up under her shirt to cup a breast and toy with a nipple. Regan couldn't stay quiet, a soft moan leaking out of her. She grasped Ava's hand, stopping it, and turned to look her in the eye.

What she saw shocked her.

She saw sorrow. She saw regret. She saw apology. She saw desire.

And she saw something else she didn't want to think about.

"I'm sorry," Ava whispered into the dim light of the room. "I panicked."

"I know," Regan whispered back. "It's okay." And it was. Just like that, it was.

Those were the only words spoken before Ava's mouth crushed against hers, kissing her with knowledge, passion, and want. Ava shifted so she was mostly on top of Regan, and she shoved Regan's shirt up to reveal her breasts, staring at them so hungrily Regan was sure she could actually feel her eyes, feel them sliding along her skin and rolling her nipples, and then Ava bent forward and took one into her mouth and sucked so hard, Regan thought she might pass out from the pleasure of it. She held tightly to Ava's hips as they slid along her thigh, leaving a trail of wetness on Regan's skin.

Sex with Ava had been incredible up to that point. Indescribably good. Their sexual compatibility was off the charts. But this? Now? Tonight? The charts were left in the dust. There were no charts; they no longer existed. There was only Ava. Her hands, her mouth, her tongue—God, *her tongue*.

Ava was everywhere. Her hands roamed Regan's body. They stroked, squeezed, even scratched a little, until Regan was literally writhing beneath her, feeling like she couldn't get enough. She wanted more but couldn't articulate a thing because it was all so much. Ava kissed her, with certainty and thoroughness as she cupped a breast in each hand and kneaded. Soft and hard. Stroking and squeezing. Shifting her body, she used her legs to spread Regan's and then practically dove down between them, devouring her with her mouth, her tongue, her fingers.

All Regan could do was hold on. To anything. She grabbed at the headboard. The covers. Her pillow. No longer able to differentiate between what part of Ava was touching what part of her, she became awash with pleasure. It was all one enormous burst of wonderfulness that took up every inch of her body and soul, and then she was coming. Colors burst behind her eyelids like fireworks as every muscle in her body tightened and she arched up off the bed. Somewhere, vaguely, she could feel Ava holding on to her, but her tongue was still moving, still stroking, still pulling sounds and spasms and absolutely mind-blowing joy from her body. She covered her own face with a pillow, knowing somewhere in her brain that she needed to let it out, and she screamed with pleasure. She didn't groan. She didn't whimper. She screamed into the pillow as her body took over, riding out the orgasm as long as possible before her muscles finally gave out and dropped her back to the mattress, like a heavy sack of flour.

"Jesus Christ," she whispered, panting, eyes still squeezed shut. "Jesus fucking Christ."

A low chuckle came from between her legs as Ava rested her cheek against Regan's inner thigh. That was when she realized Ava's fingers were inside her, and her body contracted once, just to remind her.

"That was amazing," she managed to croak out. "*You're* amazing."

"And *you* are beautiful." Ava slid her fingers out slowly, causing another small muscle spasm that made Regan gasp a soft laugh.

"Come up here," she said, body still humming as she turned on her side so she could rest on Ava's shoulder. Her body felt weighed down, like her limbs were filled with water, suddenly tired. She sighed happily against Ava's bare skin. "That was...unexpected."

Ava yawned. "Had to. Couldn't help it."

"Hey, I'm not complaining. I was just surprised." They should talk about this. Regan wanted to talk about it. But she also wanted to simply hold Ava, to enjoy feeling her weight, her skin, listen to her soft breathing—

Shit.

Ava was already asleep. And while Regan really wanted to have a discussion—because what were they doing? And what were they going to do when the retreat ended in less than two weeks?—she also couldn't bear to wake Ava up. This was a time she loved, this post-lovemaking cuddle, this closeness. This was the time when the feelings she knew she was developing for Ava settled warmly inside her and snuggled up, keeping her from moving, keeping her from even wanting to move.

She inhaled deeply and let it out in a long, slow breath. Talking could wait.

❖

Regan woke up alone.

Sun streamed through the window, which caused her to lie there, face in the pillow, and blink in confusion for a moment. She was rarely in bed when the sun rose, but this retreat had messed with her usual schedule...not to mention all the sex she'd been having. Her body was clearly exhausted if it was now letting her sleep past sunrise.

The bathroom door was open, the light off. Ava's bed was still neatly made. Reaching her hand to the other side of the bed told her it was cool; Ava must've left a while ago. Her fingers brushed a piece of paper, and she lifted her head to examine it.

You looked too peaceful to wake up.
Went for a run.
Ava

She'd signed her name with a crudely drawn heart next to it, and it made Regan smile as she rolled over onto her back and reached for her phone on the nightstand. It buzzed with a text as she held it in her hand. Kiki.

Checking in. How's things?

The relief Regan felt confused her at first, but then she realized that Kiki was part of her regular life. That she represented normal in a time when normal seemed really far away from her grasp, and for whatever reason, she needed to touch normal right now.

Hey, you, she typed back. *Getting off work or heading in?*

The gray dots bounced as Kiki typed her answer. *Just got home. Rough night.*

Regan knew better than to ask for details. *Rough night* usually meant she'd lost a patient. Maybe more than one. But Regan didn't push. Kiki would give her details if and when she was ready to, so she simply said *I'm sorry* with a sad emoji.

Cheer me up. Tell me about all the sex you're having. That was followed by an eggplant emoji, which made Regan laugh because Kiki used it to refer to anything that had to do with sex, even if it was between two women with no "eggplants" involved.

She sent back a sweating emoji, a sun emoji, and anything else she could find that might represent the word *hot*.

Wow! was Kiki's response. *That's a lot. I was half expecting you to tell me it had ended.*

Regan didn't want to text. She wanted to talk. She grabbed a shirt and threw it on since she was still naked from last night's session, and then she hit the FaceTime icon. She gave Kiki no time to say anything when her face appeared on the screen, she simply said, "It has not stopped. If anything, it has increased. She came in last night after dinner and didn't say a word, just basically ripped my clothes off." Even saying the words and remembering the previous night started her center throbbing and made her skin flush with heat. She swallowed.

Kiki squinted into the phone. "Oh my God, I can see it on your face. It's right there, plain as can be. She's gotten to you. You *like* her, don't you?" Kiki's tone was a combination of shocked disbelief and gentle happiness.

Trying to lie, or even downplay, to Kiki was useless. She knew Regan too well and could read her like a book. All Regan could do was sigh, and then, to her fucking horror, her body betrayed her and her eyes welled up.

"Oh, honey," Kiki said, pushing her face close to the screen. "You *do* like her. It's okay. Don't cry." The reason Kiki had become a nurse in the first place was her innate desire to help people, so the teasing was shoved aside to make room for genuine concern. Her voice went soft. "I assume she's not there with you. Can you tell me what's going on?"

The wetness had decided not to stay in her eyes, and she swiped at her cheek. "You're right. I just really like her," she said quietly, then cleared her throat. "It's been a long time since I trusted somebody, you know?"

"Believe me, I know." Kiki's smile was gentle, a reminder that she'd been there through Regan's last disaster of a relationship with a woman who wouldn't know faithfulness if it walked up to her on the street and slapped her across the face. "What makes you trust this one? I mean, you're not in the most ideal of circumstances."

Regan nodded. "That's true. And I don't even know what it is. Maybe it was her owning up to what happened all those years ago and feeling bad about it? I'm not sure." A sigh. A gaze off toward the window. "All I know is that I'd like to see her after this is all over with. Keep seeing her, I mean."

"Have you talked about that?"

"Not yet." Regan shook her head. "I meant to last night, but…" She rolled her lips in and smothered a grin.

"Got a little busy, did you?" Kiki laughed.

"*So* busy."

"Where is she now?"

"She went for a run while I was still asleep. Left me a note."

"Does it have a heart on it?"

"It does."

Kiki barked a laugh. "OMG, you two have it bad."

And now Regan was laughing, too. "Right? It's outrageous how this has all transpired."

"It really is." Kiki's expression slid back into seriousness. "Just be careful, love. Okay? I know you really like her, but take care of you, yeah?"

"Yeah. I will. Promise."

They caught up on a few more things and then Regan spent a hilarious moment talking to Artie on FaceTime. The cat could not have looked more bored if he'd tried, and it only made Regan laugh. She finally said her goodbyes and hung up, and not two minutes later, the door opened and Ava walked in.

Jesus fucking Christ.

Flushed and glistening and still a teeny bit out of breath, and holy shit, Ava looked good enough to eat.

"Nope." Ava held up a finger and chuckled softly. "I know that look, but I ran into both Becca and Hadley downstairs and they're both waiting for us so they can help with our big ideas." She toed off her running shoes, then strode to Regan's bed and grasped her chin in one hand. "We have no time for hanky-panky." She kissed Regan's mouth, and her lips tasted salty. "Sadly." She headed for the bathroom. "I'm gonna shower." She stopped with the door almost closed, met Regan's gaze, and said, "You look really cute when you just wake up."

The door clicked shut.

Regan flopped back onto the bed with a groan and the goofiest grin on her face. She could feel it. "This woman is gonna be the death of me," she whispered to the empty room. "I just know it."

❖

Hadley had proven to be a good assistant in the kitchen, but she was an even better brainstormer. She and Regan had been in Regan and Ava's room for the whole morning and well into the afternoon, trying to come up with a bake that represented her joy in July Fourth for tomorrow's contest.

They'd finalized their idea around four o'clock.

"I think this is gonna be awesome," Hadley said, sifting through the papers spread out on the floor between the foot of Regan's bed and the foot of Ava's.

Regan scanned them all: lists, sketches, idea notes, visualizing the cake, the cream puffs, the tiny apple pies, the sugar art...It was a lot. But if they could pull it off, it'd be amazing. A July Fourth picnic made of desserts, complete with a lawn, an American flag with rainbow stripes to add some Pride, a picnic table, and fireworks.

"Baked art isn't my forte," Regan said. "I'm better at standard desserts that look like they're supposed to, not like something else entirely." She looked up at Hadley and grinned. "But if we can pull this off, it's gonna be pretty fucking cool."

"We can totally pull it off." Hadley held up a hand for a high five, and Regan slapped it. "Nice work, Chef."

"We'll see." Regan started piling the papers and closed her laptop. "I'm starving. Food?"

"Are you kidding? My stomach has started eating itself."

Regan tossed their work in a haphazard pile on her bed and they headed downstairs.

The teams had scattered that morning. Vienna was in her and Maia's room, while Maia was in the living room to the right of the stairs. Paige and her assistant sat at one end of the dining room table, and through the window, Regan could see Ava and Becca sitting in the grass, a laptop in Ava's lap and a notebook in Becca's. They weren't close enough for Regan to make out expressions, other than Ava wasn't exactly smiling, but then Becca said something and gave her a nudge and there was that smile.

The buffet table had an array of food and drinks, from sandwiches and chips to cookies and muffins. Bottles of water, cans of soda, beer, and wine were also available, the wine on the buffet, the bottles and cans in a large bucket of ice on its own stand next to it. Regan grabbed a bottle of water first, cracked it open, and took a long drink from it, not realizing just how thirsty she was until the first sip hit her lips. Chocolate chip muffin in hand, she sat down at the table just as Paige closed her notebook and smiled at her assistant, whose name Regan couldn't pull from her brain.

"Success?" she asked.

Paige shrugged and gave her an uncertain smile. "I think so? What about you two?"

Hadley sat down next to her with a bag of potato chips and a Coke. "We're gonna kick ass tomorrow."

"Wow," said Paige's assistant. *Violet!* Regan thought. That was her name. "Pretty sure of yourself."

Hadley looked to Regan, then back. "Yup." She sipped from her Coke, watching Violet the entire time. *Okay, so a bit of competition between the assistants, I see.*

Maia and her assistant, who Regan did remember was named Rose—she took a second to be amused that two of the assistants had flower names—came in from the living room just as the front door opened and Ava and Becca entered.

"Looks like we all needed about the same amount of time," Madison said in her usually cheerful tone. "How are we feeling about our projects?"

Responses were varied, from grumbles to nods to excitement.

Ava met Regan's gaze and smiled gently, then nearly knocked over her water onto her laptop, catching it at the very last minute. "Okay, I'm gonna take this up before I destroy it by accident."

Becca smiled at her. "I'll do it."

"You sure?" Ava asked. Becca had been doing small favors and things for her since the retreat had begun, and Ava had mentioned to Regan that she didn't want to take advantage, especially when they weren't in the kitchen.

"Absolutely. You chill. Be right back." And with that, Becca grabbed the laptop and headed for the stairs.

Vienna and Bethany came in just then, Vienna jerking a thumb over her shoulder. "That girl almost took me out on the stairs." But she shook her head and laughed softly, which made Regan happy. Vienna had seemed a bit...on edge for the past week or so, and seeing her smile was a nice change.

Vienna grabbed herself an apple and sat down next to Ava, then bumped her with a shoulder. Ava grinned at her, and it was clear to Regan that a friendship had deepened with their dinner the night before.

"What time did Liza say the fireworks were?" Madison asked.

"Not until after dark," said Paige, who checked her watch. Then she sighed and looked around the table. "I was gonna ask if anybody wanted to go out to happy hour, but I'm freaking exhausted." She laughed gently.

"Me too," Madison added. "I say we stay put. We can make our own happy hour." She met the faces of the assistants. "You guys are staying for the fireworks, right?" When they nodded, she continued. "Yeah, so let's do our own happy hour and have dinner and just chill. It's our day off and we have to work tomorrow, so let's relax. Yeah?"

The room agreed and Regan had to force herself to be outwardly cheerful. Not that she didn't want to hang out more with her fellow pastry chefs. She did. But she knew what she really wanted was more alone time with Ava, and she also knew she had to calm the hell down and also participate in the retreat. It was why she was there in the first place.

Take a breath, Callahan. She'll still be in the same bed with you tonight.

Smiling and shaking her head at her own self-deprecation, she looked up and met Ava's eyes across the table. Her expression was knowing, and it occurred to Regan that Ava might actually be feeling the same way. It was something she hadn't really thought about, and it made her warm from the inside.

Becca arrived and sat back in her chair.

"You get lost up there?" Ava teased.

Becca blushed slightly. "I used your bathroom. Hope you don't mind."

Ava shrugged and then May came into the room and got their

attention. She filled them in on dinner, the schedule for the night and the next day, and then exited just as silently as she'd arrived.

"I swear to God, I've seen her in a horror movie," Maia whispered, eyes wide as the others laughed.

Vienna had a bottle of wine in one hand, corkscrew in the other. "Who's in?" she asked.

And the night off began.

❖

It was clear that nobody really ended up cutting loose that night. There was plenty to drink. Lots of wine, loads of beer, even a small bar set up on the patio with a small assortment of liquors. But Regan noticed the retreat attendees seemed to be a bit more serious about tomorrow's bake. Was it because there were less than two weeks left in the retreat itself and they wanted to make the best final impressions they could? Or was it because in less than two weeks, one of them was going to be a hundred grand richer, and they wanted to have a clear head for the work ahead?

No idea. All she knew, as she nursed her second glass of wine, was that she'd mellowed nicely, her body feeling warm and relaxed. She'd noticed, though, that Ava seemed the tiniest bit…she wasn't sure of the right word. Worried? Concerned? Stressed? Some variation of one of those things? She poured another glass of wine and carried it over to her.

"You okay?" she asked quietly, handing her the glass.

Ava grimaced as she took it, and somewhere in Regan's mind came the comment that even when she was unhappy—frowning or grimacing—Ava was still fucking stunning. A shake of Ava's head had her looking more worried. "I'm not thrilled with the idea Becca and I came up with for tomorrow."

Regan wasn't proud of the relief that coursed through her right then, knowing Ava's stress wasn't about her. Or them. "I'm sure it's fine."

Ava sipped the wine and gave it a moment before saying with softly steel words, "I don't want fine, though. I want great. I want spectacular. And what we have isn't it." She took another sip, then groaned, her irritation clear. "I'm better than this, damn it."

"Can I help in some way?" Regan hated seeing her like this. Uncertain and frustrated. Doubting herself.

Her offer seemed to land where it was needed, and she could see Ava's shoulders relax just a little. When she met Regan's gaze, it was with a soft smile as she reached out and ran her hand down Regan's arm. "No. That wouldn't be fair. But I appreciate you offering. You're very sweet." She leaned against her a bit, just enough for Regan to feel it, and blew out a breath. "I'm just gonna have to suck it up and work on it tonight until I come up with something I feel better about. I'm sorry."

"What are you sorry about?"

"That we won't get a chance for some time tonight." Ava's voice was very soft, her expression saying she was very aware of those around them and their proximity.

Regan lowered her voice to match. "Babe, you do what you need to do. Don't worry about me. You want to feel confident going into tomorrow. I get that." She waited until Ava looked at her again and said, "I'm a big girl."

Ava's smile of relief was all she needed. The night righted itself just as the first fireworks were shot off. A collective gasp went around the yard as the retreaters, the assistants, and even the remaining staff stopped what they were doing to gather in the yard, sit on blankets, and watch.

Regan had snagged an extra blanket from their room, and now she spread it out on the grass for her and Ava. Vienna and Maia sat next to them on one side, the others behind them, and they all lifted their faces to the sky.

Vienna leaned close and said under her breath, "For a private display, this is pretty goddamn good."

Ava nodded and Regan had to agree.

Apparently, so did Madison. "These are some pretty impressive fireworks," she said from behind them, just as a huge one burst into a bright green star far above their heads. A couple of assistants sat nearby and vocally agreed, as three fireworks in a row burst above them in red, then white, then blue. The women oohed and aahed and then laughed at the cliché of it.

The display went on for nearly a half hour before the big finale of bangs and booms and flashes that pretty much every fireworks display Regan had ever seen in her life ended with. As she sat there next to Ava, close enough that their thighs and shoulders were touching, and as she covered her ears with both hands, the way she had during the big booms since she was a child, a thought raced through her head on a loop.

There's nowhere I'd rather be right now.

She looked at Ava, at the colors and light on her face, on her wide eyes and creamy smooth skin and dark hair streaked with red and green from the fireworks above. She saw the soft smile, the gentle lines that smile created in her face, and when she turned that smile to Regan, the thought hit again.

There's nowhere I'd rather be. Nowhere.

Ava's expression said she might've had an idea what Regan was thinking, but she didn't have a chance to say so before Becca appeared. She squatted down next to Ava and said something that Regan couldn't hear over the sound of the fireworks. Ava gave her a nod, then turned to Regan.

"All right, Becca's got an idea that might be better than what we came up with, so we're gonna go see if we can hash it out." She frowned and tipped her head to the side.

"It's okay," Regan said, a hand on her arm. "I don't want you feeling guilty." She used her chin to gesture toward Becca, who was already heading for the door inside. "Go. Come up with something awesome."

"Just not as awesome as yours," Ava teased as she shifted to her knees.

"I mean, I didn't wanna say..."

Ava leaned in close to her ear and whispered, "I really want to kiss you right now, but I won't. It's probably better to leave you wanting anyway." With a wink, she pushed herself to her feet, waved good night to the others, and went in after Becca.

Regan followed her departure with her eyes, and her gaze was snagged by Maia, who frowned and ran her own fingertip down from an eye in an impression of a tear. Regan playfully smacked her.

"Shut up," she said but couldn't keep the smile off her face, no matter how hard she tried. Which wasn't really very hard.

Chapter Sixteen

Ava had slept like the dead, but it didn't feel like it when she'd woken up. She and Becca had worked on a new design until after two in the morning, then she'd tiptoed to her room, stepped out of her clothes, and crawled into bed with Regan, spooning her from behind. Regan's body was warm and soft, and Ava had snuggled in and fallen asleep immediately, but when Regan's alarm had gone off at six, Ava felt like it had been four minutes instead of four hours.

She'd shaken it off, though, as she'd done so many other times in her working life, and now stood behind her counter in the kitchen.

"Kinda mysterious," she whispered to Becca, who stood beside her as they waited for Liza to come in and start them off.

"Right?" Becca replied.

Across the aisle, Regan stood with Hadley, hands clasped in front of her, looking sharp in her white chef's coat. She glanced Ava's way and gave her a little grin and a wink, and Ava's body shot her memory back in time to about forty-five minutes ago when she'd been in the shower with Regan, her back pressed against the cold tile, Regan's fingers pushing in and out of her until she came so hard, she had to clamp a hand over her mouth to keep from letting the entire mansion know she was having a major orgasm. The memory alone had her throbbing and wet, and she grinned back at Regan, then looked down at the floor as she shook her head subtly. The flesh between her legs was deliciously sore.

"You okay?" Becca asked on a whisper.

Ava nodded and met her eyes. "I'm great. Yeah. You?"

"Ready to knock this out of the park."

There was no more time for pumping each other up, as Liza Bennett-Schmidt entered the room, followed as always by May in her black pants and white button-down shirt. "Good morning, chefs," Liza said, holding her hands out to the sides. She also wore her chef's coat—not nearly as well as Regan, Ava absently thought—and May carried an iPad. "I trust you are all rested and ready?"

Murmurs went around the kitchen.

"Excellent. I also trust you all have designs or notes or sketches or whatever you need for this project. For the record, your success with this bake will be a large part of who I decide to donate my money to." It was only the second time she'd mentioned the money, and Ava could feel everybody in the room perk up, stand a bit more at attention. Even Vienna, who had said the other night that she didn't care about the money, seemed to straighten up and stand taller.

"Just to ensure there's no leaking of ideas—by osmosis or by glances at other kitchens—we're taking precautions."

May snapped her fingers at the doorway, and suddenly staff members entered in single file, carrying large white muslin screens between them. As they proceeded to set them up around each kitchen area, Ava gave Regan a little finger-wiggle wave just before a screen was dropped there, blocking Regan from her view.

"Seems a little drastic," she murmured out of the side of her mouth.

"I was gonna say the same thing," Becca murmured back, and then they laughed softly at the silliness of talking out of the sides of their mouths when they were the only two inside their little muslin box.

"Screens are set." They heard Liza's voice, though they could no longer see her. "You have all day to make your bakes. I will wander through from time to time, but you have until five o'clock this evening and then we'll do a presentation for everybody to see."

"Gonna be a long day," Becca whispered, and Ava nodded in agreement.

"Your bake starts...now," Liza commanded, and the sounds of sudden movement could be heard in the air of the kitchen.

Ava turned to Becca. "Ready?"

Becca answered by raising her hand in the air. Ava slapped it in a high five. "We got this," Becca said, and they were off.

The strangest thing about the setup was all the noise that she couldn't see happening. When she was working in Pomp, she had her own area within the kitchen where she made all her pastries and desserts. But she could still see the rest of the kitchen, watch the chefs and sous chefs making salads and chopping ingredients for soups and grilling steaks or chicken or pulling baked racks of lamb out of the oven. It was all right there for her to watch as she listened to the soundtrack of a working restaurant kitchen. This? This was just…odd. All the sounds and none of the sights.

Time ticked on. Their cake went into the oven first, as was the plan. Ava wanted to make sure it was fully cooled before she frosted and decorated it.

Liza came through at the two-hour mark, strolling in with her hands clasped behind her back to scan their station. Ava didn't like the way she had to fight not to squirm when Liza was nearby, but she managed. Chef looked at their design on Becca's iPad. She pressed a finger on the center of the cake, which—much to Ava's relief—sprang back perfectly. She studied the batter in the mixing bowl, then stuck a spoon in and tasted. She gave one nod but said nothing, and Ava's brain wanted to know if it was a nod of *Perfect* or a nod of *Terrible, of course she screwed it up.* Liza wasn't telling. She stood there for another moment, scrutinizing and making Ava as nervous as possible, before finally exiting behind a screen, not having said a word. Ava wasn't proud of the breath of relief she let out, and when she glanced at Becca, they grinned at each other.

"Let's go," Becca said, and scrolled the iPad for what was next.

She wondered how Regan was doing. They'd been ordered not to share their ideas, so they hadn't. But Regan had seemed just as keyed up that morning as Ava was, just as happily tense. Part of the reason for the shower sex—*Tension release*, Regan had claimed—and it had worked for a while. But Ava could feel her shoulders tightening up on her as she worked, stirring, mixing, chopping, piping. She took a moment and reminded herself to breathe. In slowly through the nose, out even more slowly through the mouth. She did that a couple of times and felt more centered. Baking under pressure was rough. It happened fairly often at Pomp. Somebody wanted something on the fly or a customer had a food allergy of some sort and couldn't eat the item on the dessert menu, so Ava'd have to make something at the very last possible minute. Pressure and stress. Like now. Like today.

It was nerve-racking.

And it was exhilarating.

❖

If you asked her, Regan would say she never really worked under pressure like this. With a time limit. But that wouldn't exactly be true, since there had been multiple times that she had to hurry and make something on the fly—cookies to fill a suddenly cleaned-out display, a wedding cake at the very last minute that had been left off the schedule for whatever reason. But it wasn't how she usually had to do things, so this was kind of nerve-racking.

But it was coming together. She and Hadley were very much on the same wavelength, and once the cake was done and frosted a lovely spring green, complete with texture to make it look like grass and blue wavy frosting along one side to represent a creek, Hadley started on the mini brownies they'd use to make a small picnic table as well as cornhole parts.

She was excited to see the others' bakes. They were all such different people with such differing personalities, she was almost looking more forward to seeing the rest than showing off hers.

Ava's was one she especially couldn't wait to see. In the time they'd spent together, she felt like she was finally starting to get to know Ava—despite there being so much more she wanted to know. And what she was learning, she really liked. Ava was smart, and nothing turned Regan on like intelligence. She was also super creative. Her patriotism bake would be nothing short of spectacular. Regan was certain of it. Maybe tonight, they could talk some more. Just talk. Learn about each other. Find out about things like hopes and dreams and pasts and futures. She hadn't been kidding when she talked to Kiki about wanting to trust again. Despite their past, Ava was starting to feel like somebody she could.

"Brownies in," Hadley said quietly. "Should we start the sculptures?"

This was the part Regan could admit was her weakest: making food art. Making food look like something else. But Hadley had assured her that she was good at it, so together, they set about using fondant and cake scraps from after they trimmed it and the rice cereal bars Hadley had made while Regan made the cake and shaped them into other things. A tiny apple pie, plates, cups, a bag of chips, a bowl of potato salad, a cooler with cans in it. Everything in miniature. Everything totally edible. Hadley was in charge of the tiny details.

It was meticulous work, but worth it. To Regan, this *was* July Fourth: a picnic with all the picnic foods, cornhole, walks near the water, fireworks.

Speaking of fireworks, they were her job, and she got to work on the Isomalt, getting ready to stretch it and do her best to make it look like bursts of light in the sky above her picnic. She used clear and colored it, some red, some blue. The rest would stay clear. She and Hadley found some clear sticks they'd use to "put them in the air," and Regan sent up a quick prayer to the baking gods to help her not break them.

She was working on shaping one when Liza came around one of the screens. "Chefs," she said by way of greeting.

"Chef," they responded in unison.

"And how are we doing?" Liza had her hands clasped behind her back as if resisting the urge to touch things, or maybe to help. She peered over Regan's shoulder, which, no, didn't make her nervous at all, for fuck's sake.

Feeling herself starting to sweat, she forced herself to focus and work and pretend one of her idols wasn't hovering over her, judging her every move.

Finally, Liza moved over to Hadley's area, where she was putting the lid on the cooler of tiny cans. "Interesting," she said as she watched for a moment, and Regan had to force herself not to roll her eyes. Would it kill the woman to offer some encouragement? Hadley did a commendable job of keeping her hands from shaking. Regan made a mental note to compliment her on that later.

Liza watched for another moment, said, "Mm-hmm," and was on her way. Hadley looked at Regan and they both blew out breaths, then laughed quietly with each other.

"Holy fuck," Hadley whispered, and that pretty much said it all.

They got back to work.

❖

They were all nervous.

All you had to do was look around to notice, and that's what Ava did, now that the screens had been taken away and the assistants sent off to another room. Nobody spoke. The entire kitchen was silent. But everybody was moving in some way. Maia's knee was bouncing up and down like a jackhammer. Paige was chewing on a thumbnail. Madison spun the silver ring on her middle finger. Vienna sat perfectly still unless you looked very closely, and then you could see the muscle in her jaw working as she clenched and unclenched her teeth. And Regan? Regan was adorably—and literally—twiddling her thumbs. Her fingers were entwined and her thumbs rolled around and around each other. She glanced across the aisle and gave Ava a wink.

Liza's crew had taken the bakes away just before taking the screens, so nobody got to see anybody else's project. Liza was going to have each one brought in on its own, one at a time, and the bakers could talk about them and about their process.

So they waited.

Finally, Liza came strolling in, looking very satisfied with herself. Ava was kind of amazed at how her view of the famous chef had changed over the past weeks. Seven weeks ago, she didn't think *looking very satisfied with herself* would have been a way she'd describe Liza Bennett-Schmidt, her idol. But today? Definitely. Her ego was much, much larger than Ava had expected. And her kindness? Kinda lacking. But she shook those thoughts away and did her best to focus on the learning she'd done here. Because there had definitely been a lot of that, regardless.

"Chefs," Liza said.

"Chef," they parroted back.

"How do you feel?"

Nods, shrugs, and a couple of *goods* went through the room. They all looked exhausted but also relieved. Ava knew she was. Relieved to have this day over. Presenting was the easy part.

"Well, you've shown terrific creativity on this project. I'm very impressed with most of you."

The *most of you* didn't bode well, but it was also unsurprising. It seemed Liza always chose one of them to focus her negativity on with each project, and Ava hoped it wasn't her turn.

"Our first bake is from Maia," Chef Liza said, and two staff members carried in Maia's bake. "Maia, would you come forward and tell us about your work?"

"Sure." Maia glanced across the aisle at Vienna, who gave her a thumbs-up.

At the front of the room, she turned to face her peers, just as Liza said, "I see you found your bandanna."

"Yeah. I tore the whole room apart and then yesterday, it just... appeared."

"Weird," Liza said.

"Right?" Maia asked, and their gazes held for a beat before Maia began her presentation. "To me, July Fourth has always meant a weekend at my grandparents' cottage on the lake." Her bake had a lake as the central focus, a cake with a dip in it and covered by blue Isomalt to give the impression of glimmering water. There was a dock protruding into the lake, a couple canoes, and a small cabin. All very detailed. People were fishing, and two figures bobbed in the "water."

Ava was just thinking about how impressive the detail was when Liza said, "Well, your people look a little toy-like."

"I mean, they're miniature, so they kinda are," Maia said softly, absently tugging at the bandanna around her neck. They didn't normally respond to Liza's critiques or try to defend themselves, so Ava was surprised to hear Maia's voice, as quiet as it was.

Liza nodded as she studied Maia's work. "Your piping here on the edge is a little messy. Nice work on the dock, though." She circled, then pointed. "One of your canoes is cracked."

Maia's lips tightened into a thin line, and her throat moved as she swallowed. But she stood there, hands clasped behind her back, and listened.

"Overall, a bit amateurish, but not terrible." Liza waved a hand and the staff guys took the project away. The others clapped, and for Ava's part, she was trying to let Maia know how good her work was. She suspected the others felt the same.

The next three were Paige, then Vienna, then Madison. Ava thought all their bakes looked spectacular, especially Vienna's barbecue, complete with a miniature gas grill that looked so real, Ava expected to feel heat coming off it. Liza systematically pointed out a couple positive things and more negative things on each of them, but the other chefs clapped each time, and Maia even whistled at Vienna's.

"Ava, you're next," Liza said, and the staff members carried her bake out and set it on the display table. Regan gave her a little thumbs-up as she headed toward the front and took her place near her project.

"To me," she said, forcing cheer into her tone, "the Fourth of July represents family and gathering, and all I kept thinking of for that was a big picnic in the park. Right? Lush green grass, all the regular picnic foods, games like corn hole, and then, once it gets dark, fireworks."

Liza circled the bake, taking in the details. Ava stood still, hands clasped behind her back, and tried not to sweat through her chef's coat. "Your picnic table is a little unsteady." She poked it with a finger, but it didn't collapse or fall over. "Nice work on the Isomalt. Your fireworks are impressive. How'd you get them to stay up like that?"

Ava pointed to the clear sticks Becca had found somewhere. "Just these. They worked well."

Liza nodded. "Mm-hmm." She took another lap around. "Nice frosting. And your piping is consistent. Good work. Very, very good work." She waved a hand, and the staff guys came in to whisk her project away.

Almost instantly, her heart began to ease up on the pounding, and she headed back to her spot. But when her eyes met Regan's, the expression shocked her. Regan wasn't smiling. Her eyes were dark and cloudy, and her face had lost all color. Ava mouthed *Are you okay?* just as Liza called Regan's name.

Regan closed her eyes for a moment, then seemed to have to force herself to walk to the front of the room. She didn't look at Ava. What in the world was going on with her?

It only took another few seconds for the answer to that question to become perfectly, horrifyingly clear.

"Oh, my," Liza said. "What have we here?"

Ava stared. Regan's bake looked exactly like hers, complete with Isomalt fireworks in red and blue, and tiny fondant foods on the picnic table made of brownies.

Oh, no. Oh, no, no, no...

"Pretty sure I specifically said not to share your ideas with anybody," Liza said, and there was something about the tone of her voice. *She knew,* Ava thought. *She saw both our bakes from the beginning. She had to know we were making the same thing, yet she never spoke up.*

"I didn't," Regan said, her voice so soft, Ava almost didn't hear it.

"No? Then how did you come up with Ava's idea?"

"I—" The battle in Regan's head was clear on her face, and Ava watched it play out. Regan cleared her throat. "I followed your instructions. I guess we just had the same idea."

There was only one explanation for what had happened. The assistants. Either Hadley had stolen Ava's idea or Becca had stolen Regan's. And since this idea had been a suggestion from Becca...

Jesus Christ.

Ava thought back on the tiny details. The cornhole—Becca's idea. The fireworks—Ava's suggestion, but the Isomalt was Becca's. Even the tiny foods on the picnic table. Ava had wanted to add people, but Becca thought they'd be too difficult and suggested they focus on food instead.

Becca had stolen Regan's idea and passed it to Ava as her own.

Oh, God.

She was stuck. The last thing a chef did was throw their sous chef under the bus. It was considered cheap and unfair and an asshole move, and when there was an issue, the chef took the fallout, similar to a captain going down with the ship. Plus, Liza would take way too much pleasure in frying her like an egg if she blamed Becca. But she was sure that's who was to blame. She couldn't even begin to get into the why of it yet. She was too stunned.

"I don't tolerate cheating, even in a retreat where there are no grades." Liza shook her head, and there was something about her expression. "You came here to learn, and stealing isn't something I teach." With the wave of her hand, she dismissed Regan, but Ava still watched her face because there was something...

And then Liza met her gaze, and it hit her.

She's enjoying this.

Liza Bennett-Schmidt quirked one corner of her mouth just enough for Ava to understand. She liked the turmoil. She fed off the discord.

What the fuck?

Regan hurried back to her station, eyes on the floor, face flaming red. Ava kept her eyes on her, pleading for her to look up, but she wouldn't. Ava saw a drop fall from her cheek and realized she was silently crying. Her heart squeezed in her chest.

"Well." Liza stood before them, doing her best to feign a concerned expression, but it was too late. Ava had already seen behind the mask, and she knew. "That's not how I expected this day to go. I don't have the words to express my disappointment."

For the first time, Ava looked around at the others. Madison looked at the floor. Vienna gave her a small smile. Maia glared in Regan's direction. Paige looked at Regan, too, and just shook her head in slow disapproval.

They thought Regan was guilty.

Liza turned and left without another word, which was new. She probably needs to go have a laugh and doesn't want to do it in front of us.

Ava hurried across the aisle and reached for Regan, who flinched away. "Regan, I am so sorry," she said on a whisper. "I had no idea—"

But when Regan finally looked up at her, there was fire in her eyes. Anger. Rage. "How could you?" Her eyes flashed, and her hands balled into fists. "How could you do that to me?"

"I didn't—"

"I trusted you, and you know what? I *knew* I shouldn't. I *knew* it." The words were filled with venom and pain. "I *knew* you were too good to be true." She shoved past Ava and hurried out of the room, not looking at the others, who were all doing a terrible of job of acting like they hadn't been eavesdropping.

"It wasn't her," Ava said to the other four. Her voice was quiet, and a wave of shame rolled through her. "She didn't steal my idea. I stole hers."

Madison gasped, then covered her mouth with her hand.

"Not intentionally," Ava clarified. "But I think Becca did."

They had likely all been assistants or sous chefs at some point, so the skepticism was clear. Sous chefs caught the brunt of the rage of head chefs constantly. And while they were generally not blamed for mistakes publicly, they were often verbally pummeled in the privacy of the kitchen.

"I know. I know," Ava said, shaking her head. There was a beat, and then the others started to gather their things. Distancing themselves? Maybe. Ava couldn't blame them. There was still a hundred grand up for grabs, and who wanted to get caught in the turmoil of a cheating scandal? She braced her hands on her counter and wanted to laugh. This wasn't culinary school or a reality TV show. It was a simple retreat. For *learning* a craft. She hadn't come there to compete with others. She'd come to improve her own skills. But Liza Bennett-Schmidt had turned it all into something quite a bit different while they weren't paying attention.

When she glanced up from her counter, everybody was gone. She ran her tongue around inside her cheek. "Okay then," she said on a sigh and gathered up her own stuff. With one last glance around the kitchen, she said aloud, "I need to figure out how to make this right."

CHAPTER SEVENTEEN

The way the rest of them had looked at her.

Regan swallowed down the lump in her throat, beyond hurt that these people she'd been sharing space and meals with for the past six and a half weeks had instantly decided she was guilty of stealing somebody's idea.

She had to give herself a mental shake on that, though, because if her project had come out first, would Liza have assumed *Ava* had stolen from *her*? Probably. And the gang would be looking at *Ava* the way they'd looked at her.

"Fucking luck of the draw," she muttered as she pulled out her suitcase.

And Ava. How could she do that? How could she steal something—from Regan of all people—and pass it off as her own? And then just stand there and let fucking Liza Bennett-Schmidt lambaste her in front of everybody without saying a word?

She was stuffing clothes into her suitcase when the door opened.

Fuck.

She did not want to deal with her right now. Or maybe ever again.

"Regan, listen, please. I—what are you doing?"

She couldn't look at Ava. Didn't want to. Didn't want to be reminded of how pretty she was or how she'd begun to find herself lost in those dark eyes or how she'd started to feel safe in those arms. She kept packing. "What does it look like I'm doing? I'm going home."

"What? Why?" Regan shot her a look and Ava had the good sense to look chagrined. "I mean, can you let me explain? Please? Don't go. I think I know what happened."

Regan kept packing and said nothing, so Ava went on. Her words were urgent, her sentences were run-on, like she couldn't take a breath. "Remember when Becca took my laptop up here for me yesterday I think you'd left your notes out, she saw them, and I don't know took pictures? Then she came to me with the idea and we ran with it, worked on it together or so I thought but now, I think she might've had all of it in her head because of what she found of yours, and she kind of led me along..."

Regan had to take a breath. She had to count to five to keep herself from unloading like a cannon. She reached five and looked at Ava, finally. When she spoke, she did it slowly. "Seriously? That's your play? Getting an underling in trouble? Again? I probably should've predicted that."

The barb hit its mark. She could tell by the zap of pain that shot across Ava's face. It didn't make her feel good, though, and she returned her attention to her packing.

"Would you please just wait?" Ava's voice had gone soft. Pleading. Like she knew Regan wasn't buying her explanation.

"Wait for what?" Regan snapped, throwing the last bunch of clothes in. She shook her head. "The last person I was with fucked me over. Badly. It's taken me more than *two years* to get my shit together and feel like I could trust somebody again." She closed her eyes. "I should've known better than to let that somebody be you. You already showed me who you are. Years ago. But I let some good sex cloud my judgment." Okay, that was a low blow, she didn't have to see the tears well up in Ava's eyes to know it. But she couldn't stop herself. No more deep breaths. No more counting to five. She was too angry. Too embarrassed. Too hurt.

"I'll fix it," Ava said, but her voice had lost conviction and the tears had spilled over. Regan looked once and couldn't look again, so she kept packing. "I'll fix it," Ava said again. "Please."

Regan shook her head. "To be honest, I'm glad to go home. I miss it. I miss my cat. I miss my regular life. This fucking fairy tale had to end at some point, right?" She just needed her stuff from the bathroom. Her stomach roiled so badly, she thought she might throw up.

"I—" Ava seemed to have lost steam now, Regan could tell from her body language. Her shoulders slumped. The tears continued to fall as she cried silently and watched Regan continue to pack. Regan wished she'd leave, let her collect her freaking toiletries in peace, but she stood there and looked—she had to admit it—devastated. It didn't take long, thank fuck, and Regan was zipping her suitcase.

As she swung her backpack over her shoulder and raised the telescoping handle on her suitcase, she hazarded a glance at Ava, who was looking at her feet now, as if she couldn't bear to watch Regan walk out the door. Regan almost scoffed aloud. Wishful fucking thinking.

But then Ava tried once more. She raised her watery eyes to Regan and whispered, "I wish you'd just talk to me before you go. Just talk to me."

She was almost tempted. Almost. But the words pushed out of her before she could falter.

"I have nothing more to say to you."

❖

Hauling eight weeks' worth of clothes and toiletries down the grand staircase gracefully was next to impossible, and it was only in that moment she remembered the driver or some staff member had carried them up. At first she was worried about losing her balance and tumbling the whole way down. Then, after struggling for half the distance, she absently wondered if she should take the dive because it would certainly be faster. It was hard to make your point by stomping off when you were dragging fifty pounds of luggage with you.

When she finally made it to the bottom—after much bumping and banging—Regan wasn't thrilled to see the rest of the gang in her peripheral vision hanging out in the dining room to her left. She'd hoped to avoid them—still hoped it as she headed for the front door before she heard her name. They'd known her—become her friends, she had hoped—over the past weeks, but they had convicted her without bothering to ask her anything. At all. *Fuck all of 'em.*

"Ms. Callahan?" It was May, in her boring black pants and boring white shirt and super-boring bun. But was that something in her eyes? Sympathy? Understanding? Regan didn't have long to figure it out before May continued. "Chef would like to see you for a moment in her office." She held an arm out, indicating the way was behind her.

She didn't have to go. There were no rules now. Regan was her own woman and she could damn well leave if she wanted to fucking leave. She stood there for a moment. The others were watching from the dining room—she could feel their eyes on her. A sound above her told her Ava was standing at the top of the staircase. May waited.

With an irritated sigh and a muttered "Goddamn it," she let go of her luggage and followed May down the hall in a direction she'd never been. They seemed to walk endlessly, turning corners and hurrying down halls—because May did not stroll, she walked with speed and purpose—until they finally reached the office of Liza Bennett-Schmidt.

It was surprising, to say the least, and Regan found herself gaping, gawking like she was in some museum or gallery. While the rest of the house clearly spoke of wealth, it was also a bit...stodgy? Was that the word? Wood and velvet and burgundy. Dark and heavy. Rich, yes, but dark and heavy. Liza's office, however, was more like the kitchen they worked in—modern and bright and sleek. The walls were white, the windows floor-to-ceiling, looking out onto the gorgeously lush grounds. Regan thought about how much creativity she'd have if this was her space for ideas, if this was where she dreamed up new flavor combinations and delicious new creations for the bakery.

The desk Liza sat at was simply glass and chrome. No drawers to speak of. Not a single smudge or fingerprint on the glass—Regan found herself absently wondering if Liza ever even touched it. Her chair was big and looked supremely comfortable, not to mention ergonomic. She wore a dark skirt, her legs crossed easily, red pumps on her feet. Dark-rimmed glasses sat perched on her nose as she looked over the rim of them at Regan. Her gorgeous auburn hair was pulled back in a ponytail, less severe than her bun, and she looked amused, if nothing else.

"I'm disappointed in you" was the first thing she said to Regan, then she pulled off her glasses and used them to indicate the chair in front of her desk.

"My idea gets stolen, and you're disappointed in me." Regan sat with a sigh. "Of course."

Liza tipped her head to one side, a sly smile on her face that Regan couldn't read. "What will it take for you to stay?"

Regan shook her head.

"There are less than two weeks left, and there's still the money."

"Right. Because you're going to give that to the person you think stole somebody else's work."

Liza waved a hand and scoffed, like she'd said the silliest, most meaningless thing. "If there's one thing I've learned in this business, it's that some people will do anything to get ahead. Even if it means stepping on others."

"I've met a few people like that," Regan said. "And I am not one of them."

Liza sat forward and put her forearms on her desk, as if she'd just had a grand idea she wanted to share, like she hadn't heard her at all. "All right. What if I give you your own room? I suspect you'd rather not be rooming with Chef Ava at this point. Would you finish the retreat then?"

Regan sighed. "I don't know…"

"I have so much more to teach you." Liza smiled like the Cheshire Cat. "And you'll be home in less than two weeks."

Regan wasn't naive. She knew her big exit was mostly based off adrenaline from her hurt and anger. Now that she'd had some time to cool down, the offer to stay was tempting. Not to mention the added break of not stressing over trying to avoid Ava when they shared a room. Also, there was the satisfaction of seeing the faces of the others and looking them each in the eye. She stared out the window at the trees, the lush green grass, the gorgeous blue sky that would turn a deep indigo as the summer day came to an end.

"I need to make it clear," she said, turning back to Liza, "that I did *not* steal Ava's idea. If anything, she stole mine. I am not a thief. In addition to that, I'm good enough to not need to steal somebody else's work."

"Oh, I know," Liza said, surprising her. "So? You'll stay?"

Regan sighed, part of her annoyed that she didn't storm out and head home like she'd intended to in the first place. She felt the tiniest bit weak over that. At the same time, she'd come for an eight-week retreat, and it had only been six and a half. There were still things she could learn from a master baker like Liza, whether or not she liked her.

And Regan Callahan was no quitter.

"Give me a new room, and I'll stay."

Liza clapped her hands once, clearly delighted, and again, there was a part of Regan that was irritated the woman had gotten her way. Liza waved behind her. Why it surprised Regan to see May standing there when she turned, she wasn't sure. The woman was like a ghost, floating along in silence, suddenly appearing in corners, and Regan would think she'd be used to that by now.

"Show Chef Regan to her new residence, would you?" Liza ordered.

"Of course, Chef." May held her arm out again, and Regan stood.

"Chef," Liza said, and Regan turned back to her. "I'm thrilled you're staying."

Wish I could say the same was what she thought, but she kept it inside. Instead, she gave a nod and followed May.

It was only after she saw that her luggage was gone and recalled Liza speaking as if the room had already been set up for a guest that she realized Liza had known all along she'd stay.

❖

Ava's heart hurt.

She was sad. Angry. Frustrated.

Why wouldn't Regan believe her?

She'd asked herself that question about seven hundred times so far, and every time, her brain threw her an image of her own face giving her a look that said *Really? You can't figure that one out?*

She'd asked May if she could speak with Liza, but May told her Liza was not available until tomorrow. "Are you all right, Chef Ava?" May had asked then. "You look a bit pale. Are you feeling well?"

"No." Ava didn't understand why she felt a sudden irritation with this woman. She was only trying to help. Wasn't she? "No, I'm not feeling well."

"I'm sorry to hear that. Would you rather have some alone time instead of dinner with the group? I can have dinner brought to your room."

Just like that, her irritation evaporated like vapor off a pond in the morning. Alone time—more specifically, to not face the others right now—was exactly what she needed. "That would be great," she said to May and thanked her.

That was nearly two hours ago. It had been close to four since Regan stormed out of the room and went home. Because of Ava. Well, because of Ava, but also because she wouldn't listen to Ava, wouldn't believe her.

Ava had been the cause of her dismissal before, so why in the world would Regan believe her this time?

But what about all we've shared these past few weeks? Isn't that worth giving me the benefit of the doubt? She felt a little anger start to simmer over that.

And this was the way her internal monologue went for hours, as her dinner sat untouched on a tray, as Regan's bed lay empty, stripped of the bedding immediately by a member of the housekeeping staff, as Ava lay on her own bed, crying silently and trying to come up with the right text to send Regan and failing miserably.

Somewhere around two in the morning, Ava's hurt started to be overshadowed by something else: that simmering anger. Because what the hell, Regan? Yes, they had a history, and Ava hadn't behaved in a happy, shiny manner during that history, but it was years ago. *Literal years!* She'd apologized several times. And hello? They'd had sex. Lots of it. Lots and lots of it. Good sex. Excellent sex. Mind-blowingly fantastic sex. Maybe Regan didn't understand that Ava wasn't a person who did that with just anybody. There had to be a connection. And eventually, feelings.

And here come the tears again.

The anger morphed back into a wrenching sadness. She'd constructed fourteen different texts and had sent none of them. Lengthy explanations. Accusatory and angry outbursts. Pleading paragraphs. At 3:20 in the morning, she'd settled on two lines.

I'm sorry. I miss you.

That was it. She hit send, then turned off all notifications on her phone.

Her eyelids felt like they were lined with sandpaper. Her nose was raw from blowing it. She was exhausted and had to try to get at least a little bit of sleep. She still had to bake tomorrow and be up in—she glanced at her watch and groaned—three hours.

And her heart hurt.

❖

Ava had fallen into a deep sleep at some point, and at the sound of her alarm, felt like she was swimming up from the depths of the ocean, pulling and pulling until she finally broke the surface. She'd slapped at her phone, sending it to the floor, and then lay there blinking at the ceiling.

She felt like death, heavy and dark. Even taking a deep breath was a chore.

She showered and dressed and stayed in her room until the last possible moment, allowing herself just enough time to grab the largest cup of coffee she could manage to carry down to the kitchen without spilling, skillfully avoiding the others until it was time to work and the opportunity for chatting had passed. She didn't want to chat. Didn't want to explain or hear anybody else's thoughts or opinions on the subject.

Let me bake.

That was all she wanted. To lose herself in sugar and butter and flour. To mix and stir and decorate. To give her brain something to focus on so her heart would take a fucking break. A deep breath helped her focus as she headed down to the kitchen. Vienna gave her a hesitant smile, as did Maia. Paige and Madison hadn't arrived yet, but she could hear chatter in the hall, and then they scurried in and to their stations. None of the assistant chefs were present. Ava tried not to glance over at Regan's empty spot, but she couldn't help it. She didn't want to see it empty, all trace of her gone like in their room, but glance she did. And the space was still set up for somebody, all the tools and appliances still there. That was a relief—to not see it empty and stark—and Ava felt just a bit lighter.

She was taking a sip of her coffee when Regan walked in, and she coughed as the hot liquid went down the wrong pipe.

Regan took her place at her station, standing tall and stoic, without looking at Ava, who was still coughing. She'd just gotten herself under control when Liza entered the room, looking authoritative and pleased with herself.

"Good morning, chefs," she said, her tone annoyingly cheerful.

"Good morning, Chef," they chimed back.

"For the rest of the retreat, you will be on your own. The assistants have finished their assignments and have gone home."

A murmur ran through the kitchen, and Ava stared at Liza, who stared back at her with the slightest of smirks on her face. Was Ava right? Had Becca stolen Regan's idea and passed it off as her own? Did Liza know that? What the fuck?

"Today, we're going to perfect our pâte à choux," Liza went on. She was referring to the delicate dough—often called choux pastry—that was the base of many pastries. It could be hard to master, though Ava was pretty confident about hers; it was one of the first things they taught in culinary school. They'd worked on it early in the retreat, but a couple folks had struggled, so clearly Liza thought they needed more training. *How is she going on with the retreat like nothing happened yesterday?*

Ava worked on autopilot. She had no choice. If she stopped, if she looked at Regan or made eye contact with Liza again, she was afraid she might fall apart. Her stress levels felt impossibly high, her anxiety through the roof. So she forced herself to concentrate on what she was doing, to ignore the fact that the woman who had come mere inches from stealing her heart and had crushed it instead stood barely ten feet from her, also seeming to focus solely on her work.

I guess this is how it's gonna be, huh?

Fine. She could do this.

She could do this.

God, can I do this?

CHAPTER EIGHTEEN

Things had changed at the retreat, and not just between Ava and Regan. It couldn't even be considered a divide. It was a fracturing. A shattering. Ava watched it happen.

Vienna—who had already expressed reservations about the entire retreat—had distanced herself from the rest of them, it seemed, even Ava. She came down in the morning, grabbed her coffee, and headed out onto the grounds. Paige and Madison seemed to be the only ones whose friendship stayed intact, and they could usually be found in a corner of a room or sitting next to each other at the table, their heads together and their voices hushed. Maia didn't really change much. She'd been kind of a loner from the start, and she remained so, but she'd nod at Regan when she saw her, or she'd sit next to Ava if there was space. Ava appreciated that more than she was willing to admit.

As for Regan, she kept her head down, came in a room to get what she needed, and took whatever it was—coffee, dinner, a cocktail—back up to her room. She barely looked at any of them. It made Ava's heart squeeze in her chest.

"Feeling a little bit like high school, isn't it?" Maia asked on Wednesday morning as she plopped down next to Ava. She took a sip of her coffee and scanned the room over the rim of her mug.

Ava sighed and shook her head. "I can't believe what a colossal disappointment this retreat has been," she said quietly. "If I didn't have a deep-seated aversion to quitting anything—even when I should—I'd go home right now."

"Yeah, but you don't wanna give Chef that satisfaction."

"You got that right." Ava shook her head and then sipped. "It's only a little while longer." Eight days, to be exact. Eight long days that felt like years stretched out before them.

"Yep. You doing okay?" Maia had been the only one to ask her that.

Ava lifted a shoulder. "Well, let's see. I thought this was gonna be an amazing retreat where I'd learn from my baking idol, I end up rooming with a woman from my past who hates me, but it starts to be kinda great, and I'm learning a ton, and my fellow retreaters are cool, and I even make amends with the woman from my past, and she doesn't hate me anymore."

"Sounds awesome," Maia said, a grin on her face as she sipped. "And then?"

"And then it all went to shit." Ava chuckled. She had to or she'd cry. "My baking idol is a bit of a sadist, I think"—Maia snorted at that—"though I am still learning a ton, so I can't fault her there. But a definite sadist who likes to fuck with people, which was proven by her weird need to out me and my ex-nemesis-turned—" She cleared her throat and looked away.

"Sex bunny? The cream to your puff? *Love-ah?*"

"What?" Ava laughed. "'Sex bunny'? Seriously. No. Never say that again." Maia laughed, too, and then Ava turned serious again, because Maia was the only person who'd had a long enough conversation with her to allow her to voice her theory. "Regan didn't steal my idea. I think I inadvertently stole hers." At Maia's furrowed brow, she went on. "I think *Becca* stole Regan's idea and sold it to me as her own, and I ran with it."

"Why didn't you say something?" There was no accusation in Maia's tone, just simple curiosity, but Ava felt the question like a punch to the gut.

"Because I was a fucking coward. I let our history get in my way—and so did she, if I'm being honest, because she doesn't believe that I didn't steal it. I told her what I thought happened, but she figured I was cutting the person beneath me loose." She tipped her head to one side, then dropped her shoulders in defeat. "Which is valid."

"Why's it valid?"

"Because it's what I did with her. Way back."

"Ah." Maia nodded. She sipped her coffee. "But you're not that person now."

Ava sighed, and it felt heavy, weighted. "No, but I guess she doesn't see that. Not anymore." Taking a sip of her own coffee, she had to give herself a moment and swallow down the lump in her throat. "I really thought she would." It came out as a mere whisper, and Maia turned to look at her.

"I'm really sorry," Maia said and squeezed her knee.

"Yeah. Me too."

"Look, all we need to do is get through the next week and we can get the fuck out of here and never look back."

"Yes, please," Ava said, with a nod and a bump of Maia's shoulder. Inside, though, the thought of never seeing Regan again made her heart pound harder in her chest and squeezed the air from her lungs. She had to give herself a minute to acclimate to that emotion as it rolled through her. The two of them sat quietly. It was so different from how it had been a week or two into the retreat, when the dining room had been a place of gathering and making new friends and laughter. Now it was nearly empty, and something about that made Ava sad.

Maia glanced at the smartwatch on her wrist and frowned. Then she took a deep breath, finished her coffee, and looked at Ava. "Ready?"

"No. But let's go." She pushed to her feet, her legs feeling almost leaden as they headed for the kitchen.

❖

Regan wanted to go home so badly, she could taste it.

She'd spent the past several days kicking herself for letting Liza Bennett-Schmidt talk her into staying. What she should have done was tell the famous chef to take her stupid retreat and her fancy single room (where had *that* been the whole time?) and shove them up her game-playing ass. Because she was pretty sure that's what was happening here, she just didn't know why. Had the chef grown bored with her millions and millions of dollars and her mansion in the hills? Did baking fail to thrill her any longer, so she looked for excitement in other ways? Mainly by manipulating people? The fact that the assistants were gone now was a curious development, and one that was very convenient for Liza and very inconvenient for Regan. She wanted to believe Ava. She did. But Ava's track record wouldn't allow it. Except now there was no Becca to confront, to ask for the truth.

Liza Bennett-Schmidt was one sneaky bitch.

"I miss her," she said quietly into the phone one night when there were only two days left of the retreat.

Kiki sighed, but not in an accusatory way. Regan knew that. Her friend was just worried about her. "I know you do. I'm sorry, babe." She could hear Kiki take a sip of whatever she was drinking before she asked, "There's no way you can talk to her?"

Regan pursed her lips, remembering the things she'd said to Ava. "I think that ship has sailed." She blew out a breath. "And just because I miss her doesn't mean I trust her." She'd spent the past week or so doing her best to focus on her work, whatever bake was on the counter in front of her, all the while taking peripheral glances at Ava to her right. Ava, who seemed tenser than ever, if the visible tightness of her shoulders was any indication. Ava, who had started the retreat with a very serious expression and rarely smiled, who then had moved to easier smiling and even outright laughter, and had now returned to serious and smileless.

It made Regan sad.

The evenings after they baked, she'd either go for a walk—which was a bit dangerous, as Ava had started running on the daily—watch a movie, or search for new baking ideas to put into play when she got back to Sweet Temptations. Anything to keep her distracted and her mind off the fact that she was alone in her big bed, that there were none of Ava's toiletries lined up neatly on the bathroom sink, none of her towels folded precisely and hanging on the rack, nobody to shoot disapproving looks at her mess of clothes scattered all over the floor of the room. She was tired of the pillow next to hers not smelling like Ava. She was tired of the loneliness and uncertainty and homesickness. She missed her apartment, her cat, and her bakery. And Ava.

"Nope." She shook her head vehemently as she stabbed at the keys on her laptop looking for something violent to watch. A good slasher film—the bloodier the better—would keep her mind off the gorgeous brunette who had captured her heart...and then stomped on it. "Man, your taste in women sucks, Callahan," she muttered as she started the movie.

❖

Leaving the Bennett-Schmidt retreat was nothing like arriving at it. Not in atmosphere and not in attitude of the attendees. Their arrival had been excited. Celebratory. Their exit was quiet. Cerebral. They each received a letter under their door in the morning from Liza Bennett-Schmidt. It thanked them for attending, said she hoped they enjoyed it and got something out of it and that she was going to sit down with all her notes to decide who'd get the money—they would be notified by mail.

So fucking anticlimactic.

Regan sighed as she lugged her suitcase down the grand staircase. Again, no Charles to carry it for her. Near the front door stood Madison and Paige, and she looked around to see if anybody else was there.

"The others left in the early van," Paige said, watching her scan.

"There was an earlier van?" Regan asked.

"Apparently." Madison shrugged. "I'd have been on it if I'd known."

"Same," Regan said. "I can't wait to get home," she said quietly, more to herself than the others, but Paige responded.

"You're so lucky to not have far to go. Just a train ride, right?" At Regan's nod, she said, "I'm headed across the country. Probably won't get home until late, barring any flight delays."

"I don't have to go as far," Madison said. "But I still have a flight."

The small talk was grinding on Regan. These were people who'd assumed she'd stolen somebody else's idea. Hadn't even asked her about it. When she'd reached the end of her patience—which didn't take longer than a few minutes, she spoke very calmly. "Listen, you don't have to talk to me and pretend like the last two weeks of being pretty much ostracized never happened. It's fine. I'm a big girl. I can take it. But I do need you both to know that I did not steal Ava's design. I have no idea how we ended up with the same one, but I did not steal hers. That's not who I am." The front door opened and Charles entered, then stopped in his tracks, clearly sensing he was interrupting something. Regan shrugged and added, "But thanks for giving me the benefit of the doubt." She turned her attention to their driver. "Hey, Charles."

"Ms. Callahan. I trust you're ready to go?" He grasped the handle of her suitcase.

"Absolutely. Get me the hell out of here." She followed him out, leaving Madison and Paige standing there, tandem expressions of sheepishness on their faces. Good. It was the least they owed her.

She climbed into the van, took a seat in the back, and kept her eyes on the passing landscape as they drove. She could feel the tension in the van, could sense that one or both of the other women wanted to say something, but neither of them did. Their trains were leaving from two different spots, and Regan hurried away from the van before anybody could say anything. It was rude, she knew, not to even offer up a goodbye, but she was so fucking over this entire experience. All she wanted was to get home as quickly as possible and let her brain— and her heart—decompress and recover from eight weeks that were supposed to have been fun and educational but had ended up being confusing and stressful.

"Fuck that shit," she whispered quietly, once she was settled on the train. All of it. The retreat, the mean-girl politics, Liza Bennett-Schmidt, who couldn't even be bothered to see her guests out, and Ava. All of it. All of them. "Fuck that shit," she said again.

The girl sitting next to her was probably eighteen, black hair with a bright blue streak, and a septum pierced by a thick silver ring. "Damn right," she said, nodding but never looking up from her phone.

Regan smiled. *Gotta love New York.*

❖

Much to her surprise, Ava *did* still have a job when she got home. But her first week back at Pomp was rough, mostly because of the hours. At the retreat, her body had gotten used to waking up early, going for a run regularly. Now she was back to beginning her workday midafternoon and working until after midnight at times. It took a toll.

One bright spot: She did find that several of the practices and hacks she'd learned from Liza Bennett-Schmidt had actually come in handy, and she used them often. "At least I got *something* out of the damn thing," she muttered at her workstation one night while making crème brûlée.

"Only back for a week and already talking to yourself," Courtney said as she came into the kitchen. "It's so sad, really."

Ava grinned as she used the handheld blowtorch to caramelize the tops of the desserts. "That's me. Sad and pathetic. Hashtag My Life."

Courtney went into the walk-in fridge and came out with a bag of lemons. "Have you texted her yet?"

Ava didn't look up, just kept torching. "No." That one word was all she said, and she continued to work until she felt Courtney's eyes on her. She sighed and straightened. Courtney was still standing there, bag of lemons in hand.

"Why not?" her friend asked. There was no accusation in her tone, only curiosity mixed with a hint of sympathy that made Ava want to grind her teeth. Courtney cocked her head to the side, clearly wondering.

Ava shrugged and shook her head. "I just…I tried. I keep typing things up and deleting them before I can send them." Suddenly, her shoes were very interesting. "I don't know what to say."

Courtney stepped closer and looked around, then lowered her voice. "You still miss her?" she asked softly.

Ava nodded and, to her horror, felt her eyes well up. "I thought it would ease up once I got home and back into my routine, but…" She swallowed hard. "It's only made me realize how lonely my life is."

Courtney leaned in even closer, then lowered her voice to a whisper. "Then fucking text her." Then she kissed Ava's cheek sweetly and bopped out of the kitchen, headed back to her bar.

Ava laughed through her nose and shook her head once more.

Fucking text her.

She snorted again and set the crème brûlées on a tray, making the presentation as perfect as possible. The waiter smiled at her with a soft "Nice" as he took them, and she stood there with a hand on her hip, watching him go, Courtney's words echoing through her head.

Fucking text her.

If only it was that simple.

Could it be? Maybe she was overthinking. God knew, she was fantastic at *that*.

Of course, in true Ava Prescott fashion, she spent the rest of her shift overthinking. To text or not to text, that was the question, and the answer was nowhere to be found. Her brain went around and around with pros and cons, and what she would say should she text, and what she absolutely should not say should she text, and by the time she punched out, she had a massive headache and couldn't wait to go home.

Jiminy was happy to see her, so that was a bright spot in her day. He'd been very cuddly since her return, and she still felt some residual guilt for having left him for that long. To make up for it, she put him first every time she got home. She opened the door, set all her stuff down immediately, and swooped him up into her arms. "This is my cat," she'd say to him, showering him with kisses. "This is my cat. Isn't he handsome? Look how handsome he is." She wasn't 100 percent sure, but he seemed to like it, and he kind of glowed proudly when she called him her cat, so she continued to do it.

Once their daily love fest was finished, she set him down and fed him. She really wanted pasta, but her level of fatigue was high, and even making something that simple felt like too much. Instead, she whipped up some eggs, tossed some shredded cheese on them, and called it dinner. She made herself comfortable on her bed with her plate and her cat and the day's mail, doing her best not to think of Regan and failing spectacularly.

She wolfed her eggs down in mere minutes, not having realized just how hungry she was, and set the plate aside in favor of the mail. Energy levels in the red zone, she promised herself she'd take a quick scan to make sure nothing was pressing and deal with the rest in the morning.

It was envelope number three, which was certified, that changed everything.

CHAPTER NINETEEN

To my amazing retreat attendees,

By now, I trust you are all home and back to somewhat regularly scheduled programming. I am so glad you all chose to attend my retreat, and I hope you learned something, took something away, and feel it was time well spent.

I have a few things to say...and a few things to confess.

First of all, each of you has my undying gratitude for attending. I've been in this business for a very, very long time, and to know there are other chefs out there who still look up to me and feel they can learn from me is a boost I need every now and again. So I thank you.

Second, I believe that baking under pressure is a skill that not enough bakers and pastry chefs excel at, so it's one of the things I try to push at my retreat. But I don't always tell my chefs. I just...fiddle with the circumstances. And I use the assistant chefs to help. I did that with most of you at some point or another, and you excelled. In fact, yours was the most levelheaded group I've had in years, so bravo! And now this is where I come clean.

Vienna, I was extra hard on you because as a woman of color in a male-dominated industry, you face even more obstacles than most. You handled everything I threw at you with grace, and you never lost your cool in the kitchen. Impressive. Very, very impressive.

Maia, I had your assistant chef take your lucky bandannas and then return them a week later. I know you were stressed, but you baked just as well, if not better, without what you consider your lucky talisman! You relied on your skills, not luck, and you succeeded, despite the stress you felt. Well done.

Paige, your assistant chef let me know that pie crust was your weak link in baking, and that's why I had you making pie so often. But you got it! By the end of the retreat, your crust could seriously rival mine. So, see? The pressure of it paid off.

Madison, you were such a delight, so kind, cheerful, and encouraging to your fellow chefs that I couldn't bear to mess with you (not that I didn't think about it!). Please don't ever change.

Regan and Ava, I owe you two the biggest kudos. In all the years I've run this retreat, I've never had two attendees fall for each other. That was a first! The pressure of keeping that separate from what we were doing and learning must've been a lot, and I apologize for abusing my power and outing you to the others. That was petty of me, but I can get a bit carried away in a retreat. May tells me all the time that I play mind games, and maybe she's right. I certainly did when I had Becca steal Regan's July Fourth idea and pass it off as her own so Ava would make the same thing. I wanted to see the sparks fly, see how you each handled such a thing. I honestly didn't think it would drive a wedge between you as large as the one it did, though. I guess that means what you had was, sadly, just a temporary fling. But still, I shouldn't have stuck my nose in. I apologize for that. (And not that you asked, but I thought you two were great together.)

All right. Now for the reason I sent this letter in the first place: the money. My financial advisor says I can do this, even though my CPA is losing his mind, but I don't care. What good is having money if you can't spend it the way you want? Therefore, I am increasing my total donation (that's what I've been told we're to call it) to $200,000, and I'm giving some to all of you. Vienna, Madison, Paige, and Maia, you will each receive $25,000. Thank you for your participation, *dedication, and success. Regan and Ava, I really messed with your heads, and I feel guilty about that, so I'm giving each of you $50,000. Again, I apologize. You really were great together.*

Checks will arrive in the next week under separate cover.

Again, thank you all for participating.

Love and baked goods,

Liza Bennett-Schmidt

PS: Please remember that you each signed a nondisclosure agreement, so don't go sharing these details...

Regan blinked at the paper in her hand. She was seated on her couch in the living room, Artie stretched across the back of it, one paw on her shoulder, as if he wanted to make sure she stayed there. She blinked some more. Read it again. And again. Each time she finished, she'd whisper "Holy shit" and read it again. The paper trembled in her hand.

Her phone started to ping, and it continued to do so until she picked it up to see texts from the other retreat attendees, various versions of their own "Holy shit." Liza must've mailed the letters so they all arrived on the same day. She remembered Paige and Madison were on the West Coast, so she wasn't sure they'd be texting, but Vienna and Maia were.

What the actual fuck? were Vienna's first words. Followed quickly by *I'ma make a group text.* And then all their texts started to show up in the same place.

I don't understand. Maia. *We all get money?*

Seems that way, Regan typed. *It also seems like whoever said Liza was a sadist was right.*

Ava did, typed Vienna.

It was definitely Ava, said a text from Madison. *Hi, guys! I miss you all!*

Along came Paige. *Yup. Ava. Also, OMG, what the heck?*

Regan grinned at her tame language, especially compared to the rest of them.

I said she was a sadist. A text from Ava, finally.

Regan's heart skipped a beat when she saw her name pop up. She actually felt it in her chest.

Looks like you were right, typed Paige. *Who does that? Seriously, what kind of person does that?*

Someone miserable in their own life? That was Maia. *So they have to fuck around in other people's?*

Makes sense, Regan typed. *But Jesus.* She sat there, phone in hand, shaking her head in disbelief.

Well, we got some confirmation. That was Vienna.

Meaning? Maia.

That we weren't all crazy! Vienna began. *She definitely zeroed in on me. We know your bandannas were taken, Maia, and you didn't lose them. We know Regan didn't steal Ava's idea.*

Told you. Regan couldn't resist typing that.

And we know that Becca is the one who did steal Regan's idea.

Told you. That was Ava, and Regan grimaced as she read the words. Because, shit. She owed Ava a serious apology. She opened a private text between the two of them as the group text continued to ping with messages. Her thumbs hovered over the buttons, then she started to type. Stopped. Started again. Stopped.

"Shit."

Everything she typed seemed trite. Lame. Not good enough.

With a sigh, she clicked back to the group.

If I didn't need the money, I'd tell her to take her check and shove it up her narcissistic ass. That was Maia, and it made Regan grin as she remembered her funky hair and no-nonsense attitude.

Paige commented, *At least now we know why we had to sign NDAs. She doesn't want future attendees knowing how much she likes mind games.*

I think the best revenge, Ava typed, *is to take the checks and do something good with them.*

I agree, Regan typed. *I know we all had plans for it and we're getting less than we thought, but we're all getting some, which is pretty cool. Use it well.*

Good plan, typed Vienna. *I said it before, but it bears repeating: Never meet your heroes. Jesus Christ.*

❖

August had come in hot.

Like, really hot. Fry an egg on the pavement hot. Surface of the sun hot. And it didn't really matter how hard Pomp's air-conditioning unit was working, there were still ovens running and burners lit in the kitchen, and not even two hours into her shift, Ava was sweating like a menopausal woman in a sauna.

Not her favorite conditions to work in, and added to Goldie and her "I hate the world and everyone in it especially my employees" attitude that day, the idea of quitting—simply taking off her chef's coat, handing it to Goldie, and telling her to stick it where the sun don't shine—was almost too tempting. After all, she now had fifty thousand dollars sitting in her bank account. She didn't *have* to stay there if she didn't want to. Not really.

The corners of her mouth tugged upward, as they always seemed to do when she thought about her bank balance. How could they not? There was a cushion now, and she'd never had a cushion before. Totally new to her. Her mother texted her every morning to ask how her fifty thousand grandchildren were doing, and it cracked Ava up every time. Maybe money couldn't buy happiness, but it could certainly buy relief.

Shoving aside that whispering desire to leave her job, she put her head down and focused on the cranberry orange scones she was making for the brunch special the next day and did her best not to sweat on them.

Fridays were always hella busy, and by the time she wiped down her counter and put the last of her equipment away at the end of her shift, she felt like a wet dishrag, limp and wrung out. She finished up, bid her good nights to the few crew members left, and pushed her way through the back door and into the hot August night.

Then stopped dead in her tracks.

"Hi." Regan leaned against the wall of the building directly across from the door, arms folded over her chest, feet crossed at the ankle, looking as beautiful and sexy as she ever had in worn jeans and a simple white T-shirt. Ava had to make a conscious effort to catch her breath and then to remember that she was still mad at Regan.

And stung by her.

And missed her terribly.

She inhaled to steady herself. "Hey."

Regan pushed off the wall. "You look nice."

Ava glanced down at her own work clothes, the flour that dusted her pants, felt the wisps of hair that had escaped her ponytail and snorted. "Oh, I'm sure. I'm sweaty and dirty and exhausted."

"I mean it," Regan said. "A sight for sore eyes, isn't that what they say?"

Ava tipped her head. "And are your eyes sore?"

"From not seeing you. Yeah. They are." There was a beat, two, and then they both burst into laughter. "Oh God, that was so cheesy."

"The cheesiest line anybody's ever used on me, hands down."

They continued to laugh for a moment, and when it died down, Regan met her gaze. God, those blue eyes of hers. Ava had forgotten how much she loved them.

"I owe you an apology," Regan said softly. "A big one."

Ava pressed her lips together to hide her surprise, not sure if she was successful. She let Regan talk.

"I am *so* sorry." Regan glanced down at her feet, then off into the distance. "I should have believed you. Or at least given you the benefit of the doubt. I let the past color the present for me, even after you swore you knew what had happened. I should have listened to you, and I'm so sorry I didn't." She searched for Ava's eyes, then held her gaze and swallowed hard enough for Ava to hear it.

Ava glanced off to her left. "It's a bummer that it took Liza telling you what I already had to get you to believe me." That hurt. She couldn't pretend it didn't.

"I know." Regan nodded and, if Ava was being honest, looked miserable. "You're right. I'm so sorry."

"After everything we'd gone through..." Ava looked off down the alley and shook her head. "I mean, I know my track record isn't spotless, but," she refocused her gaze on Regan, "after all we'd gone through."

"I know," Regan said, nodding. She glanced down at her shoes and said it again. "I know." Another beat went by, both of them silent, Ava absorbing and Regan likely waiting her out before giving in and asking, "What can I do? Is there anything I can do to fix it? Just tell me. I'll do it." She cleared her throat, and Ava wondered if she was on the verge of tears. "Anything. I'll do it. I miss you so much."

There were so many things Ava wanted to say in that moment.

She wanted to shout. She wanted to show Regan her anger and her hurt and her disappointment. She wanted to shove her in the shoulder and ask her what the fuck she'd been thinking, how she could think—after all the time and all the kissing and all the sex—that she'd actually steal her idea, that she'd do something like that to her. She wanted to scream and cry and rage.

"Take me to dinner." That's what she said instead, and she blinked once, twice, actually surprised by her own words.

Regan flinched in surprise as well, her eyes going wide. "Really? Dinner?"

"Yes."

"Okay." Regan nodded. A lot. "Okay. I can do that. I'd love to do that. I'd be happy to do that. Dinner. Yes."

"Good." Ava blew out an unexpected breath of relief. "Good. Now walk me to the subway, and then text me tomorrow with a day and time."

"Yes, ma'am." Regan was trying hard to hide her smile. Ava could tell. But she did a commendable job as they fell into step together. And as thrilled Ava was that Regan had taken steps and shown up unannounced, she wasn't about to let her off the hook that easily.

They walked in silence.

It was called "the city that never sleeps" for a reason, and there were still quite a lot of people out on the streets. Driving, walking, shouting, honking horns. Definitely fewer than during the day, but it wasn't like they were walking along in their own little quiet world. Even if it felt like it.

Their hands brushed once as they walked, and it took a lot of effort for Ava to resist grabbing Regan's, feeling the warmth of it, entwining their fingers. Her brain chose that moment to toss her an image, a memory of those same fingers inside her, sliding slowly in and out, then picking up speed.

She cleared her throat.

"It's good to see your face again," Regan said quietly. She still sported the ghost of a smile as she glanced up at Ava. They'd reached the stairs down into the subway.

Ava smiled back at her, then turned to head down the stairs. "Text me." She tossed the words over her shoulder, not looking back.

"I will." Regan's voice was enthusiastic. Happy. And when Ava, against her better judgment, did turn and glance back up from the bottom of the steps, Regan was smiling like she'd just won the lottery.

❖

"Honey, what are you doing?" Ava's mom's voice was gentle, almost tender, and a hint of worry tinted the edges of it.

"What do you mean?" It was Monday morning, Ava's day off. She had her phone propped up on the counter as she gave her tiny kitchen its weekly wipe-down, even though she'd hardly used it, as she hadn't really felt much like cooking since she'd returned from the retreat. Or eating, for that matter.

When she glanced at the phone, her mother tipped her head to the side. "You know *exactly* what I mean."

Ava sighed. "It's just dinner, Mom."

"Is it, though?"

She stopped scrubbing the sink and stood up, honestly pondering the question. "I mean," she said, then sighed in what felt a bit like defeat. Her mother knew her well. "I think so? Maybe?"

Her mom's tender smile made her wish they were together and she could curl up and lay her head in her mother's lap like she used to do when she was younger.

"All I'm saying is that I want you to protect your heart. I know the feelings you started to develop for this girl. I also know how much she hurt you by not taking you at your word. By not trusting you."

"I know."

"It took somebody else telling her the truth for her to realize *you* had told her the truth."

"I know."

Her mother sighed quietly. "*I* trust you. Okay? If her apology and buying you dinner," she pointed at the screen as she added adamantly, "*you make her buy* is enough for you to give her another chance, then I can accept that. You're a grown woman, and I trust your judgment. But, baby, protect your heart. Okay? Will you do that for your mom?"

Ava nodded as the love in her mother's voice and on her face made Ava's eyes well up. "I will. I promise."

"That's all I ask."

❖

"Just be your fantastic self."

That's what Kiki and Brian had both told Regan as she got ready to head out to dinner.

"It's okay to apologize again," Kiki had said. "You do owe her that. But don't grovel. If she can't forgive you, she can't forgive you. You shouldn't have to apologize forever. But you're doing the right thing by stepping up and owning your mistake. I'm proud of you."

Regan rode the subway to the closest stop and then walked the additional three blocks to Savor, an American fusion restaurant that her friend Jason cooked in. Extra thankful the heat wave had eased up and she wasn't a sweat factory, she pulled the door open and gave her name to the hostess. A glance around told her Ava hadn't arrived yet, and she was thankful for that as well. More time to calm her nerves and rehearse the things she wanted to say.

Jason had reserved her a table for two in a quiet corner. She let the hostess know she was meeting someone, then took the menu and the wine list and made herself comfortable.

Savor was small, maybe a dozen to fifteen tables total, and it wasn't terribly busy, but it was Monday, so that made sense. She was off tomorrow and knew Ava was off today, so neither of them had work hanging over their heads tonight.

She took a deep breath and glanced down at her outfit. Simple and—hopefully—classy black pants and a red shirt with capped sleeves. Kiki had said she looked gorgeous, so she was gonna go with that, because Kiki would've never let her out of the apartment looking anything but presentable. Tucking hair behind her ear, she had no more time to think because there was Ava, standing just inside the door, and if Kiki thought Regan looked gorgeous, she wondered what adjectives she'd have come up with for Ava. Stunningly beautiful? Impossibly attractive? Alarmingly magnificent?

Exquisite.

That was the word that floated into Regan's head and stayed as Ava met her gaze, then walked through the restaurant toward her. She was nervous. Regan wasn't sure how she could tell that, but she could. She knew Ava well enough by now, and that thought surprised her a bit.

"Hi," Ava said as Regan stood up and startled them both by hugging her. She felt Ava's arms around her, though, so she drew herself an invisible point.

"You look beautiful," she said as they sat.

"Thank you. You do, too." Ava smiled at her. Another thing she could tell about Ava's face: She knew the difference between her genuine smile and her fake one, and this one was genuine.

"It's really good to see you."

Ava laughed softly. "You just saw me three days ago."

"Too long," Regan said, and realized that she had never meant anything more.

Ava held her gaze for a moment, then looked around. "This is nice. I've never been here. Have you?"

"My friend Jason is the head chef, so I try to come once in a while. And I always recommend it if somebody asks."

"Well, it smells great."

They pretended to lose themselves in the menu. At least Regan did. She needed a minute to gather herself—she hadn't expected seeing Ava in this setting to fluster her as much as it felt like it was. She cleared her throat and glanced over the top of her menu. "Wine?"

"God, yes" was Ava's instantaneous response.

They grinned knowingly at each other.

The waitress arrived and they ordered a bottle of a buttery Chardonnay, laughing about how the wine got such a bad rap but they both loved it.

Ava put her forearms on the table and leaned forward a bit until Regan met her gaze. "Okay. It's clear that we're both nervous."

Regan nodded her agreement.

"Which is silly, really." Ava punctuated that with a shrug.

"Considering everything we've...done with each other, I agree with the silliness." She tipped her head and watched in delight as Ava's cheeks turned pink.

"So, how about we just...talk?"

"I like that idea."

"Great."

And then they sat in silence for a good thirty seconds before they burst into more laughter.

The wine came. Regan tasted and approved it, and the waitress poured, took their meal orders, and left. Ava held up her glass and Regan touched hers to it, both of them saying "Cheers."

They sipped, and then Regan set her glass down, and it was her turn to lean forward. "Okay. I'm diving in."

"Thank God," Ava said, but she grinned, and it took any bite away.

"I miss you." It was a simple sentence for a simple truth. She let it sit for a moment and waited for Ava's expression to soften, which it did, before pushing forward. "And I fucked up. I know I did. I have apologized for that, and I'm not sure it's enough. But I don't know what more I can do other than continue to apologize until you believe me." She saw Ava's face change and knew her choice of words had hit home. "And I know I didn't believe you, so it seems fitting that the tables have turned."

Ava sipped her wine and seemed to be taking in Regan's words.

"If there's something I can do to help you feel better about it, about me, please tell me. But what I want you to know is that I'm sorry, I miss you, and I'd like to see you again. We were too good together not to even try." She cleared her throat and forced herself to take a breath, to slow down, to steady herself. She wasn't going to beg. She drew the line at begging. Her glass felt heavy in her hand as she took a sip and waited. The hardest ten seconds of her life.

When Ava finally spoke, her voice was soft. "I want to be angry about you not believing me. I mean, I *am* angry about it, but you had a good reason for feeling the way you did, so I'm trying to remember that. Your feelings didn't materialize in a vacuum. I was partly responsible for them. I know that." Another sip of wine. Then she inhaled a big breath and let it out very, very slowly. "I miss you, too." She let those words hang in the air for a few seconds before she continued, and God, she was so fucking beautiful right then, Regan couldn't help but stare. Her dark eyes seemed huge, her hair as black as night, her lips glossy with wine. "Before the stolen project fiasco, I had never in my life felt the way I felt when I was with you. When it was just you and me, alone in that room and away from the world. And I realize those were extenuating—and unrealistic—circumstances, but..." She let the sentence dangle until Regan jumped in to finish it.

"But you want it back." At Ava's nod, Regan reached across the table and grasped her hand. "So do I. So let's give it a shot. Yeah? What do we have to lose?"

"Our hearts?" Ava's eyes were wet now, and Regan held her hand tighter.

"I think you're worth that risk." At Ava's audible swallow, she asked, "Do you think that I am? That we are?"

Ava's nod was immediate, and the relief that surged through Regan's body was so palpable, it made her gasp.

"I promise you," she said, still holding Ava's hand, "that I will do my best to never, ever hurt you again. You —" A lump developed in her throat, and her vision blurred from unshed tears. "You're the most amazing thing that's ever happened to me. And I will spend the rest of my life doing my best to make sure that you're the happiest woman on earth."

The waitress arrived with their entrees just then and stood awkwardly while the two of them wiped their faces and chuckled through their tears.

Regan picked up her fork and said, "You know, I knew it the second time."

Ava's brow furrowed. "The second time what?" She lowered her voice and whispered, "We had sex?"

Regan grinned. "Yes. I knew then."

"Knew what?"

"That we were supposed to be together. That I'd fall for you. I'd already started."

Ava's fork stopped halfway to her lips, and she stared at Regan for a moment before taking the bite. "Yeah. Same."

Regan's surprise was obvious, she knew. "Really?"

"Mm-hmm. Except I knew the first time." She looked very pleased with herself, and Regan realized they'd veered slightly from super serious to a little bit playful.

"Oh, I see. So you were ahead of me."

"Mm-hmm. Better get used to it."

Their gazes held, Ava smiling at her as she chewed, and Regan had the sudden understanding, like a bolt of lightning coming out of nowhere and striking her with an electric shock, that this was it.

This. Was. It.

Like a neon sign in her head telling her to stop and look and listen, to fucking pay attention. She was going to love this woman. In fact, she already did, she just wasn't ready to voice that yet. But she knew it. Deep down, she knew it.

"You being a step ahead?" she asked, adding a teasing tone to her voice.

"Yup."

"No problem."

"Really?" Ava looked surprised. "No problem? You're not gonna argue with me?"

"Nope."

"Why not?"

"Because I just realized something."

"Yeah? What's that?"

Regan leaned forward and waited until Ava's dark eyes were locked on hers. "I'd follow you anywhere."

EPILOGUE

Eighteen months later

It had been a year and a half since Regan had told Ava she'd follow her anywhere, and she'd kept her word. Ava sat now, reminiscing, thinking of all the wonderful things that had transpired over the past eighteen months, and she couldn't imagine having done a single day of them without Regan. The fiasco of the retreat had been forgiven, if not forgotten—simply because it was too crazy to forget, and also, it had been where they'd *really* met, despite their shared history—and they'd been there for each other during some big life changes. Six months ago, Regan's boss had retired, and she'd used her retreat money to buy the bakery. She was over the moon with happiness as the sole owner of Sweet Temptations Bakery.

And now?

And now it was Ava's turn. She'd made a big life change, too, and today was the day. *The* day.

She smiled, despite all the emotions churning in the center of her body. And then she could feel it as the smile morphed into a grimace, because had she ever been this nervous?

No. She didn't think so. But it was a weird mix of good and bad, excited and stressed, worried and chill.

A glance at her watch told her she had about an hour until she opened the doors to her new dessert and wine bar, called simply Ava, and let in her very first customers, which might include a critic or two. The thought of that ratcheted up everything going on in her body right then, multiplied it all, and she pressed a hand to her stomach, hoping she wouldn't be sick. Again.

"You okay?" Regan was close, suddenly, her voice soft near Ava's ear.

Ava swallowed and nodded. "Yeah. All good."

"Nervous?"

"Unbelievably so."

"Well, you look incredible."

Ava glanced down at her black pants and smoothed her hands down the thighs. A simple white shirt and black blazer on top completed what she hoped was a look of professionalism, of somebody who knew what she was doing, who deserved to own and run this place. Her hair was loose, not something she was used to at work, but Regan had suggested that a more casual look than her usual ponytail or bun was the way to go, and she'd listened.

"Thank you, babe," she said.

As the bartender bustled, the sounds of bumping bottles and clinking glasses filling the air, Regan wrapped her arms around Ava from behind and held her tightly for a moment before asking, "Wanna take a last sweep?"

How was it that Regan knew her so well already? It had been a year and a half since they'd finished that stupid retreat, and it had been a year and a half since Regan had apologized for not giving her the benefit of the doubt, and it had been a year and a half of them learning to trust each other. But a year and a half wasn't really all that long, was it? How could Regan possibly know her so well already? How could she possibly know that taking another walk around her tiny wine bar's seating area—even after she'd done so a dozen times in the past hour or two—was exactly what she needed to do right then?

"Yes, please."

Regan held out her hand. "Let's do it." She led her out into the center of the space.

It was a great little place. Ava could admit that. Not big. Twelve tables, plus eight seats at the bar, but that was enough. It would allow her to focus on her customers, the wine, the desserts, and how they were enjoying it. It would allow her to be hands on, present. Bar to the left as you walk in. Kitchen and office in the back. It was small and perfect.

The tables were square, which would allow them to be pushed together for larger parties, four chairs at each, the surfaces polished to a lovely shine. The chairs were dark wood, comfortable. The bar was also dark wood, with an old-fashioned brass bar and a cool quartz bar top. She was only open in the evenings for now, and only four nights a week to start, so she had a rotating staff of three bartenders, four waitstaff, and herself, who would make all the desserts. Regan had offered to help if she needed it.

She let go of Regan's hand and wandered slowly through the dining room, ran her fingertips across the tabletops, straightened a votive here and a bud vase there. She adjusted a barstool that wasn't angled quite exactly as the other seven.

"Don't judge me," she said as she felt Regan's eyes on her.

"Wouldn't dream of it," Regan said with a tender smile. She stood next to the bar, leaning with her arms crossed over her chest, looking gorgeous as always as she watched Ava perform the same ritual she'd performed countless times already. Regan had taken the next day off from the bakery, letting her staff deal with it, so that she could be there all night for Ava's opening and not have to then wake up at three in the morning.

Ava straightened a framed painting on the wall. Hands on her hips, she looked around at the décor. It was soft and subtle, the colors earthy, the art abstract. The lighting was dim, but not so dim you couldn't see the color of your wine, its legs, or the filling in the tart you were eating. Because Ava wanted nothing more than for her customers to see the deliciousness they were experiencing. She and Regan had created the menu together, and she couldn't wait for people to taste it.

Moving behind the bar to the cash register and iPad there, she checked the program, scanned the reservations one more time. Full house.

"It's gonna be lit here tonight," Regan said as she approached. "Opening night at Ava's gonna be *lit*."

Ava laughed softly at her excitement. "I hope so."

"Listen, while you were out here worrying if the tables were shiny enough, your little staff and I tasted everything on the menu."

"You did?" She hadn't known that.

"We did. We tasted the tarts and the cream puffs. Fantastic. We tasted the chocolate lava cake and the carrot cake. Divine. We tasted the soufflé." She did a chef's kiss. "Exquisite. People are going to be blown away by how good everything is. And the pairings on the menu? Brill."

"You've done so much for me here," Ava said, feeling a tiny surge of relief that was quickly overshadowed by the rise of love she felt for Regan. "I couldn't have done any of this without you. You're pretty amazing."

"*You* are pretty amazing." Regan looked at her with such love and pride that it brought tears to Ava's eyes. "Oh God, no, that's a good thing. Stop crying, you weirdo, you'll mess up your makeup." She laughed softly and used her fingertips to gently catch the tears that spilled over, smiling the whole time. "You don't want to greet your adoring public with mascara streaks on your face."

"My adoring public, huh?"

"Absolutely."

"You sound like you know them."

Regan nodded. "I do. I know all the public. All of them, and they love you. Just like I do." She kissed Ava softly on the mouth.

"I love you, too."

"Good. Now, let's give your tiny staff a pep talk and open this baby up. What do you say?"

Twenty minutes later, Ava stood at the front door, Regan right next to her, holding her hand. Ava turned to her, met those blue eyes she'd grown to love so deeply. "I couldn't have done any of this without you," she said again, quietly enough that only Regan could hear her. "You're my rock and my strength, and I'm so grateful to have you here by my side."

Regan's entire expression softened. "Now you're gonna make *me* cry."

"No crying." Ava squeezed her hand. "I just wanted you to know that we're in this together."

Regan squeezed back, lifted Ava's hand, and brushed a kiss across her knuckles. "Always."

Ava looked over her shoulder at her staff. The waitstaff and the bartender were all facing her, eager and ready for the night. "Ready?"

Nods, smiles, and murmurs buzzed through the dining room.

"I'm so glad you're all here," she said and hoped her pride in them showed. With one more squeeze of Regan's hand, she turned the lock and opened the door.

"Here we go."

About the Author

Award-winning author Georgia Beers has written more than forty novels of sapphic romance. She resides in upstate New York, where she was born and raised. She strongly believes in the beauty of an excellent glass of wine, a good scary movie, and the unconditional love of a dog. Fall is her very favorite season.

She is currently hard at work on her next book. You can visit her and find out more at www.georgiabeers.com or search her on Patreon.

Books Available From Bold Strokes Books

Coming Up Clutch by Anna Gram. College softball star Kelly "Razor" Mitchell hung up her cleats early, but when former crush, now coach Ashton Sharpe shows up on her doorstep seven years later, beautiful as ever, Razor hopes the longing in her gaze has nothing to do with softball. (978-1-63679-817-2)

Firecamp by Jaycie Morrison. Going their separate ways seemed inevitable for two people as different as Fallon and Nora, while meeting up again is strictly coincidental. (978-1-63679-753-3)

Fixed Up by Aurora Rey. When electrician Jack Barrow and artist Ellie Lancaster get stuck on a job site during a blizzard, close quarters send all sorts of sparks flying. (978-1-63679-788-5)

Stranded by Ronica Black. Can Abigail and Whitley overcome their personal hang-ups and stubbornness to survive not only Alaska but a dangerous stalker as well? (978-1-63679-761-8)

Whisk Me Away by Georgia Beers. Regan's a gorgeous flake. Ava, a beautiful untouchable ice queen. When they meet again at a retreat for up-and-coming pastry chefs, the competition, and the ovens, heat up. (978-1-63679-796-0)

Across the Enchanted Border by Crin Claxton. Magic, telepathy, swordsmanship, tyranny, and tenderness abound in a tale of two lands separated by the enchanted border. (978-1-63679-804-2)

Deep Cover by Kara A. McLeod. Running from your problems by pretending to be someone else only works if the person you're pretending to be doesn't have even bigger problems. (978-1-63679-808-0)

Good Game by Suzanne Lenoir. Even though Lauren has sworn off dating gamers, it's becoming hard to resist the multifaceted Sam. An opposites attract lesbian romance. (978-1-63679-764-9)

Innocence of the Maiden by Ileandra Young. Three powerful women. Two covens at war. One horrifying murder. When mighty and powerful witches begin to butt heads, who out there is strong enough to mediate? (978-1-63679-765-6)

Protection in Paradise by Julia Underwood. When arson forces them together, the flames between chief of police Eve Maguire and librarian Shaye Hayden aren't that easy to extinguish. (978-1-63679-847-9)

Too Forward by Krystina Rivers. Just as professional basketball player Jane May's career finally starts heating up, a new relationship with her team's brand consultant could derail the success and happiness she's struggled so long to find. (978-1-63679-717-5)

Worth Waiting For by Kristin Keppler. For Peyton and Hanna, reliving the past is painful, but looking back might be the only way to move forward. (978-1-63679-773-1)

All For Her: Forbidden Romance Novellas by Gun Brooke, J.J. Hale & Aurora Rey. Explore the angst and excitement of forbidden love few would dare in this heart-stopping novella collection. (978-1-63679-713-7)

Finding Harmony by CF Frizzell. Rock star Harper Cushing has to rearrange her grandmother's future and sell the family store out from under her, but she reassesses everything because Gram's helper, Frankie, could be offering the harmony her heart has been missing. (978-1-63679-741-0)

Gaze by Kris Bryant. Love at first sight is for dreamers, but the more time Lucky and Brianna spend together, the more they realize the chemistry of a gaze can make anything possible. (978-1-63679-711-3)

Laying of Hands by Patricia Evans. The mysterious new writing instructor at camp makes Grace Waters brave enough to wonder what would happen if she dared to write her own story. (978-1-63679-782-3)

The Naked Truth by Sandy Lowe. How far are Rowan and Genevieve willing to go and how much will they risk to make their most captivating and forbidden fantasies a reality? (978-1-63679-426-6)

The Roommate by Claire Forsythe. Jess Black's boyfriend is handsome and successful. That's why it comes as a shock when she meets a woman on the train who makes her pulse race. (978-1-63679-757-1)

The Blessed by Anne Shade. Layla and Suri are brought together by fate to defeat the darkness threatening to tear their world apart. What they don't expect to discover is a love that might set them free. (978-1-63679-715-1)

Seducing the Widow by Jane Walsh. Former rival debutantes have a second chance at love after fifteen years apart when a spinster persuades her ex-lover to help save her family business. (978-1-63679-747-2)

Close to Home by Allisa Bahney. Eli Thomas has to decide if avoiding her hometown forever is worth losing the people who used to mean the most to her, especially Aracely Hernandez, the girl who got away. (978-1-63679-661-1)

The Guardians by Sheri Lewis Wohl. Dogs, devotion, and determination are all that stand between darkness and light. (978-1-63679-681-9)

Innis Harbor by Patricia Evans. When Amir Farzaneh meets and falls in love with Loch, a dark secret lurking in her past reappears, threatening the happiness she'd just started to believe could be hers. (978-1-63679-781-6)

The Mogul Meets Her Match by Julia Underwood. When CEO Claire Beauchamp goes undercover as a customer of Abby Pita's café to help seal a deal that will solidify her career, she doesn't expect to be so drawn to her. When the truth is revealed, will she break Abby's heart? (978-1-63679-784-7)

Trial Run by Carsen Taite. When Reggie Knoll and Brooke Dawson wind up serving on a jury together, their one task—reaching a unanimous verdict—is derailed by the fiery clash of their personalities, the intensity of their attraction, and a secret that could threaten Brooke's life. (978-1-63555-865-4)

Waterlogged by Nance Sparks. When conservation warden Jordan Pearce discovers a body floating in the flowage, the serenity of the Northwoods is rocked. (978-1-63679-699-4)